MIGUELITO'S CONFESSION

Miguel A. De La Torre

MIGUELITO'S CONFESSION

Dedicated to
Deborah
whose fingerprints can be
found
on this manuscript and
on
my life

Happy Havana

As far as the old cop was concerned, he was the only person left on earth, the harsh consequence of a self-serving attitude he embraced throughout his entire life. Often, in fits of anger, he would bellow how his only wish was to be left alone in a small apartment with his teacup poodle named Baby, away from the wife and son he had come to resent, perceiving them as a millstone around his neck. He voiced such thoughts when his mind was lucid and his body able; but now, the passage of time had reduced him to a pitiful and pathetic sack of skin and bones. Some might argue he deserved lying there alone, simply existing, oblivious to his surroundings, trying to remember what is best kept forgotten.

During his youth, he possessed a name commanding respect, if respect could be garnered through fear and intimidation. He was a very tall, small man, thin throughout his youth, slightly paunch during his middle years, and now quite gaunt. Hard to imagine that the frail fragile body taking up space once walked straight, with an iron spined back acquired through military training. His long frame did not quite fit on the single bed, so his curled-down feet hung over the bottom edge. Silver hair reached all the way down to his collarbone while a shaggy beard covered his lower face, a look he would have despised if he had self-awareness. He could have been mistaken for an aged version of *los revolucionario barbudos* – those bearded revolutionaries - he once hunted in the mountains of eastern Cuba during the middle of the last century. His chalk-like hue supplanted what was once the healthy milky complexion revealing *gallego* (Galician) ancestry. Having forgotten how to swallow weeks earlier, it did not take long before he started to literally waste away, as his leathery skin clung to his bones for dear life.

For the past twenty hours, the adult diaper he wore remained dry as his limbs grew colder, a clear indication to staff at the Happy Havana Retirement Village they would soon have another bed for some other client on their waiting list. The residence nurse had removed his dentures for his own protection, fearing he might choke if they became loose or dislodged. Besides, no one needed another malpractice suit. With nothing sturdy to frame his face, his skin sunk into his skull, creating a hollow hole where his mouth once existed. He looked like one of those World War II walking skeletons depicted in those old black-and-white concentration camp photos.

The nutrition needed to sustain life was being pumped through an enteral feeding PEG tube directly attached to his stomach, bypassing the esophagus. This was but one of the many tubes and wires keeping him alive. Months earlier when he was more cognizant and still had a few ounces of strength, he tore at all the tubes and wires fastened onto his arms as if they were vipers with venomous fangs sunk deeply into his veins, sucking the very essence of his departing life. He was determined to rid himself of these serpents, believing they'd been affixed by some fiendish imaginary antagonist. In his mind, one of his nemeses from long ago must have kidnapped him and was now extracting a torturous revenge. He wasn't sure which old commie adversary was responsible. Maybe they all came together to conspire against him? Or maybe it was his own family trying to hasten his death so that they could inherit all his imaginary wealth. Who knows? Regardless as to who was behind his torment, he was determined to be tube-free and not subdued. But his constant thrashing and resistance led the residency staff to increase his morphine medication and restrain him with bed straps for his own protection, and their peace of mind. Eventually the dementia progressed to the point where he lost all contact with reality. Oblivious to his surroundings, he forgot about his confinement and the coils of tubing.

His last moments among the living were spent in room 28, not far from the nursing station down the hall. The walls of the room were pale light blue on the bottom and a dull oyster white on top, chosen because studies showed such colors induce serenity. When originally painted, the room may have very well made its occupants feel tranquil and safe; but after two decades of neglect, the walls were discolored and depressing. A window adorned with dirty yellowish curtains overlooked the endless highway construction projects of the Palmetto Expressway which contributed to Miami's nightmarish traffic jams. Room 28 resembled the other identical fifty-five mass-produced rooms of what was called a retirement village, a marketing euphemism for a building where the aroma of despair and death mingled with the pungent stench of human waste which lingered in the nostrils of those visiting comatose relatives, hours after they departed the facilities. This "retirement village" is where those who could no longer reason for themselves went to die.

He may have felt he was totally alone in the room, but in reality, a faded polyester navy blue curtain separated him from some unnamed roommate. Still, neither he nor the stranger in the bed next to him were aware of each other's presence. The management team at Happy Havana discovered it was possible to maximize profit by adding a second bed and recently began considering a third; so, did it really matter if the old cop lacked privacy? For what it was costing his son to provide his father with the semblance of medical care, one should have expected better. But truth be told, there is much profit to be made in dying. Besides, who would listen to the cry of the old, assuming they have the means by which to make themselves heard?

Saving nothing for a rainy day, the old cop had refused to purchase any type of insurance which could have eased the financial strain his care took. "*¿Para qué?*" he often snarled,

"What for? So that my wife can enjoy the money with some future lover? *Que se joda* – fuck those who come after me. That is why I have a son – to take care of me in my old age." If prudent, he would have had a nice nest egg by now, but the lure of the horses had depleted his secret reserves of cash he kept hidden in nooks and crannies throughout the house. Important life events, like his son's wedding, had to be planned around the starting gate timetable. He always assumed one day he would hit it big and not only live a life of leisure and luxury but be able to pour riches upon his boy. Even though the idea of leaving an inheritance for his son was absurd, he truly believed he loved him, and what better way to demonstrate love than with money. Whenever he hit a number and had a few spare bucks in his pocket, which was not too often, he never hesitated to slip a Benjamin to his son so he could enjoy an evening of carousing.

In his mind's eye, he envisioned himself generous; true if generosity was measured by dollars. But if instead generosity was measured by time given, encouragement offered, hugs shared, and kindness shown; then he was indeed very stingy. Not surprisingly, his small acts of liberality with money were inconsequential in providing for his final days, instead burdening his surviving son with the cost of a facility barely offering adequate care. Still, with the exception of himself, his boy was the only thing he really loved in his own dysfunctional way – even though he always suspected his boy might not be truly his.

If he had had possession of his full faculties, this moment of embracing death might have been terrifying. He spent a lifetime fearing this inevitable junction in time, and now that it was upon him, he failed to fully comprehend what was befalling him, as the tangible and imaginary merged in his feeble mind. Fortunately, his dementia was so acute that while he suspected time was slipping into nothingness, he was likewise unaware of the fact he was dying. His memories jumbled against each other in disjointed fragments, like the splintered shards of glass from a cup shattered on a terrazzo floor. Often it is said that prior to death, one witnesses their entire life flash before their eyes. He, however, struggled to remember just who he was.

"Aarrrggghh, *coño, quiero café* . . . I want coffee. . . *¿por favor cafecito?* . . . please someone bring . . . someone . . . where? . . . children . . . children . . . boys . . . girls? . . . *no chancletas.* . . boys . . . how many? . . . one . . . two . . . names? . . . three . . . three . . . where they? No one . . . where *café*? . . . why son missing? . . . *hijos de puta* . . . arrgh . . . *¿por que Dios?* Why God? . . . *coño* . . . *mijo* – my son. . . which? . . . *solo - por qué?* . . . smell *café* . . . why can't have . . . *mijito, donde* . . . alone . . . hmmmm *café"*

The irony of this moment is that the old cop lived a life so afraid of dying he refused to live, always preferring the radio broadcast chatter accompanying the sport programs upon which he placed bets than talking with friends and family. Before the onslaught of his mind-eating disease, he carried the mantle of insignificance well, always doing what was right in his own eyes. And yet, he constantly worried about his final demise. Childlike fables of Hell and damnation, as illustrated by Hieronymus Bosch, filled him with dread, although he maintained an impermeable *macho* façade, barricading others from ever getting close enough to provide comfort or loving counsel. He was haunted by all he had seen and more importantly, all he had done – despicable acts designed to keep his *macho* mask firmly in place. He feared more the mask might slip and reveal his insecurities and weaknesses than being utterly alone. Though he tried to convince himself, and anyone who would listen of heroic yarns living the life of a patriot fighting gloriously against the godless evils of communism, he could never fully shake the gnawing feeling of shame associated with the exploits in which he engaged to protect God and preserve country. Why is it that all too often, the greatest atrocities seem to be committed in God's name defending the good from satanic forces?

With less than half a dozen breaths left, his eyes suddenly opened for the first time in days. For just a moment, a moment lasting the rest of his life, the fog lifted as he became more lucid. Memories rushed into his mind as long extinguished synapses sparked anew. He remembered. He has one son. He remembered an abused wife whom he never appreciated, who died of lung cancer due to secondhand smoke, one of the several hazards for anyone living with him. The pain of strained relationships became as intense as when he first felt estranged. As he grieved what was lost, he felt a presence in his room apart from the other dying soul in the bed next to his.

This presence was very much alive, more an energy than something material. He strained his eyes around the room, seeking to see through a glass darkly, but there were only smoky shades of gloom. He tried to ask who was there, but he couldn't find the strength to move his tongue and utter the words - so he groaned.

As his eyes adjusted to the darkness, he detected movement from the room's blurry edges. It seemed as if the begrimed corners were crowded with shadows. But shadows of what? Human? Couldn't tell. His eyes widened reacting to the rising fear which gripped him as he tried to focus on these figures now gaining definition. "Who or what are those," he wondered. He sensed they were not friendly, as a malicious energy rose from nothingness. He sensed danger. He wanted to shriek, he wanted to run, but all he could do was moan - "aarrrggh."

It seemed as if it took hours, maybe days for these figures to make their way out of the shadows. In real time, the entire apparition took less than a fraction of a second, but in his mind, the encounter with his fate lasted an eternity. About a dozen faces attached to puffs of air became discernable. As the shadows came closer, he began to recognize some of the figures. They were all young, menacing, angry and thirsting for vengeance. "Dead . . . how . . . no . . . *comemierdas*," filled his mind. Words fail to capture the contempt yet fear he held for them. If his mind was functioning, he would still have been just as confused for they have ceased to exist a lifetime ago. Even if he could fully remember, he would not have recalled their names, that's how insignificant they were to him. But their faces, they remained familiar even in the fog of remembering. They were such young men in the prime of life with futures before them. Such violent endings.

His eyes were the last thing they gazed upon before their lives were snuffed out; so, it is only fitting they came now to return the favor. But ultimately it was their own fault that they perished, he reasoned with himself. If pressed about his involvement with their violent end, he would have justified himself by blaming them for choosing to align themselves with dangerous ideologies. He tried to save them, he tried to provide an out from their certain doom he would have argued. But they didn't listen to him. Their obstinacy is what got them killed. It was not his fault; it was never his fault.

"*Vete al carajo* – go to Hell," he would have wanted to say if only he could find his voice. It didn't really matter, though, because the shadows knew what he was feeling. Likewise, and a bit more startling, he felt their loathing, he heard the cacophony of their aggressive and menacing thoughts. As he defiantly stared back at his tormentors, he noticed a man of the cloth at the far left of the group. He remembered the priest with the baby-face, even his name - Padre Pedro. But if he was hoping the Catholic priest would provide holy unction, he was sadly mistaken. Of all the shadowy figures before him, this one held the greatest animosity. Even though the old cop could barely move, even though he was petrified of death, even though he had lived the life of a coward, he continued to wear his *macho* mask to the end. If he had to, he would even tell God to go fuck himself to continue with this self-deception. No, he would not beg for mercy, for forgiveness, nor for grace. No, he would never admit to being wrong.

As he cursed the wraithlike shadows now surrounding his bed, he caught a glimpse of one more figure standing apart from the rest, also familiar but in a very different manner. Although his tormentors were upon him, so close he could smell their foul breaths, this particular apparition simply stood there with a menacing grin. There was neither anger nor hatred emulating from him, rather fulfillment, satisfaction, even a perverse form of sadistic ecstasy. His pearly white teeth glittered against the backdrop of deep, dark, black skin. Unlike the other phantoms who were now climbing onto his bed and pressing down hard on his chest making it difficult to gasp his next breath, this black figure did not appear to be like the others, a spirit. He had a muscular physique, not too tall, but very strong. As ethereal hands gripped the old cop's throat, the black quasi-deity remained upright like a mighty warrior-king.

"Oggún?" The old cop recognized him by his green vest and pants, flattened-out straw hat, and tiger skin bag ornamented with cowry shells. In his left hand he held a long machete. "Oggún, *baba* - father, not help?" he wondered. Why wasn't the mighty warrior disbursing his persecutors with a swing of his machete? If he wanted to, the human-eating god could smite these perturbing spirits as if they were nothing but pesky gnats. Oggún, the *orisha* who revels amid carnage, always present wherever there are accidents, killings, wars or bloodlettings just stood there, grinning. Some, like the old cop, resonated with the blood-spiller, finding comfort and pride in being the faithful child of such a formidable *macho orisha* warrior. But now, in his hour of need, the only thing the old cop felt was abandonment by the deity he had so faithfully served.

He gazed straight into Oggún's jet black eyes. And even though Oggún was doing nothing to defend his devotee from the menacing shadows, the old cop futilely looked in vain for an eluded calm in Oggún's presence. He stared deeper into those pitch-black eyes, losing himself in their depth. The darkness of those smiling eyes started to pull him in, engulfing his bed, his being, his entire existence. All he could sense was the deep nothingness closing in on him. He struggled against the current but found himself sinking deeper into the void of those inky eyes. He was drowning, no longer able to breathe as the empty night inundated him. There was no light to move toward, no tunnel with friends and family to guide the way, just the utter oblivion which only grew dimmer and bleaker. And just before all senses came to a final extinction, he caught a whiff of *café*.

Down the hall, about twenty-five yards from where he lay dying was the nursing station. Until recently two nurses would have been on duty, but cutbacks in personnel to increase profit margins slashed the "adequate" level of medical care offered to the residents of Happy Havana. Only one nurse was now required to staff the graveyard shift. Tomás Sanchez didn't mind working alone because it allowed him to be unsupervised for most of the early morning hours. Besides, the denizens of Happy Havana Retirement Village were usually not too troublesome. By the time most made it to the facility, their deteriorating mental faculties were so far advanced that they were unresponsive and easy to manage. There were always those waiting to enroll their loved ones at Happy Havana once their upkeep became unmanageable. Thanks mainly to a slick glossy brochure full of 1950s black-and-white pictures of a fictitious Cuba - a place which only existed in the fading minds of a lost generation – loved ones felt this was the place where *mami* or *papi* could feel at home, forgetting that loved ones would probably have no sense as to where they were. By conjuring up nostalgic images, Happy Havana became a final resting stop for Cubans whose bones would eventually be interned in a foreign soil, never to return to the land that had witnessed their birth.

The management of Happy Havana provided a cot for the night nurse to rest *only* when it was not too busy, so Nurse Sanchez made sure it was never too busy. Wired sensors were fastened to patients' bodies, designed, via a refurbished physiologic monitor, to set off an alarm notifying the person on duty of any radical deviations occurring in any of the four vital signs being measured: body temperature, blood pressure, pulse rate and/or respiratory rate. These hospital machines, once popular during operations in the 1990s, were reconfigured to inexpensively meet the needs of mid-level nursing homes. All one hundred and ten patients at the facility were wired-up. The alarm went off as expected moments before the old cop died, but Tomás Sanchez never heard it. Tonight, like every other night, he had turned off the sound as soon as the other staff went home.

Tough economic times exacerbated by the economic uncertainties wrought by the 2020 pandemic meant Nurse Sanchez, like most, had to work two jobs in order to feed his children and put clothes on their back, children he seldom saw. Being a single parent and making ends meet was challenging enough. He was grateful for his mother, his kid's *abuelita,* who despite her advanced age, kept the household functioning. If he could only sleep during his nightshift, then he could be sufficiently alert to work during the day as a real nurse at Jackson Memorial Hospital in downtown Miami. He did not really see an ethical problem with how he carried out his responsibilities at Happy Havana, since the patients' families all signed do-not-resuscitate orders. Besides, at Happy Havana he was more of a night security guard than a nurse, waiting for something to happen. If the alarm was to sound, indicating that a particular patient was dying, all he could do was go to their room, wait for their demise, make a note of the time of death, and then notify the next of kin. This wouldn't have been so bad if not for the fact that management, in order to save money, had purchased used and obsolete monitoring equipment. A patient shifting in their sleep was enough to set off the alarms. And while wireless patches now existed which could directly contact a nurse's cellphone at the first indication of clinical deterioration, management deemed them too expensive – even though they really weren't. It was common to receive half a dozen false alarms throughout the night. But by turning off the sound, Sanchez would be able to enjoy uninterrupted sleep. In the morning, prior to the arrival of the day shift, he could turn up the sound and check the rooms where alarms had been triggered during the night.

At 5:30 a.m., an hour and a half prior to the arrival of the day shift, Gloria Estefan's *The Rhythm is Gonna Get You*, which served as Sanchez's cell phone alarm, blasted. Before brushing his teeth and putting away his cot, he brewed *café* on the hotplate also provided by management. Ignoring his elevated BMI, he checked the pastry cardboard box from Mima's Bakery on Coral Way to see if there were any *pastelitos de guayaba* – guava pastries - left, but all he found were stale crumbs. Probably for the better, he thought to himself, especially since the appearance of the spare tire around his waist after turning thirty. The strong aroma of Cuban coffee which permeating the rooms and hallways of the facility helped mask the faint stench of decaying old people. As he took his first sip, he turned up the volume of the nursing station monitor to see what activity he missed. Only three residents required his attention – a slow night. With coffee in hand, he went to check on them. The first two were false alarms. The sensors attached to the patients' bodies slipped sometime during the night. Sanchez simply reattached them and made a note on his duty roster. If management wasn't so cheap and had gotten machines which actually displayed the time of the alarm, he wouldn't have to be guesstimating all of the time. The first alarm rang at, let's say, 1:43 a.m. and the second at, oh, 4:02 a.m.

As soon as he walked into room 28, he knew this was no false alarm. The patient just laid there, motionless, eyes wide open, staring at the left corner of the room. Sanchez lifted the patient's chart. Manuel de la Cruz. Person to contact: son Dr. Miguel A. De La Cruz in Denver, Colorado. He would have to make a call and break the bad news. "Good morning Dr. De La Cruz, I regret to inform you that your father died during the night at … at …" What time should be listed as the time of death? Sanchez felt the old cop's forehead – still warm but quickly becoming clammy. He must have recently died. Let's place the time of death at 6:03 a.m. And so it was, Manuel, a man so afraid of death that he refused to live, died before he was officially declared dead.

Oggún's Sin

"Augh!" Sweat poured down his burly body. Swish! Barriers dissipated before his formidable presence. "Augh!" Bulging muscles, pushed to their limit, flexed to the point of tearing. Swish, a path began to clear. "Augh!" With a deep breath, the fierce Oggún, small in stature but brawny in frame, lifted his trusty machete high above his head, threatening to scar the very face of the sky. Then with a burst of force, he swung his machete down hard on its mark to clear another patch of impassable jungle. Swish. With prodigious might he swung his machete, the first technical instrument he ever forged with ore taken from the belly of a mountain. As each stroke found its target, dense green vegetation scattered to the four corners of the earth. "Augh!" In synchronized rhythm he inched himself forward – minute after minute, hour after hour, week after week, month after month – meticulously cutting through the chaos of nature so that civilization could spring forth. No other deity could have made a way out of no way, clearing obstacles so that all – gods and humans - could progress forward. He may be known as the god of war, but likewise, because he is Lord of the metals, he is the god of progress and civilization. Slowly but surely the shrubbery melted away before the terrifying Oggún. Never taking a break, never resting for a moment, Oggún labored continuously until the job was completed.

When the *orishas* first began to leave their domain in the heavens for *tierra firme*, they found their path thwarted at every turn by a primal jungle of impenetrable foliage. Unable to inhabit the land in such a state, the gods questioned the worthiness of their endeavor to occupy the earth. Maybe their excursion was a misstep. Maybe they should return to the heavens where they belong. They were about to abandon their terrestrial quest when Oggún stepped forward, mocking their indecisiveness and weakness. "You may be gods, but you are as useless as tits on an old celibate hag," he taunted them. The gods never approved of his belligerent attitude; but few possessed the courage to reproach him; well aware he was a violent brute, always ready to indulge in hard drinking or revel in a knock-down fight - ideally both. Born in the bowels of the earth, the quarrelsome Oggún made few friends and many enemies. The gods, not being fools, knew better than to tangle with the most powerful among the warrior deities, as strong as the iron he ruled over. It was safer to keep their annoyance to themselves.

As the gods stood idle, unable to navigate the earth, Oggún swaggered to the front of the pantheon, and haughtily bellowed, "It seems as though I am the only one with large enough *cojones* to clear a path through this brushwood thicket." They looked away in shame, knowing he was right. If anyone could triumph over the dense jungle, it would be Oggún. He removed his green vest, stretched his muscles, and lifted his sharpened machete. Some of the goddesses murmured appreciatively as they watched him strip down to his loincloth, a small garment barely covering his potency. He noticed their attention but brushed those thoughts aside and focused on the arduous task at hand. A job needed to be done. Swish "Augh!" Swish "Augh!" Swish "Augh!" Never turning away from a fight or a task, no matter how insurmountable the impediments appeared to be, he worked unceasingly for months.

Due solely to the strength of his unrelenting brute force, a path, with time, was cleared. Thanks to Oggún, the gods were given passage and thus able to inhabit the earth. *Osin-Imole* they spontaneously shouted once the task was accomplished, for he was indeed the first of the primordial *orishas* to come to earth. His back was stiff and sore as a result of his arduous labors, his muscles ached, and his joints felt excruciating pain. Exhausted, as perspiration poured from his body, the broad-shouldered Oggún strutted before the other gods. The goddesses who had watched his steady, repetitive motions savored their private delicious thoughts, especially the young goddess of love and desire, Ochún, who had not moved her eyes from his manhood the entire time. She contemplated the possible consequences of having Oggún as a lover in light of her own petite frame. Still, she continued to feed her fantasies.

Although many resented Oggún's machismo, the gods still showed gratitude for his toil, awarding him the city of Ire-Ekiti to rule, a city occupied by humans which stands to this day in the southwestern hilly region of present-day Nigeria. As king of this important Yoruba metropolis, Oggún distinguished himself as the greatest blacksmith ever to have existed. He could have enjoyed ruling in peace over Ire-Ekiti till the ends of time, but as the father of tragedies he could not resist crossing boundaries which no one – not even a deity - should ever cross. Unfortunately, like all his human devotees would discover, including the old Cuban cop Manuel gasping for his very last breaths, Oggún lived at the mercy of his most basic and violent instincts. Those dispositions, mixed with a false sense of invincibility, made him and many of his disciples, catastrophic heart-wrenching figures.

Not too far from Ire-Ekiti lived two of Obatalá's avatars, or alternate personas. The father of humanity, Obatalá, head of the *orisha* pantheon, chose to settle down and live on the earth which he created. Because of the complex spiritual nature of the *orishas*, they might have as many as twenty or thirty avatars. Some have none. Obatalá has forty-five, some which are male and others which are female. Two of these avatars, the male Ayáguna and the female Yemmu represent two different manifestations of Obatalá. Ayáguna, who is recognized for waging an aggressive and fearless battle against evil, represents the violent side of the otherwise peaceful Obatalá; while Yemmu, his mate, as the feminine side of Obatalá, was the primordial mother who birthed the sun during the Winter Solstice. Together, living on a large spread of farmland cultivating yam outside of the bustling city of Ire-Ekiti, they sired several children, among them their first-born, Oggún. Oggún often visited their yam farm where he always found a welcoming tasty home-cooked meal. But as seasons passed, his visits became more frequent, almost daily, especially when his father Ayáguna was out working in the fields.

As weeks drifted into months, Oggún's feelings toward his mother turned to lust as the once peaceful home became a house of overbearing tension where a deafening silence suffocated its inhabitants. Refusing to believe a nefarious act could occur under his own roof, Ayáguna tried hard to ignore the averted glances as an expanding cloud of dread and apprehension smothered the joy and gaiety which once filled his home. Besides, if anything was truly amiss, he would know. He relied on his enchanted white rooster Osún to inform him of all that was going-on whenever he was absent. Osún's sole purpose and responsibility was to provide Ayáguna with an account of each day's activities. When Ayáguna returned from a hard day of work, the magical bird never had anything new to report. And yet, something was obviously very wrong.

"Could it be that his wife Yemmu was showering too much attention on their moody and insolent adult son?" wondered Ayáguna. "But why would this make her distant, not just from Oggún, but also from her other children? Why did she refuse to keep his bed warm at night?" Ayáguna could have sworn he noticed a mixture of dread, repulsion, and shame in her eyes every time he romantically reached out for her, so he decided to approach his other son, the mischievous Elleguá, to subtly question him. Maybe it would have been better to approach Yemmu directly, but in patriarchal societies, the norm seems to resolve family problems among men, even when it concerned women. Ayáguna believed that if anything was out of the ordinary, surely the young Elleguá, who stayed home all-day playing games and eating sweets, would know. But how could he ask questions without betraying his nagging doubts and suspicions? Getting a straight answer from Elleguá was never an easy proposition, for his son seldom spoke plainly, preferring the language of riddles and conundrums

Elleguá, always lurking behind closed doors, was well aware of the sexual violence Oggún repeatedly visited upon their mother. He would hear her sobs each day after Oggún, satisfied, left the house. Elleguá was no fool, even though he played one. As brother, he knew Oggún's violent temper firsthand, and even though he was a warrior in his own right, he was no match for the formidable god of war. But brute strength is not the only weapon which can be used to overcome an opponent; a lesson never quite learned by Oggún who preferred fists and armaments over measured dialogue and diplomacy. Elleguá knew that victory is always best savored when achieved without violence, but it would take a cunning plan.

Elleguá sensed his father's reluctance so instead designed a ruse to reveal the truth. Elleguá was not like the other gods. An impish and mischievous trickster with a puckish grin, his fellow *orishas* and humans alike were cautious of any type of contact or interaction with him. Although he was as whimsical and capricious as fate, he nevertheless was a great defender of justice. He was prone to cause chaos so that stability could reign, lie so that truth could be discovered, steal so that the poor might eat. One night after dinner, when Yemmu was in the kitchen cleaning up and Osún the rooster had gone reveling, Ayáguna approached Elleguá who was sitting by the fireplace chewing tobacco. Elleguá put on a glum face to elicit his father's concern and draw him into conversation. In Elleguá's mind, it was the only way to bring an end to the abuses suffered by his mother. Ayáguna did notice Elleguá's dour demeanor and asked, "Why are you so sullen *omo-mí* – my child?"

"Oh *baba-mí* – my father, I'm afraid something terrible is occurring every day when you leave the house and go out to work in your fields."

"What could possibly be so terrible?"

"I fear your wrath. I'm afraid of what you might do if I told you. Please don't be angry with me." Crocodile tears began to trickle down Elleguá's face.

"*Omo-mí*" Ayáguna gently tried to reassure his son, whom he knew needed no reassurance. "You have nothing to fear, just tell me what is concerning you."

"I don't know. I'm afraid you might . . ."

"*¡Basta! – Enough!*" Ayáguna snapped, already tired of Elleguá's incessant games. Catching himself, Ayáguna lowered his voice and spoke in a controlled tone. "Tell me what you know," he slowly and calmly threatened, "before you discover a reason to truly fear."

"Well, every day after you head for the fields to work, my older brother Oggún shows up. He . . . he . . .," Elleguá pauses for dramatic effect, pretending to be unable to finish the sentence.

"He is also my son, he's always welcome at my home." Ayáguna responded attempting to fill the silent pause without betraying his rising suspicions. Then he asked the question whose reply he dreaded hearing. "What could be so terrible about him visiting his mother?"

"But *baba-mí*, once he arrives, he takes away all my food and gives it to Osún, your messenger. After the rooster eats all his food, and then mine, he gets very sleepy and falls into a stupor. Haven't you noticed how fat Osún has been getting?"

Ayáguna blinked. Now that he mentioned it, he *had* noticed Osún's recent weight gain. Elleguá continued, "Once Osún is sound asleep, Oggún throws me and the other children out of the house. I try to spy on what's going on, but he closes all the window shutters and locks the door."

"What about your mother Yemmu? What does she say about all this?"

"I don't know," Elleguá lied, "Oggún keeps her in the house, locked behind closed doors. I press my ears against the window shutters, but all I hear is what appears to be a violent trashing with *iyá-mí* – my mother - shrieking at first, followed by what sounds like her gently sobbing. I'm concerned she might be in some type of danger."

Ayáguna began to suspect what he was hearing but remained cautious; after all, Elleguá was a notorious trickster. His son continued, "*Baba-mí*, I don't know what is going on after I'm thrown out of the house, but I have a plan to find out." And with that, Elleguá whispered his proposal into Ayáguna's ear, setting a trap by which to ensnare his abusive brother and rescue his mother. Ayáguna listened carefully and nodded.

The next morning, even though Ayáguna tossed and turned throughout the night, he awoke quite early, before the sun made its daily appearance. Usually before a long journey he would linger in bed enjoying the pleasures his wife had to offer; but recently, physical intimacy had been lacking. Ayáguna leaped out of bed and started to put on his long white linen clothes. In a matter-of-fact tone he commanded, more than requested, that his wife pack enough food to last him three days. He mumbled something about having to travel to a neighboring village.

Yemmu left the comfort of her warm bed to assist her husband as he prepared for his journey. She cooked him a bowl of long-grain white rice with no salt to which she added some chopped up cocoa butter and stirred until it melted. Then she boiled four eggs for about seventeen minutes, peeled off the shell and chopped them lengthwise, placing them on top of the mound of rice. For dessert, she packed eight small meringue cookies. As soon as his knapsack was packed along with a change of clothes for the long trek, Ayáguna said his goodbyes, picked up his staff and horsetail flywhisk, and left the house, walking briskly down the middle of the dusty dirt road. But after traveling just a few kilometers, far enough to be out of his farm's sight, he ducked into the deep forest which lined the path and quietly backtracked. About an hour had passed before he found himself at the back door of his home. He wanted to peek through the window, but all the shutters were boarded up, just as Elleguá had described. Holding his breath, he tiptoed to the front of the house. Of course, Elleguá heard the wooden planks under Ayáguna's feet squeak in protest to the weight pressed upon them, but he continued whittling a piece of wood, pretending he didn't notice his father sneaking up behind him.

"*Omo-mí*," Ayáguna whispered, is Oggún here?"

"Yes *baba-mí*," responded Elleguá, pretending to be startled by Ayáguna's appearance. Then, as if to prove everything he told Ayáguna was true, he pointed to the eastern corner of the porch. Looking in the direction to which Elleguá gestured, Ayáguna saw Osún the rooster curled up like a ball contentedly napping while the other younger children played in the front yard. As Ayáguna began to accept Elleguá's truthfulness, rage began to get the better of him. The corners of his vision grew gray and blurry as he shook off lightheadiness. He felt hurt and betrayed by his messenger Osún, whose loyalty had been exchanged for a bowl of porridge. He strode toward the front door, no longer worried about being heard by those inside. He didn't even slow down to see if the door was locked. Lifting his right foot high he kicked in the door; wood splinters flew in all directions.

There was an eerie silence as the dust began to resettle. Walking into the darkened room required a few seconds for his eyes to adjust. But as they did, he spied two stationary figures coming into focus. Paralyzed from shock by the exploding door, neither Oggún nor his mother Yemmu moved. There they were on the floor in the middle of the room, frozen, with Yemmu on all fours being mounted by Oggún. "Like a common bitch," Ayáguna thought to himself, quick to blame the victim. Once they realized Ayáguna stood before them with blazing eyes, gazing upon their shame, both mother and child felt fear and trepidation to the very core of their being. Trembling, they scurried to separate corners of the room, cowering before Ayáguna's wrath, attempting to cover their nakedness with whatever discarded scraps of clothing which had been thrust aside earlier during Oggún's heat of passion. It was a sight which had never been seen before: the mighty and fierce Oggún panic stricken, scurrying like a frightened mouse.

Yemmu, fearing her husband's wrath, begged for mercy – not so much for herself, but for her son who, despite his abuse, she still cared for. Misunderstanding her pleas and seeing her only as a willing accomplice to this crime, Ayáguna began to curse her out loud, holding her responsible for the injustice her son visited upon her. As far as Ayáguna was concerned, his honor had been stolen by the *taking* of his woman, his property, and that's all that mattered. He had caught another man, even if it was his own first-born son, plowing in his fields, directly challenging his authority as head of the family. Regardless of his wife's well-meaning motherly intentions to protect her son, she too had to be punished. But rather than cursing her directly, he decided to cause her greater misery and anguish by damning her next child. Staring at her as though he could see through her very being, he swore that the next fruit coming from her womb would be buried alive. Furthermore, her other beloved baby boy Changó would be banished from the house and forced to live with Dadá, goddess of the gardens, who made her home high on the tops of the palm trees. Yemmu felt faint as the room began spinning around her. She struggled to maintain consciousness as she begged for mercy. But her words were wasted on her enraged, stone-faced husband who was more concern with his stolen honor than how she was dishonored.

This was more than Yemmu could bear. Tired of being reduced to an object at the whim of the male *orishas* in her life, she looked to the heavens and prayed to the source of all *ashé*, from whom all the *orishas* receive their power – Olodumare - from whom came all life, energy and being. She begged her spirit to depart her body and allow another manifestation to take its place. Suddenly recognizing he might have jumped to his conclusions and judged too harshly, Ayáguna attempted to retract his curse, but it was too late. The words were uttered and thus were destined to become reality. Olodumare, upon hearing Yemmu's request, immediately called her essence to his heavenly abode. Instantly, as tears burst from her eyes, streams of water rushed out of every orifice in her body, filling the room with great swilling waves threatening to drown everyone by her sadness. All the male *orishas* present clung to each other, choking and spluttering. Then just as quickly, the waters subsided, and a new spirit occupied Yemmu's body. Standing up before Ayáguna with a regal dignity, she introduced herself as Yemayá, the queen of the seas and the mother of all life, since from her waters all life finds its origins. Obatalá may be the seed of life, but it is Yemayá who germinates that seed within her watery womb. From this day forward, only Yemayá would be the one who could punish her children. She would be a safeguard and a refuge for all women who are misused and abused by men. She would be a comfort and a source of strength for all maltreated women trapped in violent relationships.

When Ayáguna saw the havoc he inflicted on Yemmu through his rash judgement, he was overcome with remorse. He too found he was unable to bear all the misfortune which had befallen his household, so he begged for a new spirit. Olodumare the creator also heard his pleas and granted his request. As his spirit left his body it was absorbed back into its origin – the peaceful and serene Obatalá.

Witnessing the consequences which his unrestrained lust had unleashed, Oggún's terror surged. He dreaded the wrath of his father-now-as-Obatalá, and begged for mercy, asking that he be allowed to utter his own curse. The clear-headed Obatalá thought for a moment. If he relented, he was sure Oggún would devise a punishment more severe than anything the wise *orisha* could ever imagine. But he realized it was no longer within his right to pass judgement on his son, for that role now fell to Yemayá. Although she still loved her son, she tried to balance her fury with the distress caused by his ultimate betrayal and assault. Not sure what to do or say, Yemayá rallied all her resources to appear composed and in control. With frosty words, through clenched teeth, she simply said: "So be it. I will always love you, but you will never find forgiveness from me!" Oggún slowly emerged from the dark corner of the room and decreed that for all eternity he would never again know peace or rest. Rather he would unceasingly labor, day and night, in an attempt to work off the shame he has brought upon himself and his father. Interestingly enough, his mother was not mentioned within the words of the self-inflicting curse he just made. In his mind it was his father who was shamed for he trespassed upon his property. Still, this is the price he would pay for his sin, so that through work, he might regain his salvation and redemption. Furthermore, he would divulge the secrets of making iron to all of humanity so he would no longer be the master of anything, not even metals.

Obatalá was not fully pacified. The rooster Osún, who had been awakened by all the commotion, now stood at a safe distance behind, trembling at what fate might befall him due to his silent complicity. Without dignifying the rooster with even a glance, Obatalá, sensing his presence simply stated his duties as messenger had come to an end. From this day forth, those responsibilities are to be bestowed upon Elleguá. And because Elleguá had been denied food, from now on no god will ever be allowed to eat without Elleguá first being fed. This means that any sacrifice lifted to any god or goddess must first go through Elleguá, who gets to first taste the *ashé* being offered. Furthermore, from this day forward Osún would serve Elleguá and would feed on whatever Elleguá chooses to provide.

Disgraced and deeply humiliated, the dejected Oggún left his parent's house, never to return. He sought solitude deep in the forest. Self-exiled, he cut himself off from all the other gods, choosing the life of a hermit. This, of course, had dire consequences for humanity. Yes, all war ceased, but this did not mean that, by opposite effect, peace reigned – for peace is never simply the absent of conflict. Sometimes peace can be more deadly. Without the guidance of the god of metals, civilization and progress came to a halt. Chaos soon ensued. But Oggún could have cared less. He only selfishly dwelled upon his own misery, and if others ended up also wallowing in their own despair, so much the better.

Padre Pedro

On this particular day - the day before the celebration of the birth of our Lord and Savior – the aim was to get a young Catholic priest to reveal the names of dangerous malcontents within his parish. Not everyone was resolute in doing whatever it took to serve and protect. "Naïve cowards" the young cop thought, "so many lacked the fortitude for this type of work, totally ignorant as to how high are the stakes." Manuel de la Cruz, a sergeant with the bureau, was a patriot *en la lucha* – in the struggle - for the very soul of Cuba. Franco's Spain, Novo's Portugal, Batista's Cuba: a trinity established by God Almighty against the global satanic threat of communism. His actions were absolutely essential to preserve Christian civilization and family values for the corner of the earth where his precious island lay. He was justified before the authorities of both Heaven and la Habana to carry out this duty, regardless as to how distasteful it might appear to others. Men like him, he was convinced, arise in every generation to shield the righteous from a political fate worse than death.

Extreme measures were required to prevent *los comunistas* - the communists from gaining control. So, the sergeant simply blocked out the blood-curdling shriek, followed with a sobbing whimper that would normally send chills up the spine of anyone possessing a conscience that was close enough to hear. Most who claimed to be human are conditioned – either by society or genetics – to exhibit empathy when in the presence of another in agony. Manuel, however, displayed numbness while inflicting pain. He had become so desensitized to the howls responding to torture that they no longer affected him nor impacted his psyche. He was able to sleep soundly at night. But it was not always this way. The first time he employed advance interrogation techniques on a prisoner, he indeed felt revulsion and nausea. In fact, the periphery of his vision darkened as he felt his essence separating from his body. The tormented cries being uttered just two feet away sounded muffled, as if they were coming from another room. Feeling faint, he nonetheless mustered all his willpower to avoid giving in to the lightheadedness. His machismo simply would not allow surrendering to his humanity. So, he clenched his jaw and kept at the task at hand – seeking information by whatever means necessary.

With the passage of time and the repetitiveness of interrogations his heart formed the necessary callouses which safeguarded him from feelings of compassion or regret, callouses which grew thicker with each new interrogation.

This is how good men become beasts, by normalizing horror. If he ever paused long enough to question his actions, ideological fascist falsities quickly arose to cloud his self-questioning, serving a useful purpose in justifying activities and soothing consciences. Manuel may have been queasy during that first interrogation, but now he would say he felt nothing. But this was not exactly true. Inflicting violence elicited a new sensation which emerged to replace buried sympathetic emotions: sadistic pleasure. Over time, the screams of each suspect simultaneously calmed and excited him, for he knew he was closer to achieving the climax of arriving at the truth. "You have to respect them when they resist," the cop often thought to himself, "but eventually, their doggedness dissipates."

What most of the public failed to realize was that their beloved Cuba was precariously teetering on the edge of annihilation. Why do his compatriots refuse to see that not far in the Sierra Mountains were bands of malodourous bearded guerrilla rebels bent on the obliteration of the Cuban way of life? The Castro brothers, along with that *comemierda* Ché, were, in Manuel's mind, the incarnation of a different type of trinity, an unholy one – the incarnation of Satan, Lucifer, and the Devil himself. They were merciless terrorists refusing to play by the rules, leaving those in authority with no other option but to fight them with whatever means are required to maintain and sustain the good. Never mind that the authorities which Manuel blindly followed had overthrown an elected government and instituted a brutal dictatorship. Those threatening what the powerful had established as the rule of law had to be crushed. God would surely forgive him, if not reward him for being a frontline warrior in the trenches fighting in hand-to-hand combat against God's enemies. He was, after all, doing God's work an instrument of God's wrath in punishing infidels – especially when unbelievers dressed in religious garb.

With furrowed brows Manuel, through those greenish blue eyes, looked down with contempt at the strong-willed cleric. Strapped to a chair, Padre Pedro, the baby-faced priest fought the nauseating waves of throbbing pain emanating from his now swollen right hand index finger, a pain which spread to every nerve receptor in his body. In routine bureaucratic fashion, Manuel completed a procedure once popularized during the medieval Catholic Inquisition, a technique he had executed numerous times intended to loosen tongues by first loosening fingernails.

Beneath the priest's index figure was a metallic contraption that looked something like a splint used to set a broken bone. However, at the end of this splint-type gadget, coming over and above the fingertip, was an apparatus resembling a miniature set of pliers. The young cop gently attached these pliers to the priest's fingernail. With a firm tug on the splint, he was able to remove the entire nail quickly and efficiently. At times the nail would crack and only a portion was removed but it really didn't matter – the results were the same – excruciating pain. The nail itself, like hair, is dead material incapable of sensation, but underneath there are a significantly high number of nerve endings located within the nail bed, making this small tender area among the most sensitive zones of the human body. The pain was so intense that the poor priest soiled himself before losing consciousness. Normally it would take about six months for the cleric to regrow a new fingernail. Unfortunately, he barely had sixty minutes left.

People like Sergeant de la Cruz are not born monsters, they are prepared for the role, a training which teaches monsters to gaze into a mirror only to see a true patriot as the reflection. At some point in his life, he had to learn how to compartmentalize and justify his actions as a self-preservation mechanism, a survival strategy which allowed him to look in the mirror and not feel repulsion by his reflection. *"Hijo de puta,"* Manuel thought to himself, realizing this priest was not going to talk so easily despite his missing fingernail. In a way, he admired the priest's machismo, remaining tight lipped when others in his predicament would have betrayed their own mothers by now. *¡Cojonu como Maceo!*[*] Manuel thought. But there was no time for respect. With the rebel advancements, the cop needed answers fast. He would have to bring the questioning to a "conclusion" if necessary. No loose ends, not now. He ordered his men to revive the priest as he left interrogation room three. His men would prepare the priest while he headed toward the cubicle which he shared with two other investigators for a smoke. Sitting at his desk he

---

[*] Ballsy like [Antonio] Maceo!

leaned back on his chair, lit a cigar, and took a deep drag, relishing the pleasure it brought him. He has been smoking since he was eight. Although a relatively young man, he already developed that yellowish nicotine stains between his index and middle fingers. Staring at the ceiling, Manuel debated what to do with the wayward priest.

With only a sixth-grade education, Manuel originally joined the army to escape his parent's poverty. The year he was born, 1926, was also the year that the sugar boom collapsed devastating most of the population, including the de là Cruz family of Camagüey. His parents never recovered from economic ruin, barely surviving lean years of hunger. Once discharged from the armed forces he was recruited as a corporal for the not-so-secret police, the infamous *buró de investigaciones* – the Bureau of Investigations. The agency, which had close ties to both the CIA and the FBI, was headed by Batista's "golden man," *el coronel* Orlando Eleno Piedra. *El coronel* was a trusted man, proven by the large amethyst stone pinky ring he wore. These rings were given as gifts by Batista to his closest devotees, signifying they were men of true distinction. Manuel, a loyalist, felt somewhat cheated for never receiving such a ring despite all he did for the regime, all the blood he spilled in its name. Notwithstanding his jealousy, he served *coronel* Piedra faithfully, doing whatever needed to be done to preserve law and order, even if it meant extracting confessions from obstinate clerics.

It was almost 4:00 in the afternoon and the sergeant wanted to be done with this annoying *cura*, this stubborn priest. He was taking his latest love interest Celia - a *mulata* with long caramel legs which never ended - to the Capri Casino to celebrate *Noche Buena* – Christmas Eve. Although the front man serving as the casino's owner was the movie actor George Raft, rumors had it that the Mafioso "Fat the Butch" from New York's Westchester County ran the casinos at the Capri. The police didn't really care as long as they had *una mordida*, a taste of the pie. All Manuel knew was whenever he flashed his badge, he was treated well, was served free drinks, and given a few extra $5 red chips with their distinctive three yellow stripes painted diametrically on opposed edges of the coin. Tonight, he was determined to score big, both at poker and with Celia.

Although racist eyebrows had been raised when his family heard about the affair with a *mulata*, he really didn't care what they thought. When it came to the pleasures of the flesh, he considered himself enlightened, repudiating the Cuban adage, *juntos pero no revueltos, cada cosa en su lugar.*[*] There were occasions when it was beneficial to "scramble up" with blacks, especially if they were beautiful *negras y mulatas*. Besides, with enough power and money anyone could be whitened in Cuba, as was the case with *el mulato lindo* – the pretty mulatto, as President Fulgencio Batista was charmingly known. But whitening darker skin only went so far. Even though Batista, an Afro-Chinese was the second most powerful man on the island - after the United States

---

[*] Together but not scrambled, everything in its place.

Ambassador Earl E. T. Smith - he still was unable to gain membership to the elite Havana Yacht Club. His application continued to be blackballed by Cuba's white upper-class.

Half-jokingly, Manuel would tell his fellow law enforcers at the station that he suffered from a made-up sickness afflicting the veins in his penis that could only be cured by engaging in sex with a *negra*. It seems many young white Cuban boys had this particular affliction. In Manuel's mind, sex with *negras* was always a bit more savage, more animalistic, maybe because those types of women were closer to the heat of the jungle. Maybe it's because they lacked proper family morals. Or maybe it was just chemistry. Who knows? All he understood was that by the time they hit puberty, like a switch being flipped, they all seemed to turn into seductive temptresses. Celia was no different. He would not have been surprised to discover she placed a spell upon him through that Santería jungle black magic she practiced. Regardless, all he cared about were pleasures he envisioned for tonight.

Normally he would have gone out to celebrate *Noche Buena* with Marta, the woman with whom he had lived. For the past three *Noche Buenas* they had spent the evening together dancing *merengue* at popular clubs around the middle-class neighborhood of Vedado. But then she had to go and get herself pregnant last year. He quickly broke off the relationship, even though she kept insisting, through tears, that the child was his. Sure – only God knows how many men she screwed. No way was she going to pin her carelessness on him! He heard she gave birth to a boy two months ago and called the baby Miguelito. Who knows who the bastard's real father was? Who cares?

He looked forward to enjoying the night, but this annoying priest was cock-blocking him, delaying his embrace of Celia. He wished he didn't have to deal with the church because he considered himself to be a good Catholic, but if truth be known, lately it was crawling with communists; *comunistas* like Padre Sardiñas who was serving as chaplain for the rebel army at the military rank of *comandante*. Then there was Padre Madrigal, treasurer of Castro's July 26 Movement or Padre Chabebe who could be counted upon to relay coded messages to the rebel forces through his religious radio program. And of course, the Catholic student leader José Antonio Echevarría who participated in the attack on the presidential palace back in March of last year. At least that *hijo de puta* was eventually cornered and shot by some of Manuel's friends. *Uno menos* – one less, Manuel thought.

Like roaches, you may see one and crush it, but you know there are hundreds more in hiding. How many more of these communist-duped so-called Christians were using their churches and homes as underground headquarters for the Revolution? He had to find out. God knows, and maybe Padre Pedro does too. Manuel had no doubts that the good priest was part of the M-26-7 network. One of his parishioners who the sergeant had previously interrogated had implicated him. Not much force was needed with that one – what a *maricón* Manuel thought. A good beating with a bull-penis cane followed by extinguishing his cigarette on the prisoner's thighs was more than enough of a motivator. "*Coño*, the guy would have sold out his own family just to get out of there," Manuel chuckled. As the sergeant took one last drag of his cigar before lighting another, his aides informed him the priest was conscious and ready. He headed toward the interrogation room determined to finish with this priest in short order. After all, Celia was waiting.

"*Buenas tardes Padre*," Manuel began as he walked into the pale green room with reddish-brown droplet stains on the walls and floors, memorials to previous occupants. Using the tone of a polite and respectful altar boy, he continued: "I hope you were able to rest." The priest murmured something, probably a prayer, the young cop couldn't quite make it out. "Would you like some water? You must be thirsty." With great gentleness he lifted a glass to the priest's lips and allowed him to sip. Upon removing the glass from his lips, the sergeant noticed some water dripping down the priest's chin, mixing with the tears flowing down his face. With the tenderness of a loving son, he removed the cotton white cologne-scented handkerchief from his back pocket and wiped away both water and tears. "You know Padre, we have something in common. I am also called *el cura*. Do you know why? Because sooner or later everyone confesses their sins to me. And when they do, I offer redemption. They get to go back to their family as if nothing happened. But if they refuse to confess . . . well Padre, you know, they descend into Hell. And there, not even God almighty can save them. Now Padre, *por favor*, we know you are sympathetic to the *comunistas* – that we can forgive as long as you turn from your evil ways. We also know your church is being used as a base of operation by the communists to destroy our country – that unfortunately cannot be forgiven . . . unless . . . unless . . . you come clean and tell us who they are and where they live. Not only will you be absolved of your sins, but you will be saving your country – doing God's work. What do you say Padre? Who are these traitors polluting the House of God?"

Padre Pedro had difficulty finding his voice. He was terrified. The pain emanating from where his fingernail once resided made it difficult to concentrate. Nevertheless, as if God's Spirit provided him with momentary inspiration filling him with courage, he firmly replied, "You are."

Manuel was momentarily taken aback. "So, the Padre has *cojones* under that cassock after all," he thought to himself. "You have to admire that," he admitted approvingly with a slight smile. He had done enough of these investigations to know that this one wasn't going to talk anytime soon. True, all of them eventually talk given enough time. Unfortunately, time is something Manuel lacked. Unbeknownst to Manuel, the priest actually knew nothing and truly had nothing to report. Even if he did know something, it really wouldn't matter all that much. If truth be told, Padre Pedro abhorred politics and had always been leery of communists. He was one of the 2,500 Catholic priests, out of 3,000 on the island, who was a Spaniard, trained during the Franco dictatorship and highly influenced by the bitter Spanish Civil War victory over communism – a war which clothed itself in heavy religious overtones. The only reason he was in Cuba was because he was being punished. He was in ecclesiastical exile, cast out from his homeland for pissing off a bishop when he questioned the Church's close ties with the Spanish government. Not that he was a revolutionary. Padre Pedro simply questioned the Church linkage to the Franco regime, or any other regime for that matter, as an unwise association. He believed that whenever church and politics mixed, the church ended up on the losing side of that equation. Still, he was in full agreement with the 1937 pontifical encyclical *Divini Redemptoris*, which understood Catholicism and Marxism as mutually exclusive. And while the document was written as a reaction to the excesses of the Spanish Civil War, Padre Pedro felt it was a solid pronouncement warning against the evils of any type of atheist movement which could engulf the world, if not the Church herself.

"Padre, Padre, we should probably do to you what you are doing to Cuba – making it blind with false ideologies." Clinching his cigar between his lips, the sergeant thought of calling one of "Batista's eye specialists," those who mastered a particular technique used to intimidate people. The eye of the one being interrogated was removed. The investigator would then deliver the eye to the family members or accomplices. They were then encouraged to speak, lest they too face a similar fate. The prospect of losing their own eye usually led them to betray anyone and everyone. But why bother, time was running out and a night of festivities with the delectable Celia awaited. Making up his mind at that very moment, the young cop unholstered his 38 Colt police-issued revolver, pushed it against the base of Padre Pedro's skull, and gently pressed the trigger.

If the Batista regime were to fall, no doubt Manuel would be marched up against a wall and shot for actions such as this. Patriots of one regime quickly become human rights violators in the next. And a change in regimes was definitely possible. Rumor had it that Santa Clara, the capital of Las Villas province and the fourth largest city in the Republic, was vulnerable to rebel attacks. If they were to succeed there, then there would be nothing standing between the *comunistas* and La Habana. Although almost four thousand soldiers were being sent to finally crush the rebel's small forces, Manuel simply didn't want to take any chances. Always a cautious man, witnesses like Padre Pedro could complicate his life if the rebels were to succeed. He sensed the mood of the public was growing more boldly against Batista. Best to tie up loose ends now he thought. That is why three days ago on Sunday, when there were fewer people working at the police station, he broke into the personnel office and took his own file out of the cabinet. He wanted to make sure no documentation existed linking him to the work he did.

Looking at his watch he noticed it was 6 pm. If he wanted to pick up Celia on time he had to leave now. He had to go home, get a bite, bathe, and get ready for a night on the town. Ordering his subordinates to clean up the interrogation room, he quickly went to his office to collect a few items. Straightening the tie of his ill-fitted police uniform which hung like a tent on his thin frame, Manuel adjusted the police cap upon his head which covered most of his blond hair while discreetly concealing his receding hair line. As he left the notorious Police Station #5, he noticed small groups of people by the main front door with pictures of family members or loved ones. They just stood there holding a picture of someone who had disappeared, hoping anyone leaving the station might provide them with some information. He strolled by a group of four older women wearing black and gray dresses that might have been fashionable twenty years earlier. Devout, they were holding rosaries and silently praying as their fingers rubbed each individual bead. Accompanied by an older priest, they stood in vigil hoping against hope for any news concerning their beloved pastor. From the corner of his eye, Manuel caught a glimpse of the grinning image of Padre Pedro in the photo. He stopped and looked around. There were no other police officers leaving or entering the building at the time, not that it would have mattered.

Looking at the picture of the smiling baby-face priest with jet black hair and bedroom eyes flashing a toothy smile, he shifted his gaze into the eyes of the oldest woman, and he held out his hand with his palm facing upward. He needed some extra pocket change for tonight's revelry and God was obviously providing him with an opportunity. Quickly one of the women searched in her purse and found five pesos which she quickly placed in his palm. He looked around one more time then gazed back at the woman while slightly moving his hand up and down to indicate more was required. The two other women opened their purses, and each pulled out a few more pesos and also placed them into his open palm. Quickly closing his hand into a fist and shoving the money into his pocket he looked into the blue eyes of the oldest of the three, her hair completely white as opposed to the other two who were simply graying. Without ever saying a word, he just shook his head from side-to-side and walked away. No words were needed, the women clearly understood the message. Their cherished priest was no more. As the young cop strutted away, turning the corner, he could hear their sobs turn into wails, pleading with a silent God for an answer as to why he allowed such tragedies to occur. A waste of tears for a communist wolf in sheep's clothing, the sergeant thought. Oh well, he couldn't be bothered. His thoughts turned to Celia and the cure she would soon be providing for his illness.

Out of Africa

"Aaaaah." Pure pleasure. The sound of relief. The sound of surrender tinged with ecstasy. The blazing sun may be at its highest point in the sky baking the hot, humid, and sticky African day; but in the refreshing cool clear waters of the Osun River, she found the perfect antidote for what ailed her; specifically, the pounding tension migraine which made it difficult for her to concentrate, let alone strategize. "What am I going to do?" the perplexed goddess asked herself. She was deeply troubled by the plight faced by her precious devotees. Rage caused by their senseless quandary clouded her thinking. That she had to act was not a question. She was just unsure as to what to do. Maybe a reprieve, seeking self-care and refuge within her domain - the river – might provide enough momentary tranquility to consider possible options. Slipping out of her clothes, she eased her naked body into the energizing waters where she always found safety, security, and clarity.

She may not be the most powerful deity; nevertheless, the petite Ochún is a formidable *orisha* in her own right. Like Oggún, the god of war, she too belongs to the Yoruba pantheon of quasi-deities who serve as protectors and guides for all humanity, exercising authority over different aspects of nature, the body, and human encounters. Olodumare, from whom sprung forth all life and energy, was and continues to be the gran originator of existence. Shortly after creating Obatalá, credited with forming the land on the once watery earth, the omnipotent and omniscient Supreme Being felt compassion for the lonely deity. "It is not good for a god to be alone," Olodumare reasoned. He gathered several smooth flat stones and placed them on the dirt floor in a circle around the mighty Obatalá. Then Olodumare poured his *ashé* upon these stones.

This *ashé* emanates from the immortal and transcendent Olodumare as sacred energy, neither seen nor personified, neither good nor evil. All which inhabits life or exhibits power has *ashé*. One can find *ashé* in the energy produced by the blood of living creatures being spilled, or by the movement of water, the blowing of wind, or the consuming hunger of fire. Pouring Olodumare's *ashé* upon each stone caused them to come to life, taking on human form, some male, others female, and some in-between representing the fluidity of sexuality. One of the last stones to receive *ashé* would become Ochún. If Obatalá occupies the highest post within the *orisha* pantheon, then Ochún is ranked the undermost, the most junior of all the *orishas*. However, one should never underestimate her power despite her low ranking within the patriarchal hierarchy.

The *orishas*, at first, had no real special purpose or powers. They simply existed to serve as companions to the fatherly Obatalá. Whenever humans required divine intervention, they would have to make their supplications known to Obatalá, who would undertake a toilsome journey to the home of Olodumare, who would then give Obatalá the necessary *ashé* to answer the prayers of these mere pesky humans who were ceaselessly bitching and complaining about everything. *¡No es lo que joden, sino lo seguido que lo hacen!*[*] The process of answering their petty prayers was cumbersome, exhausting, and time consuming. Soon, Olodumare grew weary of the demands for which gods are supposedly responsible. Being an all-powerful deity was very taxing. He craved to retire from these duties. Surely there had to be a more efficient way by which *ashé* could flow to where it was needed most. One day Obatalá had an idea, a possible solution. "Release me of this onerous task," he pleaded. "Make each *orisha* an intermediary and provide them with sufficient *ashé* to answer prayers on their own so I can stop playing this never-ending role of errand boy." Olodumare considered Obatalá's proposal. Since he too was drained of the tedious process, Obatalá's plan was worth implementing.

Olodumare proceeded to divide up his powers among the different *orishas*, giving one power over metals and war,

---

[*] It's not that they bitch but how often they do it.

another the power of healing, another the power over divination, and so on. Ochún was the last to receive a domain and the *ashé* to rule. To her he gave the power over desires of the heart and flesh. All cultures know her, but by different names – whether it be Venus or Aphrodite, Freya or Rati. But Ochún is more than simply the patron goddess of love and eros, she also embodies the sacred dimensions of flowing waterways. Thus, one should never be surprised to find her lounging on the banks of any fresh-water river. And out of all the rivers of the world, the Osun River, which flows southwards through the heart of Yorubaland towards the Atlantic Gulf of Guinea, best personifies her.

On this particularly sweltering day, deeply troubled by the catastrophe befalling her followers, Ochún savored the placid river's embrace. As she leisurely bathed, she began to feel invigorated, as possible options for dealing with the wrenching tragedy her children face began to percolate. Hours slipped by before she, revived, rejuvenated, and reenergized, slowly emerged from the waters, resolute about what needed to be done. Dripping wet, her dark body glistered in the sunlight. She sat naked under the shade of the mighty ceiba trees which hugged the riverbanks. Untying her coiled-up hair, she released her long cornrow braided strands with cowrie shells tied at the tips; freeing them to cascade down her narrow back. Tenderly she adjusted her strikingly jet-black hair, allowing the ends to caress the voluptuous curves of her hips. As she sipped palm wine, she applied a captivating perfume. If a passerby would have stumbled upon this picturesque grooming scene and spied the stark-naked goddess admiring herself in a hand mirror, they - regardless of gender - would have been overcome with desire, concluding there was no other as stunning as she in all of Africa. Of course, if Ochún would have noticed the impertinent gaze of a human admirer, she would have dismissed them with a haughty glance.

As she gently adjusted her hair with her favorite tortoise shell braid comb, the numerous gold bracelets which adorned her slim wrists clinked and chimed, producing the most seductive musical enrapture ever heard by human ears, an alluring and intoxicating siren. As soon as she felt sufficiently dried by the warmth of the African sun, she stood up and put on a revealing flowing skirt whose rim was ornamented with tiny mirrors, gold bells, and cowrie shells, and tied a yellow handkerchief around her petite waist to keep the skirt firmly in place. She hid within the folds of her skirt a small gourd of *oñí* - honey. It is said that whenever she rubs her fingers, dripping with the sweet sticky fluid of her gourd, across the quivering lips of any god or human - male or female – desire is elicited, and erotic abandonment incited. After all, she is the personification of a binary female sensuality who represents love and lust.

As the youngest and most sensual of all the *orishas*, she has been dismissed as being too preoccupied with epicurean delights to care for the needs of her devotees. Yes, she does revel in nightlong dancing and parties; but she is no empty-headed party girl. She possesses a discerning intelligence and a caring heart. On this particular day she was in deep thought, anxious over the fate of her beloved children, those under her protection, and those who were not. While bathing and combing her hair she reflected upon the helplessness she felt as she witnessed them being kidnapped and sold into slavery, sent in chains to some far-off island called Cuba.

Shackled and overcrowded within the odious bowels of monstrous wooden canoes, the precious children of Yorubaland would sail toward the setting sun, never to be seen or heard from again. A minimum amount of space was allotted to ensure the maximum number of bodies could be packed into these ships. Manacled to wooden planks, entombed in stifling darkness, lying in their own vomit and shit, barely surviving the voyage, they cried out the names of their *orishas*, but their supplications never rose higher than the ship's lower deck. Or so they thought. Ochún heard their cries and was deeply moved. Several of the young maidens were kept on deck to satisfy the sexual appetites of the crew. This enraged Ochún the most. Only a goddess, unlike male deities, can ever truly understand the unique peril all women face.

How could Ochún abandon her devotees in their hour of need. She sought the advice of her sister Yemayá, the maternal *orisha* whose domain are the oceans. Yemayá recognized that even as potent as they were as goddesses, the *orishas* were nevertheless impotent to prevent this unfolding human catastrophe. "Those who possess power and privilege, whether they be deities like us or mere humans," Yemayá advised, "is to be present with the powerless in their hour of need, to simply walk in solidarity with the disenfranchised." Ochún realized what she had to do. She would accompany them in their tragic journey to this distant island. Not all the *orishas* chose this path. Of the 1,700 deities worshiped in Yorubaland, only about twenty to twenty-five travelled with their devotees to the Caribbean

Before she departed for the far-off island, she asked Yemayá for a favor, "Straighten my hair and lighten my skin complexion so it could resemble the color of *cobre* - copper. If I'm going to Cuba, then I want to go as a *mulata,* so that one day I can become the Mother of all Cubans - masters and slaves, whites and blacks, Spaniards and Africans. All Cubans will eventually join together in worshipping me." But when Ochún arrived in Cuba, she first went into hiding. If she wanted to be present among her enslaved children, she would have to put on the white Catholic mask of Spanish deities to conceal her black African face. *Ashé* made this transformation possible. Because all which exists contains *ashé,* the *orishas* as universal beings, manifest themselves in the religious symbols and figures of other faith traditions. What supposedly superior Spaniards fail to see, African slaves quickly recognize. Ochún made herself known through one particular Medieval Catholic statute white people worshipped - La Virgen de la Caridad del Cobre. She would eventually reveal herself through this Catholic empty shell on a cloudy morning ninety-nine years after the first of her devotees disembarked in chains on Cuban soil. She could have appeared to the local Spanish priest or even to the bishop but chose to make her presence known to those who had been rejected.

"Wake up Rodrigo," Juan softly said in his native Taíno language as he shook his older brother. Since the Spaniards first planted their flag upon Indigenous soil and started decimating their people, few of the original inhabitants remained. In the name of Jesús, women were raped, men thrown to the dogs to be literally ripped apart, children disemboweled. Stones and sticks were no match for swords of steel. Naked bodies did not have a chance before full solid iron plate armor. Avarice led to cruelties so unbearable, indigenous mothers chose drowning their infants in the river as a better alternative than existence under sadistic Christian rule. The de Hoyos brothers were among the few who remained since the genocidal invasion.

The sun had yet to break into the September day of 1612, and already they were running late. Starting work before the sun rose and finishing hours after it set, day in and day out, left little time for the body to fully rest. "*Coño*," replied Rodrigo, one of the few Spanish words he knew, as he rubbed the weariness out of his eyes. Laying semi-awaked in the cramp *bohío* he turned to his brother Juan who was still lying next to him. The small wood-frame hut covered by a roof thatched with dried palm leaves was barely large enough to accommodate the two boys when laying stretched out on the dirt floor to sleep. In darkness they put on some rags, the throw away clothes once wore by their Spanish overseers. While the rooster slept, the two lanky teenagers, with bellies growling with hunger, made their way, through the thick morning fog, to the shore of Nipe Bay, located in the northeastern corner of the island. The ground under their bare feet was still wet from the morning dew. Soon, a ten-year-old African boy named Juan Moreno joined the de Hoyos brothers. The three, all orphans, lived a life of deprivation among the discarded. The fact that they all had Spanish names demonstrates the success of the conquest and pacification of the island. They communicated with each other in broken Spanish, none of them spoke fluently, but knew enough to be able to work together.

When they arrived at Nipe Bay, about a mile from their *bohío*, they boarded a canoe hewed from a single tree trunk and went out in search of salt. The waters that cloudy morning was calm and inviting, even though it was hurricane season. The bay was an important source of salt needed at the town's slaughterhouses for the curing of meat. Maybe if they were lucky, they might also catch some fish to satisfy their hunger. And if they were unable to catch any fish, they hoped to find enough salt to exchange for enough food to last until tomorrow, when they would be forced to repeat this same tedious routine again, and every day for the rest of their existence, barely subsisting. *"Puta españoles,"* they often muttered under their breaths.

Around 5:30 in the morning, when Rodrigo and the two Juans were halfway across the bay rowing toward Cayo Francés, a violent storm broke out. *"Coño,* they simultaneously exclaimed, taken by surprise. The clouds suddenly darkened.

Lightening flashed as its long fingers tried to touch the waters surrounding the rickety vessel. Enormous waves were whipped up, crashing down upon them as their canoe was tossed to and fro. The howling gale threatened to capsize the canoe as water filled the hull. As the de Hoyos brothers tried to steady the vessel, the black boy attempted to bail the acuminating water. Fear gripped the three lads as they began to realize they were going to drown. At any moment their craft would simply capsize. All was lost. In desperation, they turned to their ancestral spirits for help, crying out to them in their own languages, as loud as they could so as to be heard above the fury of the storm. The indigenous brothers sought the zemis, the spirits of nature, while the black boy evoked the name of Ochún, the goddess whom his mother, before her death, often offered supplications accompanied with sacrifices. He didn't know much about this goddess from the old country, except that since his ancestor's arrival on the island, they often turned to her in moments of need. No sooner had the boys uttered words reviving their relationship to the spirits of their ancestors, then the storm - as quickly as it came upon them - subsided.

Relieved and grateful for the now placid sea, they collapsed in the boat and tried to breathe as they nervously chuckled. That is when Juan Moreno noticed in the distance what appeared to be a white bundle floating toward them. "What could that be?" they asked each other. Maybe something of worth from some shipwreck which did not survive the storm. "Maybe treasure," Rodrigo suggested.

Steering the canoe toward the object, they came close enough to make out a plank of wood upon which had been mounted a carved sixteen-inch clay statue of the Christian goddess known as *la virgin María*. In one hand she carried the baby Jesús, in the other a golden cross. Astonishingly, the statue was dry and had not even been splashed by the salty spray. Unbeknownst to the boys because they were illiterate, the words "*Yo soy la virgin de la caridad*"* were inscribed at her feet.

The de Hoyos brothers were not impressed with the Christian statue, for they soundly rejected the religion of their oppressors, and frankly, continued to do so even after this apparent miraculous event. What they did not reject however was the spiritual world which constantly uses recognizable symbols by which to communicate with mere humans. They scooped up the statue from the waters and took it to the town of Barajagua, telling everyone about their adventures and the supposed miracle they witnessed. Juan Moreno, the African boy, was the first to recognize the *ashé* of the statue. His prayers were answered by the *orisha* who journeyed with her children to this godforsaken island. How ironic that the goddess of sexual pleasure chose to masquerade as a virgin. That evening he sacrificed a yellow hen to Ochún in thanksgiving. Thanks to the two Indians and the African, Ochún revealed herself and with time became the mother of all Cubans, declared the Patron Saint of the island by Pope

---

* "I am the Virgin of Charity."

Benedict XV on 10 May 1926; but at a price some would argue was too high. *Blanqueamiento* - her bleaching.

Cuando Salí de Cuba

Manuel did not want the window seat. The pain of seeing his beloved island disappear into the horizon would simply be too much to bear. He let his newlywed Marta, whom he married almost seven months earlier, sit there instead. Her bright yellow dress, filled to the bursting by her voluptuous figure, shone defiantly over the gloom of everyone's mood on the plane. On her lap burbled their eighteen-month-old chubby boy – Miguelito, dressed in an overly-frilled baby white lace sailor shirt and dark navy pants, still dry, thank goodness. His mother beamed and cooed and kissed his fat cheeks, her cheap, yellow-painted metal bracelets jangling as she rocked him quietly, such a happy sight amid such despair.

She looked out of the window but there was little to see because the view was obscured by dark black clouds. Flashes of lightning regularly lit up the interior of the plane, giving everyone – for an instant - a pale and ghostly hue. It was as if Changó, the god of lightning, was just as angry about

Manuel's departure as he was. The plane's passengers, externally crammed together while internally being pulled apart, found themselves in an in-between space, stuck between all they knew and an unwelcoming unknown future, a future which they would occupy for their remaining years of life. So many conflicting emotions. Elation and relief about leaving in one piece, safe and alive, before it was too late. Apprehension and anxiety for what lay ahead. Anguish and grief for having had to wave farewell to families they may never see again. Distress and regret for those left behind. Dread and nervousness about the storm brewing outside rocking the plane. Confusion and shame as to what would become their new identity as foreigners in a strange and hostile land which most on the plane perceived to be an inferior culture. They felt they were being pushed toward a land of fools and loudmouths who may have abundance but lacked sophistication, rootedness, or tradition.

Marta and Manuel would eventually grow old together and die as another pair of broken-hearted Cubans. Her bright blue skies would no longer hang above their heads; or her ocean waters provide its warm loving embrace. How does one forge an identity in exile? What if one's love for la Habana remains stronger than one's allegiance to Babylon? How can one call themselves a Cuban without a Cuba? Never again able to lay on her hot tropical beaches, their bones instead interned in a cold foreign land which will never accept them, despising their very presence.

Miguelito would witness the humiliation as a small boy of seeing white teenagers spit on his father while calling him a spic. Although Miguelito left the island a baby in arms, he believes he too will eventually die unfulfilled, never having a place to call home. To live in *el exilio* – in exile, far from the land which witnessed your birth, is to never visit *abuela's* home to eat the fruits which grows in her garden. It is to live where what was familiar to one's parents is now foreign. Even if it would have been possible to resettle on the island of Miguelito's birth, it will never compare to the mythical imaginary land which his parents painted for him deep in the recesses of his brain where he learned to cherish and love the illusion as if it was real. He would call himself a Cuban because his mother, nine months after copulating with his father, happened to be living on that particular Caribbean island, a particular stretch of land which resembled a crocodile.

Like many of the passengers that day, this was the first time the entire de la Cruz family had ever flown on a plane. The ride was bumpy in more ways than one. Manuel sat next to his family in the center tan Palomar chair, silently puffing on his cigarette, gazing intently at the closed door to the cockpit, but seeing only the nothingness which lay ahead. Next to him, sitting on the aisle seat was an adolescent pretending to be a man. *El pobre*, poor kid Manuel thought, he must be leaving all his family behind in his escape from communism. He leaned over toward the teenager and gently whispered,

"Don't worry, *volveremos*."* It was more a declaration of his own resolve than a measure of comfort. The skinny boy with unkept brown hair did not acknowledge him but nervously swallowed and clung tighter to his box of Cohibas. All passengers on the plane went into exile with similar boxes, but not because they were connoisseurs. When they arrived, there would be *yanqui* aficionados waiting at the airport ready to buy their precious cargo now that it was becoming harder to get a hold of the finest cigars in the world. This would be the passengers' first profitable lesson in savage capitalism.

The Pan American DC 8 flight from La Habana to Miami was only about fifty-five minutes long. Fifty-five minutes to start a new life in a foreign land. Fifty-five minutes before becoming an alien among philistines. Fifty-five minutes to traverse between two worlds, one free, the other enslaved; but which was which? *"Pobre* Cuba," Manuel mused thinking he knew the answer. "We put our trust in the *yanquis*, a stupid people who are more concerned with quick profits, not truly considering the consequences of what was occurring just ninety miles off their shores. If the *yanquis* would not have suspended selling arms to Batista in March of '58, I wouldn't be on this damn plane."

As he sat there wallowing in his predicament, Manuel remembered he once had a desire to visit the land of the mystical *yanquis*, maybe for vacation. But now they, along with everyone else aboard, were leaving their homeland with

---

* We will return.

almost nothing. If it was solely up to him, he never would have had the courage to leave. But Marta resolvedly stated "*¡Para atrás ni para tomar impulso!*"* and that was that. So now they were on a plane with all their earthly possessions reduced to one bulging tan-color faux-leather box suitcase full of clothes and broken dreams. Despite such scant luggage, however, everyone on the plane wore their best suit or dress as if they were attending a semi-formal cocktail party. Manuel's grandfather's watch, the only family memento he treasured, had been confiscated at the airport. "*Gusanos* – maggots have already sucked us dry… *¡Basta!*" snarled the bearded airport security guard. And with an air of contempt, Manuel's watch and gold wedding ring were taken and tossed into a container brimming with the golden remains of those going into *el exilio*. He didn't care much about the ring, but the watch he would miss very much, getting angrier every time he thought of it.

All 258 seats on the plane were occupied. Everyone on board was deathly silent. A few women quietly sobbed as the plane left Cuban airspace. *Comemierdas*, it's too late for tears, Manuel thought. They wouldn't have needed to shed any if they had supported the police, men like him in their crusade against *los barbudos* – the bearded ones. He looked around at his traveling companions with disgust. How many of them hung signs on their front lawns reading "*Fidel, esta es su casa.*"† Unlike these *vendepatrias*, selling the homeland for communist

---

* "Not a backward step even to get momentum!"

† "Fidel, this is your home."

utopias, at least I fought the good fight. How could it have come to this, Manuel thought as the DC 8 climbed to a higher cruising altitude above the threatening clouds to avoid turbulence. How can he be forced to flee the only land he has ever known? He, like so many others, had been caught off guard by how quickly the Batista government capitulated. The rebel's military victories in Santa Clara seemed to have been the last nail driven into the coffin of the regime he had so faithfully served.

After Fidel's men had captured Santa Clara, Manuel, and all other patriots, saw the doom awaiting him by how el Ché exhibited his thirst for blood, specifically by how he treated the chief of police, Colonel Cornelio Rojas, a decent honorable man in his seventies. Rojas led the resistance against the rebels, ordering his men to defend their beloved city, or die doing so. He was captured protecting the police station, convicted in a kangaroo court, and marched up against a wall to be shot. But *el viejo* – the old man had massive *cojones*. Not only did he refuse a blindfold, but when the time came to give the order for his execution, he asked permission, which was granted, to command the firing squad himself. Even his executioners were forced to admire his bravery, for this is the way real men should die. Manuel fantasized about such glories for himself, although he did everything in his power to avoid a similar fate.

Manuel had hoped Batista would have displayed the same *cojones* as Rojas. But alas, it became clear that Batista was only thinking of himself and his political cronies. On December 31st, the last day of the blood-soaked year, he ordered his government and military commanders to gather at Camp Columbia to bid 1958 farewell, although it was more than just the year that was leaving. At about 2 am, he set up a paper-tiger government, resigned as president, boarded a military plane with about forty high ranking officials and their wives – including Manuel's supervisor *coronel* Orlando Piedra - and flew to the Dominican Republic. Of course, Batista's children had secretly left for the U.S. two days earlier, along with a fortune estimated at $300 million, or about a quarter of all the government expenditures of the island. The night Batista fled, Manuel was at the Capri Casino with his date Celia, welcoming in the new year. He kept returning to the Capri, even though he knew the casino's dice were loaded, the drinks watered down, and the slots rigged for low payouts. That's why he stuck to poker, which he was playing around 3 am when the news of Batista's departure, like wildfire, began to spread throughout the bar.

As Manuel continued to play his hand, thoughts of fleeing raced through his mind. Everyone who worked at the casino knew he was a cop. He could not return to his apartment because some resentful neighbors might tip off communist cells which he suspected would soon be roving the city seeking those upon whom to exert years of revenge. He had heard stories growing up of what had occurred in the aftermath of the U.S.-engineered overthrow of the Machado regime. Many people took to the streets as vigilantes, looking for former police officials and discharging their rage upon them. No, Manuel could not risk returning to his apartment just in case the bloodbath of 1933 was to be repeated tonight. With a sigh, he ignored his winning hand and folded. Asking Celia to keep an eye on his chips which he left on the table, he excused himself and walked toward the restroom. At the last minute, rather than turning right to where the bathrooms were, he made a sharp left toward the main doors and slipped out, forever leaving behind the casino and the lovely long-legged Celia.

Once outside, the usual aroma of the streets - café, tobacco mixed with sugar, rum, and sweat - now had a new ingredient, gunpowder. Because some of the firearms on the island were old, many dating to the second world war, the sulfuric smell filled the predawn hours mixing with the more modern pungent nitroglycerin, giving off an aroma which resembled burnt sugar. He could hear gunshots in the distance as old scores were being settled. With no particular destination, he started walking down Calle N making his way to *centro Habana*, wondering what to do, where to go, staying mostly on side streets and alleys. He noticed crowds gathering at the casino's front door as he left. Within minutes they would be inside overturning tables, smashing slot machines, and looting. The barbarians were now in control, convinced by propaganda that their country was turned into some type of whorehouse. He had long ago reinvented the island in his imagination to mask the reality that la Habana was an exotic space created by the United States for puritan-acting whites seeking to satisfy their repressed libidinous appetites. La Habana of 1958 served as a U.S. brothel with Mafia-controlled casinos, the sex and abortion capital of the Western Hemisphere. This is what Manuel was actually defending. Now, the people who have lived under a system which flourished at their expense unleashed decades of pent-up rage against the symbols of the former regime. "*Comemierdas*, can't they see that these casinos created jobs and brought *yanquis* with dollars?" Manuel thought.

As he passed the Cuban Shell Petroleum offices, looters were already inside. He passed a young man with a baseball bat smashing the parking meters. In the mind of this vandal, the meters signified corrupt people, like the ones Manuel supported and protected. Everyone knew the meter coins went directly to a small group of high officials within the regime. If the meter smasher would only have known that the well-dressed stranger with shining black shoes walking past him was a cop, he probably would have smashed Manuel's skull instead. Hours later, Manuel found himself on Calle Virtudes; but tonight, there were no clamoring prostitutes wearing low-cut flowery dresses, they all scattered for safer quarters.

He decided to make his way to Marta's apartment which was located west of *el barrio chino* - Chinatown. As he walked by *Teatro Shanghai* on Calle Zanja, between Campanario and Manrique, the predawn crowd were emptying the theater. They have just finish indulging their lust by watching a live sex show where a black gay man called the Man with the Sleepy Eyes - also known as Superman – deflowered a bleached-blond actress with his supposedly eighteen-inch erect endowment. No doubt the show would have made

Caligula blush. Such establishments catered to the inhibited pleasures of prude American tourists, who for a fifty-dollar roundtrip tickets on a weekend cruise, could take a vacation from their conscience, their faith, and their morality. Manuel, with his blond hair and greenish blue eyes, blended easily with the crowd of mostly North American men leaving the theater, providing momentary cover as he continued his trek westward.

Unlike the tourist surrounding him, Manuel lacked the means by which to leave the island whenever he wanted to and was angry that none of his superiors thought he was important enough to be given a seat on one of the departing planes. He felt frustrated being left behind when he and others like him placed their lives on the line. Now there was the very real possibility that he might be forced to pay the ultimate price for his blind loyalty. Thinking about all he had done for Batista left him feeling betrayed and abandoned, a sentiment that would continue to gnaw at him for the rest of his life.

Soon the crowd of Anglo men thinned as they realized the vacations from morals was unfolding amid a revolution. They quickly made their way to their hotels. Again alone, Manuel spotted more civilians who supported Castro in the streets, so he hurried his pace toward shelter – a place he could rest and think. If he didn't get off the streets soon, it would only be a matter of time before he would be stopped and questioned. Having nowhere to turn, he continued his trek to Marta's place. Surely, she would provide shelter. She did claim he had fathered her bastard son; still, he wasn't sure how he would be received, since he had broken contact with her once she told him she was pregnant. That was around last April as he recalled.

By daybreak, sometime around 6 am, he was still walking up Calle Zanja, toward Marta's apartment, noticing at various intersections how rebel city cells who just yesterday were in hiding were now trying to gain and maintain control of the streets, until at least the rebel armies made their arrival. He quickly slipped from shadow to shadow, refusing to stop, and finally arriving at the sweet-smelling building nicknamed "el cake," due to the pastry shop on the first floor. A journey which probably would have taken less than sixty minutes lasted over three terrifying hours.

As he entered the building, he heard in the distance a crowd singing "*Ya ya ya ya, te ganaste la guerra, Gánate ahora la paz, Que el que haya sido cruel, Tenga su justicia honrada.*"* Manuel would later hear what honorable justice looked like. El Che took over La Cabaña at around 4 am on the second day, an eightieth century fortress located on the eastern side of the harbor's entrance which was used by Batista as a military prison. Guards and prisoners traded places. From there the Revolution's command center was set up to begin taking control of the city. Unknown to Manuel at the time was that his own fellow police officers, along with other *batistianos* – followers of Batista, ex-soldiers, and civil servants, were being

---

* "Ya ya ya ya, you have won the war, Win now the peace, For the one who has been cruel, Have his justice honored."

systematically rounded up and jailed to await trial. If Manuel hadn't acted quickly to remain hidden, no doubt he would have joined them in their cells and in their fate. In about a week they would face firing squads after being convicted by military tribunals. The rebels may be satisfying their bloodthirst today, but Manuel prayed he would survive so that he could witness the day when it would be his turn to return the favor. He hoped he might actually live, due to his precaution, so as to eventually extract revenge. His file was not among those of his fellow police officers when the rebels stormed his station. But there was always the danger he would be recognized; after all, in his line of work, he had made more than a few enemies over the years.

Standing before Marta's door he was afraid to knock. What if she slams the door on his face? Then what? Where would he go? Fortunately for him, she was afraid of all the commotion going on in the streets and felt very alone facing the uncertainties which lay ahead. Besides, she still loved the man who would eventually raise her son and believed that once he saw the boy, he would see the resemblance and claim him as his own. Maybe this Revolution could become a blessing in disguise if it could bring them together as the family she always dreamed of having.

Due to the difficult life she lived, a single mother trying to survive in a *machista* culture, the ideal of family meant everything to Marta. Born in the hills of Santa Clara, she never attended school, remaining illiterate until she slowly taught herself how to read as an adult. When she was a small girl, her father became embroiled in a bar fight, responding to an insult to his honor. Fists flew, knives were drawn, but her father was faster than his opponent. The stabbing landed him in prison, leaving behind his wife and her three young daughters to fend for themselves. Unable to survive, Marta, the middle child, was sold to a rich family to serve as their maid, where she, as a preteen, faced both physical and sexual abuse. Years of oppression had sharpened her street smarts, making her an extremely wise illiterate woman.

Hearing a knock at the door, Marta's early morning *cafecito*, hot and frothy in its tiny yellow porcelain cup, had almost touched her lips but dropped back onto its matching miniature saucer with a clatter. A woman living alone with a newborn was an easy target for men on such a night. She glanced at her sleeping baby and picked up the sharpest kitchen knife she owned before slowly opening the door. Seeing Manuel standing there, hot and sweaty from his long walk over a short distance, caught her by surprise but she threw her arms around him nonetheless and held him tight. Manuel's terror melted away as he buried himself within the strength of her soft and perfumed embrace. He breathed a sigh of relief. In this tiny domestic apartment, with its vase of sunflowers on the little breakfast table, he would be able to bathe, eat, sleep, and think. If anyone was looking for him, they would have no way of knowing he was hiding in this apartment. He would be safe here.

Although she didn't say anything about it at the time, Marta had immediately seen the look of despair on his ashen face and the state of his clothes when she opened the door to him at six in the morning. She understood Cuba's state of affairs very well, what had been happening in the hills, and how the situation had now arrived right to her doorstep. As the days went by and Manuel stayed put, she continued to say nothing about his abrupt arrival, keeping their conversation light and casual. There was nothing to do but patiently wait until Manuel found his strength and his backbone.

At first, if Manuel ventured out, it was only at night when he could move in and out of the shadows, a way of traveling that, oddly enough, had always made him feel safe and comfortable. It was too dangerous to walk the streets in daylight where he might be spotted. By January 7th, he realized all was lost. Fidel made his triumphant entry into la Habana, and the U.S. officially recognized the new government. *Comemierdas*. Manuel knew he had to leave the island, but how? He began growing a beard to help hide his appearance. This would buy him time, but at any moment he could be caught. Safety was now contingent on his renewed relationship with Marta, so he swallowed his pride and began to shower attention on the baby. Miguelito would become his ticket out, avoiding *el paredón*, a rendezvous with a firing squad. In fairness, he did try to love this child as best he could, even though he never fully accepted him as his own. He would raise Miguelito, putting food on the table and clothes on his back, teaching him what it meant to be a macho. He never hit the child, although physical blows might have been more merciful than those which were emotional and psychological.

Grudgingly, he had to admit he developed a real affection for the child, which earned him loyalty from the child's mother. Marta believed Ochún, the goddess of love, had finally heard her petitions and accepted her offerings.

The next evening Castro gave his first national speech from Camp Columbia, the same spot from where over a week earlier Batista departed. As he was pleading for peace and unity, someone released two white doves, one of which landed on his shoulder. An "act of Providence" is how Cuba's oldest daily newspaper, the conservative *Diario de la Marina*, would describe the event on its front page the following day. For the Catholics in the audience, or who were watching by television, it was like when the Holy Spirit had descended as a dove upon Jesús after his baptism. But for followers of the *orishas*, it was reminiscent of when Obatalá, the fatherly *orisha* of peace, tranquility, and harmony, appeared as a dove hovering over the physical brawl taking place between his two warrior sons Changó the god of thunder and Oggún the god of war, bringing an end, however temporary, to the brother's feuding.

Peace was an illusion quickly denied by January 13th, when Castro decreed that the trials of Batista's criminals would continue until all of them had faced justice, with justice defined as a firing squad. The sports stadium, able to hold 18,000 spectators, would be used for public military tribunals, where the people cried out *¡Paredón!* To the Wall! Three months later, almost five hundred people met their fate lined up against that wall, many of whom were Manuel's colleagues and acquaintances. Gradually, after a few months, the executions began to taper off. By then, Manuel, sporting a full beard and convinced he was safe, started venturing out again during the day. He even managed to obtain a janitorial job at an office building. But during his off hours, he became engaged in counterrevolutionary activities. It was Manuel's job to assist in the coordination of acts of sabotage throughout La Habana. He had left many bombs at churches that were supportive of the Revolution. In reality, he was not the one who actually left the bombs. He would send Marta, carrying baby Miguelito, to attend the church service. No one would have suspected a mother and child. Once the Mass was over, she would depart with the baby, leaving behind the baby pouch containing the bomb under the pew. They never told Miguelito, once he was an adult, if any of these had exploded, only that most of the time they were attached to a warning note demanding that the church stop supporting the Revolution, or else, the next time it would explode.

Their involvement in counter revolutionary activities meant it was only a matter of time before they would be caught. Marta kept insisting they should flee before they too would be marched up against a wall to face a firing squad like so many of Manuel's colleagues. Then what would happen to her precious child? The G2, the new Cuban political police, had already begun to close in on him. They didn't know his name yet, but they knew that there were some people on the island in league with the CIA for a possible U.S.-backed invasion.

Fortunately, he was never recognized, although once he thought he was spotted on a bus by four old women wearing black and gray outdated dresses. They kept looking at him intently, as though they were trying to remember him, whispering among themselves. As soon as the bus made its next scheduled stop, Manuel, always overly cautious, hopped off. He noticed as the bus pulled away, the eyes of one of the women, still gazing at him from the bus window, widened, as if she finally remembered – but it was too late. As the bus rolled away Manuel slipped into a side street, making his way back to Marta's apartment, committing to never being so careless again. The day he was spotted, he decided to listen to Marta and begin making arrangements to leave the island. But leaving as a single man would be difficult. If he was married and had a child, it would be easier to obtain a tourist visa from the U.S. government. On September 8, 1959, Manuel finally married Marta and Miguelito ceased technically being a bastard – although those who would later know him as an adult might insist otherwise.

His family, though, were not too keen about accepting Marta as a de la Cruz, believing he was marrying down. When his paternal grandmother first set eyes on the boy, she lifted his shirt and turned him around to examine his lower backside, checking for the hereditary pair of freckle dots. All de la Cruz men have this birthmark, she had announced. Once she saw the small discoloration of his skin, she declared the child's father was Manuel and grudgingly accepted the boy as her grandson. Unbeknown to her, those same marks faded by the time he was a toddler. The rest of Manuel's family were not so convinced and throughout Miguelito's youth he continuously heard rumors about his dubious paternity. His father's sister Adela made it a point to make sure he would know the truth even though a ten-year-old boy should not have to hear such things. Manuel's side of the family never forgave Marta for tricking him into marriage to make the pregnancy respectable, whether the baby was his or not. At the dawn of the Cuban Revolution, however, Marta and her baby were Manuel's ticket off the island.

They say that behind every man there is a great woman. In reality, in front of every great woman there is a man blocking her. Because of Marta, Manuel mustered the courage and resolute to leave the island for the unknown. He may have been the supposed head of the household, but it was her who would become the driving force. It was always Marta and Manuel, never Manuel and Marta. And while she orchestrated the departure of the island for the United States, it was because she feared what would happen to Manuel if he was ever caught rather than a desire to live among the *yanquis*. She never really trusted them, getting to know them better while serving their meals and living off their tips at the hotel where she worked as a waitress. The U.S. may have freedom and wealth, but if truth be told, she always thought their affluence came at too high a price. These poor North Americans, she would ruminate, think themselves rich, but all they have is their money which contributes to the poverty of their soul, a paucity caused by their covetous eye which always look to own that which belongs to others.

Once Manuel was officially married, it took months to obtain the fake letters of reference attesting to his upright moral character and a tourist visa for his new family. With visas in hand by the end of March 1960, he called his old contacts at Pan American Airlines and reserved two seats on the next flight out of the country, which would be the very next morning, April 1st. Around the same time, the Eisenhower administration was giving a green light for the eventual military overthrow of the Castro's regime. Operation Mongoose became a covert plan orchestrated by the CIA, better known by the students of history as the Bay of Pigs fiasco. Although the de la Cruz would be living in exile when the operation to overthrow Castro took place, Manuel's counter-revolutionary acts served as an important component in setting the groundwork for the invasion, even though it failed. As he was preparing to leave, the U.S. embassy was closing and diplomatic ties between the two countries were reaching the breaking point.

Lightning flashed and the plane shook again. Manuel continued to stare forward but could not resist an occasional admiring glance at the pair of lovely long legs topped-off by the stewardess' short skirt brushing past him to check on other passengers. He's not sure what to expect once they landed, but beneath his anxiety was a flicker of enjoyment each time he smelled that foreign American perfume wafting by. He never bedded a *yanqui*, he thought, an oversight he looked forward to correcting. How long will this exile last, he wondered. How soon before the *yanquis* invade and get rid of this monstrous regime. Each year he would defiantly toast the coming New Year with "next year in La Habana;" suitcases psychologically packed in his back closets ready to return at any given moment.

The pilot announced they would soon be landing so they better buckle up. Manuel took a deep breath to brace for the uncertainty which laid ahead and recorded all the details of this flight into his trained policeman's memory. Miguelito, on the other hand, slept peacefully, unaware and unconcerned in his mother's arms.

Rats and Roaches

His mother Marta sat on an old wooden stool in the middle of a stark room which accommodated a couple of mismatched pieces of donated furniture. She was weeping. "*¿Por qué Dios mío? ¿Por qué?*"* The room was dark and grey, as if it was dusk with none of the lights yet turned on, either to save on the cost of electricity or as a result of some unpaid utility bill. Although Miguelito at the time could not understand what made the room smell the way it did, he would never forget the pungent, musky aroma of rat droppings mixed with the strong ammonia of their urine. Decades later, when he traveled on subways or walked past an alleyway, an accidental whiff would immediately trigger his self-shaming anxiety of never being able to be fully clean. The stench of childhood poverty never quite washes away regardless as to how financially secure one becomes later in

---

* "Why my God? Why?"

life. What Miguelito retained more than the sensory stimuli was a feeling of helplessness, of knowing something was terribly wrong beyond his capacity to comprehend. Until then, he had only cried in the typical ways of a child. But this was the first time he witnessed his mother crying, and as her grief became inextricably mixed together with the retch-inducing odor to which he had become accustom, he knew that the safety he had always felt by her embrace was now somehow in jeopardy. Mami's crying meant she was vulnerable, and if she was defenseless before a cruel world, then Miguelito's wellbeing could never be assured. For the first time in his life, he knew existence to be scary, and so joined her with his own tears.

With his toddler eyes and understanding, he gazed around the dark ugly room which served as both living, dining and bedroom, and saw the cause of her anguish. The ceiling and walls appeared to be moving, or at least this is how a three-year-old boy interpreted reality. As he watched more intensely, it became obvious that the ceiling wasn't *actually* moving, but rather hundreds, if not thousands of roaches were rapidly crawling all over the ceiling as a writhing and convulsing indoor sky of horror. On an old nightstand below, even the statue of the lady with the three men in the boat to which his mom lit a daily candle, took on a few extra passengers, who were waving bon voyage with their antennas, as if wishing Miguelito and his mother a fond farewell.

New York slum buildings were notorious for being a haven for all sorts of vermin. Generations of poverty-stricken tenants stretching back to the late nineteenth century would use flour and water to create a sticky paste to hang decorative wallpaper in a vain attempt to add beauty to dismal habitation. Each new tenant simply covered over the existing wallpaper of the previous occupant with their own aesthetic representation. But over time, a tasty perpetual food supply had formed between the generational layers of these papered walls, ensuring the wellbeing of future roaches.

When the de la Cruz family first arrived at the States as refugees and moved into a slum apartment, there didn't seem to be *that* many roaches. While the lights were turned on, they hid safely within the edible walls, waiting for the opportune time to make their appearance. Unfortunately, like natural disasters, pandemics, and political upheavals, there is never a convenient time for calamity to strike. The platoons of roaches were awakened from their slumber when Marta first ignited the apartment's stove. The blast of heat quickly spread throughout their tunnels, making them run for their cockroach lives, bursting forth from their hiding place, scattering out into the room. There were so many roaches it seemed as if the ceiling was an ocean whose waves lapped against the bordering walls. This fragment of a memory remains so real, so vivid that if Miguelito were to close his eyes some six decades later, like an old black-and-white 35-millimeter film, he could still see the scene projected behind his eyelids.

Although quite young, this image was forever seared into Miguelito's consciousness, and no doubt it will probably be the last thing he recollects as the last electrical discharges in his hippocampus fire off while he lays on his deathbed waiting for the next stage of existence – if a next stage even exists. Miguelito continued to wonder in later years if this horrific scene was even an experience he actually remembered. After all, reality and the imaginary always seem to blur, fusing and confusing what occurred with what we convince ourselves occurred. Maybe this vivid memory was but an intense recounting of an event retold to him by Miguelito's mother, so shocking that he unconsciously reclaimed it as his own story.

The triumph of the 1959 Cuban Revolution occurred less than three months after Miguelito's birth. Shortly after the revolution, his father – a cop - became a marked man. The de la Cruz family left the island with just one suitcase each. Arriving in Miami in April 1960, they made their way to a freezing New York City, far from the warmth of the Caribbean but where jobs existed nonetheless; jobs needed by his parents if they hoped to survive in a new inhospitable land. In New York they discovered Third-World slums grinding against First-World neighborhoods. The poverty of the Global South for them existed at 428 West 56 Street, apartment 4-B, a tenement built the year in which the twentieth century began, just two blocks away from the docks in Hell's Kitchen. This was before Hell's Kitchen became the trendy neighborhood it is today. Three years before the de la Cruz family moved into the building, Larry Kent and Carol Lawrence were photographed nearby for the iconic album cover for Leonard Bernstein's new musical "West Side Story."

Miguelito learned how to count on the old rickety staircase leading to and from his apartment on the fourth floor. With each step he took going up or down, he would proudly say a number in Spanish, although not necessarily in chronological order: "*Uno, dos, tres, cinco, nueve, ocho, diez.*" The long-standing building with its century-old façade still stands today, with the inside completely remodeled and updated in 1989. But in 1960, this was one of the many rat- and roach-infested tenement "homes" intended for the darker disposable residents of the city. There was only one bathroom per tenement floor to be shared with the other floor's inhabitants. The conditions were so unsanitary that Miguelito's parents made him pee in an old cracker tin can in their apartment rather than use the floor's sole bathroom. It was safer too, because most of their "neighbors" were pimps, sex workers and drug addicts, living in their own single-room cells. Over time, other immigrant Latino families ready to serve as disgruntled soldiers in capitalism's reserve army of laborers, found themselves in this callous arctic city. They moved into the neighborhood, nudging out, one by one, the previous generation of immigrant residents.

On hot summer days someone would open the fire hydrant and the filthy, dirty cracked sidewalks speckled with cigarette butts and reeking from dog turds would become a magical waterpark. But no amount of childhood imagination could mask the thick air of desperation which hung heavy upon all, a malodourous city smell choking all who vainly clung to hope. Empty refrigerators slumbering on the corners like the broken bodies of the unemployed, and alleys littered with used syringes and wasted lives described the only neighborhood Miguelito's parents could afford. Immigrants in those days were not receiving government assistance. It would be years before it became advantageous - for Cold War propaganda purposes - to support and help those fleeing from communism. For now, being among the first wave of Cubans coming to the shores of New York City meant there was no succor, just the random kindness of strangers.

The de la Cruz family was imprisoned in these slums for about three years. On this particular day, the earliest moment of life Miguelito could remember, his mother worked like a dog to clean the apartment, seeking to drown-out the putrid smell of rodent feces with bleach. She was expecting guests that evening and regardless of economically being forced to live in murky conditions, she wanted everything to look as spotless and decent as possible. Spending more than they could afford, she bought a slab of pork to brine in a marinade of garlic, cumin, citrus and beer, which would be roasted for four hours in the yet-to-be-used oven. Despite the bleak tenement surrounding, she sought – if just for a fleeting moment - to recreate the middle-class existence she had finally achieved back in the old country. However, when she stepped into the living room shortly before her guests were scheduled to arrive, all she saw, despite her efforts, was a sea of parasites all over the ceiling and the walls, taunting her and reminding her that regardless of how hard she tried, in this country, she would always be a filthy spic; a cockroach people living among the cockroaches.

Before ever developing the ability to remember, it was made all too clear to Miguelito that he did not belong. Just two months after immigrating to the United States, they received an official government affidavit dated June 14, 1960, a document which neither he nor his parents could read. Marta and Manuel would receive their own individualized letters. These correspondences were typed on very thin onion-skin paper with the heading: "United States Department of Justice, Immigration and Naturalization Service." While Miguelito mostly babbled, Marta and Manuel fretted. "*¿Que es esto?* – What is this?" they kept asking themselves throughout the sleepless night, full of dread as to what these letters might signify. Once a translator was found a few days later, they discovered the terrifying news. "*¿Qué vamos hacer?* – What are we going to do?" They were being placed on notice that they overstayed their tourist visas. Assigned case number A12 051 881, Miguelito, who had no sense of time, was informed he had entered the country a few months earlier, on April 1, and had remained past April 30 – after his tourist visa expired - without proper authorization. Citing Section 242 of the Immigration and Nationality Act, the letters informed Miguelito and his parents that unless they could show just cause as to why they should not be immediately deported, they would have to leave the country posthaste.

If this event had taken place in 2020 rather than 1960, there probably would have been no letter. ICE agents in military gear would have busted through their front door before the start of the day to deliver the news in person. As bad as anti-Latiné sentiments were during the 1960s, hatred for the immigrant has only gotten worse as more sadistic government tactics have been implemented by both conservative and liberal Administrations. Rather than a request to voluntarily appear before a magistrate, the de la Cruz family would instead be dragged away in handcuffs. Miguelito, no doubt, would have been torn from his mother's arms and locked in a cage along with so many other "undesirable" children along the border. And it would not matter that he had lighter skin coloring than the other children in the cage; the lifetime emotional scars which would have been carved into his psychic would have been just as damning. How ironic, that during the Jim and Jane Crow era, where discrimination and violence were the norm, the idea of toddlers behind bars remained a somewhat abhorrent act even among racists. Now, it has been normalized and legitimatized.

Fortunately, Miguelito was not an undocumented child in 2020 when immigration laws became more vindictive. In lieu of forced expatriation, the de la Cruz family were ordered to voluntarily self deport. Instead of leaving, they quickly moved out of the slums and into a black ghetto seeking to live in the shadows until they could obtain the elusive green card. Besides living with the fear of deportation, Miguelito's father had to live with the indignity of being abused by employers who paid him off-the-books. One of the jobs Manuel obtained was working at the 1964/65 World Fair being held in Flushing

Meadow. He was hired to wash dishes at one of the 110 restaurants on the fairs' grounds, cleaning and scrubbing into the wee hours of the morning. And while the pay was not sufficient to feed his family; Manuel subsidized his income by cleaning out the fountains. When no one was looking during the early morning hours before the gates opened, he and other Latino dishwashers made their wish of feeding their family come true by taking the coins tossed in by tourists making wishes.

The binding legal deportation document received, and the humiliation his father endured of having to live off scraps proved to Miguelito how whites, including the schoolhouse boys who would eventually chase and terrorize him, constantly viewed him: as some "thing" and not some "one", a being existing outside law and order. Before Miguelito ever achieved self-awareness, he had already been defined in the Anglo imagination as not belonging, an imposition upon the generosity of a so-called philanthropic nation.

For almost two years, little Miguelito would live as an *illegal* – as if any human could ever be illegal in the sights of God. Unaware of being relegated to the shadows of the slums and ghettos, hunger and poverty were simply accepted as the legitimate norm. His family would not emerge from these hidden projects of shame until December 2, 1961 when Fidel found himself under economic threat from the hegemonic power to the north. After his regime nationalized U.S.-owned oil refineries without compensation, the U.S. retaliated by placing an embargo on the island on October 1960. It was meant to last a few years in order to pressure and subjugate a proud people. Six decades later, the only thing the embargo accomplish would be to make the difficult lives of Cubans on the island even more challenging. A need for financial assistance was desperately needed if Castro's revolution was to survive.

Although Soviet economic aid began on February 13, 1960 with the purchase of 425 thousand tons of sugar, this support was not enough to keep the economy afloat against U.S. economic aggression. Ironically, it would now be more profitable for the revolution to become communist. During a television address on December 2nd Fidel declared: "I am a Marxist-Leninist and shall be one until the end of my life." With less than fifteen words, the revolution's economic and political survival was assured. David, with the assistance of the Soviets, stood up to Goliath, with his slingshot being medium-range and intermediate-range ballistic nuclear missiles. Originally not wanted in the U.S., now the de la Cruz family became convenient political props for Cold War theatrics, pawns with propaganda value. Losing swagger in its own backyard, Uncle Sam frantically needed powerful images of freedom-seeking Cubans to retell the story. Manuel, the henchman of a brutal dictatorship was transformed overnight into a freedom loving patriot seeking to breathe the fresh air of liberation and democracy which was only found in the United States. What God fearing country would send fellow fighters *en la lucha* – in the struggle against the evils of communism back to the atheist island gulag? Cubans would be welcomed with open arms. Even the elusive green card was finally obtained.

Eventually, Miguelito's mom abandoned his father (the first of many times) and moved "up" to a low-income black neighborhood, across the freeway from LaGuardia Airport in East Elmhurst Queens on 23rd Avenue. The two of them lived in the attic of an unheated three-story old wood frame house owned by an Afro-Nuyorican single mom. Rats and roaches were also waiting for them in their new home – but fortunately, not as many as found in the slums! After his parents reunited, when Miguelito was about six, they all moved into a poor working blue-collar Italian/Irish neighborhood called Jackson Heights, and yes rats and roaches continued to be their household companions. Both his parents worked several jobs for decades just to rise to the economic level of poor whites, forcing Miguelito to be a latch-key kid decades before the term became popular among whites. No matter how hard his parents tried to shield him from penury, they were unsuccessful. Television reminded him that he simply didn't belong, nor would he ever.

Watching *Leave it to Beaver* and comparing June Cleaver to his mom demonstrated something was terribly wrong with his *familia*. The images on the small black and white screen were not his experience, leading him to the only reasonable conclusion, that his *familia* and his *gente* – his people, were somewhat defective, low-class, inferior. How else could he explain their poverty and disenfranchisement? Hours and hours of television, day after day reinforced this idea. His character was clearly deficient because he did not live like the kids on the television shows. His Latino body did not look like theirs. His parents did not act nor dressed like the people in *Leave it to Beaver* reruns. The fictional Cleaver family were real "Americans," the de la Cruz were not, they were imposters, they couldn't even speak the language. How he often burned with embarrassment with his parents' inability to master English as they struggle to manage family life in a new country and within a new cultural setting. "Tell your parents," the used car salesman in the ill-fitted suit with yellow teeth would command, "that I personally will insure nothing will go wrong with this '51 Chevy beauty. Trust me, nothing would go wrong." Every time they interacted with society, Miguelito was forced to serve as interpreter, as if he was now the parent. He would be forced to translate the bad news spoken by landlords, law enforcers and government officials. The condescension for his parents conveyed in the voices of white gatekeepers needed no translation, a disdain which rubbed off on the translator who wanted to be like the gatekeepers.

Yes, at times he purposely mistranslated their vulgarity to lessen the blow, to somehow protect his parents. His vain attempts to be their shield against an Anglo world only accomplished greater misunderstanding and hardship. Whenever he failed to properly translate legal terms or complex financing concepts, which happened often, his parents suffered. They became easier prey for swindlers and hucksters. Learning they were taken advantage of; they directed their anger at the child for his poor translating skills.

Not yet seven, Miguelito carried the shame and blame for *la familia's* inability to advance and succeed in a new world. "Why couldn't they just learn the language? How hard could it be?" Miguelito often thought, "After all, I learned, even though I was forced to repeat first grade." He was humiliated by them and by the culture they represented. He wanted to be white. Oh, to have been born with blond hair and blue eyes he often mused, as self-loathing and self-ethnic hatred took root.

The de la Cruz family eventually moved to a block west of Junction Boulevard off 35th Avenue. This was over a decade before the Pooper Scooper Law was implemented, making it a challenge to walk down the sidewalks and not step in dog shit. There, Manuel, who had once been a tough cop in Cuba, obtained the stereotypical Latino job of superintendent of a six-story tenement building. Miguelito's first job, at eight-years-old was mopping the floors of the building with a mop taller than his own body, shoveling the burned trash from the incinerator twice a week for biweekly rubbish pick-ups, and clearing the sidewalks of snow during the winter, all for $5 a week. "He needs to learn the value of a buck," his father would tell the building tenants who were surprised to see a child doing arduous labor." After two years, he saved enough money to buy a small black and white portable television to which he would now be glued all day, constantly reminding him he was a perpetual outsider. The de la Cruz family was among the first Latinos on the block. Miguelito was definitely the first Latino ever to be enrolled at Blessed Sacrament, a

Catholic elementary school, which made him wear navy blue ties with the school's initials embroidered in gold: B.S.

By day he was a Catholic who prayed the rosary daily, but at night he gave homage to his *orisha* Elleguá. During this time Marta and Manuel became a priest and priestess of Santería. While on the island they rejected the religion as something *para los negros* – for blacks, they found that in exile it became a way of belonging. The Irish Catholic Church down the street was simply unwelcoming to Latinés. Like many whiter Cubans, they found more than spirituality within Santería, they found community among other displaced Cubans. This faith tradition, originally based on the spirituality of the Yoruba people's violent separation from their homeland, from their culture, and from all which provided them with meaning, was comforting to the de la Cruz couple who were now struggling with their own displacement. Those first Africans sought survival on an island hostile to their *orishas* by concealing their gods behind a thin veneer of Medieval Catholicism. This explains why Marta and Manuel's small apartment in Jackson Heights was so cluttered with statues of Catholic saints, the envy of Blessed Sacrament Church down the street from them.

Marta and Manuel would impress upon their son that the rituals they performed at night were a mystery best kept secret. An illiterate beautician and an uneducated superintendent by day were chosen by the *orishas* to help process the mysteries of the universe and share these with the human world. Anglo society ignored and discarded these two

Latinés as child-like, a drain on the body politics, a stone rejected; but in the universal scheme, they were exalted way above those wrapped in the privilege of their whiteness because they possessed *el conocimiento* – the knowledge. They were supernaturally charged to restoring harmony by reestablishing a balance of *ashé* between the spiritual and material, bringing the one coming for a healing into a full state of wholeness. They told Miguelito that if the boy were to reveal to the Irish priests and nuns at the Catholic school which he attended how from their apartment live chickens were sacrificed to the *orishas* every now and then, they would become agitated and confused, failing to understand how God really works. Furthermore, if they were to discover Miguelito's parents had *el conocimiento*, the boy might be expelled from the school. "But what are we? Aren't we Catholics?" Miguelito would ask his parents. "We are apostolic Roman Catholics, but we believe in our own way," his parents would respond. "People won't understand that *ashé* flows through all religions," his parents assured the boy.

The neighborhood where the de la Cruz family lived was, to say the least, rough. The Irish and Italian classmates would take turns beating Miguelito up after school, several times a month. Even as an adult he carried those wounds, emotionally as well as physically. There is a scar over his right eye from one particularly vicious beating where he was outnumbered three-to-one; and a greenish disfiguration on his upper right thigh (the Irish kid was aiming higher) where he was stabbed with a very sharp pencil (the point broke off and is still visible under the skin). Miguelito's adult body would continue to carry the scars of childhood violence. To survive, he had to learn it was advantageous to throw the first punch. Pacifism is seldom a successful strategy for the schoolyard where the children of desperation play.

Relegated most of his early life to dirt, violence, and poverty, not for his skin hue but because of his ethnicity, made his mind susceptible to the lure of whiteness. He grew up feeling shame whenever he engaged with Anglos, feelings internalized as he learned to see himself through the eyes of those seeking to keep him on the margins; regardless as to how much he tried to assimilate. Even as he attended college and was a successful young businessman, he still felt shame concerning his humble beginnings, shame for being a Latino. He lacked the social capital which comes with economic privilege which could have led him to feel at ease in public gatherings. He may one day become an internationally recognized academic author and tenured professor; but it would never be enough. As colleagues recited their academic pedigree, name-dropping the Ivy League schools from which they obtained their diplomas, it was always distressing to confess being a product of Miami-Dade Community College, which was all he could afford, working full-time to pay his own tuition, taking four years to complete a simple two-year Associate of Arts degree. It didn't matter how many scholastic initials he would gather after his name or how many groundbreaking books he would eventually write. Shaking off the imposter syndrome rooted in a life which has known more want than he would ever care to admit, continued to contribute to the straitjacket of shame his mind insisted on wearing.

Maybe Miguelito should know better once he reached adulthood, but in reality, he has continued to live under the tyranny of his memories responsible for accepting an imposed false identity by those who define him as dirty and inferior. **Such concerns haunt him. He would always be** the trapped scared small boy who doesn't belong, relegated to squalor, ashamed that he is not white enough, believing he deserves to live among the rats and roaches. He remains the young man condemned to seek acceptance from a society which confuses technological and military superiority with cultural or intellectual superiority. And now, even as he approaches his senior years, he finds himself amid a death-dealing struggle to liberate a mind so imprisoned that he seldom notices his own complicity with oppression. Rats and roaches – forever.

In the Beginning

Before there was time, *ashé* existed. *Ashé* was, is, and will always be the essence of Olodumare who possesses many avatars. Because *ashé* flows throughout the entire world, it takes forms within different cultures. Muslims recognize Olodumare as Allah, Hebrews call him Yahweh, Christian worship him as God. Olodumare has worn many masks throughout the centuries as diverse cultures paid him honor and respect: Ba'al, Zeus, Jupitar, Odin, Brahman, Qurtzalcoati, Wakantanka, Dangun, Lac Long Quân. Unimportant if the faithful gather in mosques, synagogues, cathedrals, forests, or open fields. Less important if they even recognize the power behind their culturally based apotheoses. Neither created nor begotten, Olodumare is the beginning of all the different creations within all the different timelines. As creator, ruler, and judge, he is immortal, omniscient, omnipotent, holy, profane, and beyond the mere human's ability to totally comprehend.

Initially, there was only blue skies above. Below, for centuries, nothing existed but molten fire. With time, the vapors created by this global inferno filled the skies, forming large hazy clouds. Desiring to create a new earth, one which could sustain life, Olodumare converted the clouds into water and extinguished the raging fires. Those places where the flames ferociously burned were left with lower elevations; so, as rain fell, they filled with waters, creating the great oceans of today. Olokun was among the first and most powerful *orishas* created by Olodumare to occupy this marshy waste. No land existed upon which gods or humans could dwell, only water. In the huge crevices between the cooling rocks, the fountain of all life on earth, the feared and revered *orisha* Olokun was born. A world of water became the dominion of this emerald colored non-binary *orisha* whose top half is simultaneously male and female. Their bottom half consist of an enormous fish tail, comprised of long placoid scales so deadly that just one bony plate was sharp enough to cut a human body in half. They found great joy swimming through the different oceans, finding an unbound and unrestrained freedom liberating.

One day, within this empty world of water, Olokun laid their body across the earth and cried out, "My womb is aching!" They were in pain, excruciating pain by a womb so full it was at the point of bursting. If that which was flowing within them was not birthed soon, they would die; for so much cannot be confined within one body, even when the body belongs to a deity. Once the pain reached the point of unbearableness, their womb burst forth all forms of sea creatures, great and small. With loving care, like a mother bear fiercely protecting her cubs, they safeguarded their domain from any and all outside threats. Not much time passed before Olodumare realized he made a terrible mistake in giving Olokun full reign of the earth he was trying to create. He had to find a way of reclaiming the plan he originally envisioned.

When Olodumare attempted to correct this shortcoming by creating a habitat which could support a new creation upon land, he found himself in constant combat with the great marine serpent and siren for the domination of the planet. "How dare Olodumare take back what was originally given to me?" Olokun screamed to no one in particular. "Such selfishness. No way! Not going to happen. He will not trespass on what belongs to me. He will have to kill me first!" Whenever Olodumare attempted establishing a foothold, Olokun would swallow it up with water. Frustrated in his inability to overcome Olokun, Olodumare turned to the head of the Yoruba pantheon, Obatalá, who represents the highest level of existence. Obatalá, the first *orisha* ever to be created, had a muscular physique. His ebony bulging muscles contrasted with bright white wooly hair and long beard. Always dressed in the purest and whitest dashiki, he shone as the sun brightly reflected off his continence. He could have been mistaken for a black rendition of Michelangelo's God in the *Creation of Adam*.

At this time, all the *orishas* lived contently in the sky, unconcerned and uncaring as to what took place in the watery world below. But like Olodumare, Obatalá was saddened by the absence of an earth teeming with life. So, he set out to create. Dangling himself from a long gold chain, forged from the trinkets borrowed from the other *orishas*, he lowered himself from the sky. Getting the reluctant *orishas* who were quite comfortable with their heavenly abode to depart with their shining ornaments was no easy task. Promises of future satisfaction in the form of *ashé* offered by potential devotees was barely enough to convince them to part with their gold and commit to the project of creation.

The golden chain swung uncontrollably as the muscular Obatalá clung up-side-down, holding on tightly by the soles of his feet. They bruised easily as he attempted to steady himself against the swaying caused by the wind. Inch by inch, carrying a snail's shell stuffed with soil and a five-toed white chicken, he slowly shimmied down the chain. Precariously hovering over the waters, he spilled some loose soil from the shell. As soon as the soil touched the water, he let loose the chicken who immediately started to do what comes natural to chickens, scratch into the spilled earth which had solidified upon the waters. Solid ground was established wherever the loose bits of earth had been scattered by the hen's scratching. As larger piles of soil converged, mountains were formed. Where the edges of smaller piles came together, valleys were forged. Little by little, Obatalá trespassed on Olokun's realm, slowly but surely expanding solid ground over their domain.

In time, enough solid ground had been created so that Obatalá could release the golden chain and descend with his own two feet onto *terra firma*. The solid ground upon which his foot first touched became the center for the city of Ilé-Ife. Olokun was infuriated when they realized what occurred. They instinctively assessed this newest threat of encroaching land upon the water. Furious, they swam in circles. At first slowly. Then, as their rage rose, their swimming picked up speed. Faster and faster, they swam. When it became impossible to swim any quicker, the enby broke new barriers. As they swam, the waters mimicked their tempest anger. Their wrath and the fury of the sea became one and the same. Tidal waves developed and were unleashed, swallowing everything in its path until their rage flooded the entire planet. As unrelenting waves crashed upon the recently created land; human beings and animals, gripped with fear of being dragged under the waters, ran toward the tall ceiba tree, finding refuge on its branches. Humans and animals that did not climb fast enough drowned, becoming offerings for Olokun. As the flood waters grew higher, they dug their nails deeper into the bark to lift themselves by a few extra inches. Only those who scurried to higher branches, survived. The primordial potentate of the ocean depths come close to preserving their watery kingdom through a rage which was only exceeded by their vanity; and it was this character flaw which would prove to be their undoing.

When all seemed lost, Obatalá had an idea on how to restrain and tame Olokun. Knowing their love for jewelry,

Obatalá gave them the long golden chain as a gift recognizing her victory over him, the same one which he used to lower himself from the sky. Attracted to the glitter of shining metal, Olokun allowed themselves to be wrapped in the chain. Before recognizing trickery was afoot, Olokun was bound and cast to the depths of the ocean. With them confined and secured, the flood waters receded, and land once again emerged. Bound in gold and out of sight, slowly going mad, they spent centuries wailing and gnashing their teeth.

They can still be found at the sea's floor. Although imprisoned, it would be a mistake to dismiss this powerful *orisha* as impotent. They continue to be fed the *ashé* of all who drown, claimed as sacrifices to the imprisoned *orisha*. During the Middle Passage, they were kept well fed. While Yemayá would come to claim the oceans as her domain, Olokun, chained to the ocean floor, continues to rule the depths. Their anger can still be felt through attempts to reclaim the land in the form of tsunamis, tidal waves, and rough seas, which overturns boats, causing shipwrecks which drown sailors. Every so often Olokun's anger may cause a regional flood here or deluge there, but never again, thanks to the golden restraints, can the entire planet be inundated.

Once Olokun's threat was neutralized, Obatalá continued his task in creating. Surveying creation, for as far as he could see, all that existed was arid dry land, void of vegetation. He dug a hole and planted a palm nut. Within seconds, a fully matured tree sprung forth from the rich fertile soil. From this sixteen-branch palm tree located in the center of Ilé-Ife, the world's creation spread outward. As the mature tree dropped palm nuts onto the ground, they instantly grew to maturity, repeating the reproduction cycle until complete forests covered the land. One by one, some of the other *orishas* became curious with this new land Obatalá created and left the sky to join him. Unfortunately, so much vegetation sprung forth that their path to occupy the planet was blocked by this dense primordial undergrowth. Oggún, with his mighty machete would make a way and launch the process of civilization.

As the *orishas* settled in their new abode, the time came to create humans who would worship them, offering up *ashé* in the form of sacrifices. Olodumare, who was not interested with such trivial matters, turned to Obatalá, commissioning the mighty *orisha* with the task. He began by fashioning humans out of mud, letting these creatures to dry in the sun, although originally, he did not form their heads. Upon completing the design of their bodies, Olodumare, in his earthly manifestation as Olofi, breathed upon them, giving them life. This is why the Yoruba word for breath, *emí*, is also the word for souls. Without their heads, these new human creations struggled about aimlessly. Correcting his error, Obatalá set out to finish his creative undertaking by forming and then giving his creatures heads; hence he is worshipped as the patron of people's physical heads, ruling over their thoughts and dreams. Whenever their minds are confused or troubled, he provides lucidity and serenity.

Not originally fastening heads to bodies was not the only error made by Obatalá. While laboring to form human bodies,

Obatalá would tire from the tedious work. Arms, legs, torso . . . repeat . . . arms, legs, torso . . . repeat . . . arms, legs, torso . . . repeat . . . so boring . . . repeat . . . so tiresome . . . repeat . . . arms, legs, torso . . . repeat . . . maybe a shot of palm wine might ease the tediousness . . . repeat . . . maybe another . . . repeat . . . legs, arm, torso . . . repeat . . . one more drink . . . repeat . . . torso, arms . . . repeat. As time went on and one too many respites were taken, Obatalá became intoxicated. With his senses impaired, the bodies he was creating started to reflect deformities, explaining for ableists, why some humans are born with physical disabilities. Remorseful by his lapse in judgement once he sobered up, he swore never again to partake in alcohol. As penitence, he committed himself to become the patron of those born with disabilities. Woe onto those who abuse the disabled, for the most powerful of all the *orishas* defends and protects them.

After the birth of humanity, Obatalá took on the avatar of Ayáguna, and took another avatar Yemmu for his wife, and built a hut on a large spread of land where he cultivated yam. Creating is tiring, even for a god. What good is it to create a whole new world if you don't get to live in and enjoy it, taking in the scents of the forest, being moved by the buzz of the hummingbirds, feeling the seashore sands between your toes. Walking away from creating on a global scale, Obatalá as Ayáguna now just wanted to feel the sweat on his brow and the ache of an outstretched arm as he tilled the soil to bring forth yam.

Obatalá's creation followed suit as these new humans also started building huts and cultivating farms. With time, Ilé-Ife became the most prosperous city-state in the world. There they lived together, humans and *orishas*, as equals before Olodumare. But covetousness is a powerful motivator and disruptor. Humans soon demanded that their differences and desires be acknowledged. Some called for larger properties, others clamored for more cattle, still others wished that their bodies had either darker or lighter skin. So many entreaties, many of which were frivolous. At first Obatalá ignored their petty supplications. But the constant trickle of demands wore thin on his patience. He decided to punish them by granting each their desires, no matter how ridiculous or unjust. Those who had pleaded for more land or larger herds began to look down at those with less. To complicate matters, Obatalá, in anger, created different languages, making communication and unity more difficult. Suspicion and distrust soon followed. People began to group themselves by skin tone and language, eventually moving away from Ilé-Ife as they sought new land to inhabit where they could create homogeneous societies. Soon they forgot the old gods and created newer ones in their own image, but the *orishas* felt no threat of displacement. They simply poured their *ashé* into the empty shells of the new deities being created by humans.

As humanity spread across the face of the earth, creating new cultures and societies, Obatalá, as Ayáguna, settled into the domestic and simpler life of farming until his familial tranquility was interrupted by Oggún's rape of his mother

Yemmu. After letting Oggún choose his own punishment and banishing his younger brother Changó to live on top of the palm trees with Dadá, he cursed the next child to come forth from Yemmu's womb by swearing to bury the child alive. Ayáguna did not directly carry out this act but commanded his son Elleguá to do the deed shortly after Yemmu gave birth to Orúnla. Elleguá, the perpetual trickster, took Ayáguna words literally. He found a ceiba tree infused with its own *orisha* and buried his brother up to his neck beside the tree, under its shadow. As years slipped by, feet and roots intermingled, making it difficult to determine where one began and another ended. The commingling of two souls formed a oneness where, like an old marry couple, one could always finish the thought or sentence of the other. That is where Orúnla stayed put, learning the secrets of divination from the ceiba tree. Soon, his skills as a diviner became well-known and his fame spread throughout the land. People would travel for days to have their destiny revealed by Orúnla. In exchange for his services, they would feed and care for the immobilized buried *orisha*.

Meanwhile, Ayáguna, now again as Obatalá, went on with his daily affairs, believing Elleguá had faithfully carried out his orders. As the years slipped by, and assuming Orúnla was dead, he began to feel tremendous remorse and regret for the curse he had made in a fit of rage. Upon hearing of Obatalá's compunction, Elleguá decided it was time to liberate his younger brother. "*Baba-mí*," the sly Elleguá one day said as he approached his father. "Come with me for I have something to show you which might lift your spirits." Taking his father to the ceiba tree, Elleguá revealed his brother, now a young man, who was very much alive, although buried up to his neck. Obatalá was filled with joy and forgave Orúnla, even though it should have been the other way around. He immediately released him from his grave after so many years of imprisonment. Seeing his son emerge naked from the earth, his father quickly clothed him in a body-length green and yellow dashiki. But after spending a lifetime beside the ceiba tree, who had served and nourished him as a mother, Orúnla found it difficult to leave her. Sensitive to Orúnla's separation anxiety, Obatalá chopped down the tree and from it made a round wooden tray upon which Orúnla could forever determine peoples' destinies.

Divination's purpose is not necessarily to foretell the future, even though it is quite capable of doing so. Its purpose is to inquire as to the harmony, or lack thereof, existing between an individual and the spiritual world so that the seeker might find a more fulfilled and meaningful life by becoming better aligned with their destiny. Santeros like Marta and Manuel would follow in Orúnla's footsteps whenever they cast sixteen cowrie shells upon a divination board, employ *el conocimiento* to help people regain their balance with their assigned fate. By discerning oracles, they became the vehicle by which humans could determine if they were on the right track. They seek Orúnla's guidance to warn against evil spells or spirits designed to wreak havoc to an otherwise satisfying destiny or warn how a person's own deteriorating character might create negative consequences in the future. Marta and Manuel were able to peer into tomorrow thanks of this system of divination designed by Orúnla.

All of creation agreed that there existed no greater diviner than this tall, socially awkward *orisha* – socially awkward since it had been difficult for him to learn social graces from a tree. But once it came to Olodumare's attention that someone else had dared to devise a divination system, he mocked the impudent *orisha* for his audacity. "There were too many charlatans already," Olodumare thought. "Only I can predict whether the future of any particular human was harmonious with their predetermined fate." Still, Orúnla's reputation as a master diviner continued to grow and spread. Feeling threatened, Olodumare decided to put a stop to the foolish chatter and devised a plot pretending to have died. When Orúnla would come to pay his last respects, Olodumare planned to expose Orúnla's forecasting as faulty. But Elleguá, who can usually be found hiding behind doors eavesdropping, overheard Olodumare's scheme and quickly warned his younger brother of the trap. The day Orúnla was scheduled to go and pay his last respects to the supposedly deceased Olodumare, he instead proclaimed Olodumare was very much alive, thus exposing the scheme. Impressed, Olodumare apologized, acquiescing to Orúnla's mastery of divination, and made him the guardian of all of existence's secrets by allowing him to be the only *orisha* present when each individual *ori* – the disembodied human consciousness - received their destiny.

Divination is important if humans wish to have a flourishing life. Death has a name – Ikú. He disposes of life, and whether one believes this true or not does not matter. No one's dance card is full when it comes to Ikú; for all will twirl in his arms in the end and feel the icy chill of his unwanted embrace. He lurks in the graveyard, where he abides under the jurisdiction of the *orisha* Oyá who is in charge of the cemetery's gates. All humans have a fixed number of days before they must return, through Ikú, to the source of all life. Whether rich or poor, valiant or coward, loved or despised, all must journey on diverse roads where nonetheless leads their body to the same unescapable destination – becoming food for the worms. As much as one might wish to avoid, ignore, or postpone the inevitable, death guides us toward an inexorable cuddle. Some die before their time, laying alone in a bed struggling to remember that which is best left forgotten. Others must exorcise unforgotten memories before they can ever rest in peace.

If a person is facing death before their appointed time, Ikú's attention can be diverted, providing an opportunity to see another dawn. But while one's rendezvous with Ikú can occur prior to its preordained date, it simply cannot surpass the predetermined time chosen for a final breath. Suicide, retribution from an *orisha*, an evil spell or curse cast by an enemy, accidents to quench Oggún thirst, or the harassment of a troubled spirit – all of these can reduce the number of days destined for life. And for those who die prior to their allotted time, they remain on earth as roaming spirits until their original expiration date arrives, while those who live out their entire allotted time immediately face judgement for either fulfilling or falling short of their assigned destiny. Hence Orúnla's oracles are so important, warning of impending danger and seeking to restore harmony so one can fulfill what is expected of them during their allotted time on earth.

In the beginning of an illusionary time, before humanity was birthed, every *ori* prostrated itself in humble submission before Olodumare, the giver and author of destinies, to negotiate what would be their assigned fate once embodied. Each *ori* received their specific destiny, designed to unfold itself through the multiple lives which the *ori* would experience. The act of discovering the destiny originally negotiated is revealed to seekers coming to Marta and Manuel for a consultation by means, like Orúnla, of casting the cowrie shells. Once their future is unmasked, they are able to realign the current life they are presently living with what was preordained. Only harmony with one's assigned destiny can bring about health and wealth.

Orúnla's presence when each *ori* received their destiny allows the *orisha* to accurately know their fate and thus can consequently communicate what is best for any particular individual. And while these destinies are preordained, they are not determined. Individuals do maintain free will to realize their potential by living in harmony with their destiny, or by choosing to ignore their destiny, never reaching the fullness of their life. Destinies can always be changed by appealing to the *orishas*. Happy destinies can be safeguard and unhappy ones can be rectified by consulting Orúnla who is familiar with everyone's assigned fate.

When a person dies, their *ori* - their head, as spirit or soul - stands before Olodumare, who calls upon the individual's guardian spirit, the *eleda*, to give testimony. This *eleda* provides a record attesting to the faithfulness of the departed, now as the *egun* – the spirit of the ancestral dead. Did the *egun* fulfill their destiny by maintaining the rituals of the religion and in keeping secret the mysteries of the faith? After testimonies are heard, Olodumare and Orúnla pass judgement. If the *egun* fell short, they are reincarnated into the body of a new human life, returning to the same family line. A father becomes one's grandson. Woe to the barren woman, for society would unjustly blame her as preventing the return of ancestors. For only by returning can an opportunity of succeeding be provided to please the *orishas* through this new life. The process of reincarnation continues multiple times until the *egun* achieves complete faithfulness to their destiny, that is, they arrived at perfect harmony between their *ori* and the original fate negotiated with Olodumare at the time of the original birth. No stigma is associated with reincarnation, for it is a jubilant event signifying another opportunity to get life right. The only shame is refusing harmony and choosing to live a self-indulging life, refusing to evolve into a self-actualized person.

The wise Orúnla may have been able to determine what is best for humans, but when it came to himself, especially when it came to dealing with women, he was found lacking.

As could be expected, buried up to one's neck for so many years meant that Orúnla was inexperienced when it came to women. Once able to walk around and enjoy the world, Orúnla fell strongly in love with the older queen of the sea, Yemayá, who had a taste for the potency of younger hard male bodies. He fell head-over-heels for her. She patiently taught the younger *orisha* how to satisfy a mature woman. Together they formed a blissful union living in matrimonial harmony. Usually, after hours of passionate love making, while trying to catch their breath lying in the dark on their sweat-soaked bed, she would coo into his ear, "*Mi amor* – my love, how do you actually discern the future?" But as persistent as she was, Orúnla simply swatted aside her pesky inquiries. "Only men," he thought to himself, "have the foresight to see into tomorrow. This gift is not intended and can never be for women."

One day, while Orúnla was away attending to the needs of some of his devotees, Yemayá rifled through his notes where she discovered the secrets of his divination abilities and decided to go into business for herself. Word soon spread concerning her mastery of the secrets of divination. Some even claimed she was a greater diviner than Orúnla himself. When the young but very wise *orisha* finally returned home months later, he was surprised to find a long line of strangers leading up to his house, where he discovered that all these people had come to have Yemayá, not him, divine their future. He was shocked that a woman had become more popular than he had ever been. "Why would my love betray me like this," Orúnla thought. "My beloved ceiba tree would never have betrayed me. It was always faithful to me, accepting me unconditionally. Maybe trees are just more preferable than women? Maybe it is best to remain grounded in the reality of the earth than living in ethereal world of emotions like love? Because years buried by the ceiba tree taught him patience and self-control, he was able to constrain his anger. He did not thunder like Changó, nor erupted in rage like Oggún.

The reserved *orisha* quietly ended their relationship and sent her back to her watery domain alone. There can be no marriage once mutual respect is lost and the bonds of trust have been broken. Yemayá pleaded for forgiveness, promising never to again divine anyone's future, but her begging made no difference. No longer the master of the secrets of divination, he devised a new oracle which forsook the cowrie shells. *El conocimiento* of the tablet of *Ifá* would be reserved only for his priests whom he would teach how to read. They would only be men, *babalawos*, to ensure no woman would ever again obtain access to its secrets. This new system of divination became so superior that even Yemayá, on occasion, sought her former husband's talents.

For centuries the *orishas* dwelled upon the earth. They brought forth an earth teeming with life, a task accomplished through the use of their sacred instruments. As humans populated the planet, spreading to the four corners of the distant lands, the *orishas* decided to return to their heavenly abode. But before departing, they taught those humans who had committed to be their devotees how to use the sacred instruments. Even though they are gone, whenever their children wish to communicate with them, they can do so by employing the same instruments through which the earth's foundations were laid - the same instruments used by Marta and Manuel for the purpose of divination in their rundown apartment in Queens. As the *orishas* returned to the heavens, one-by-one, they left their *ashé* embedded in the rocks, the forest, the streams, in short, in aspects of the material earth and the forces of nature – rain, winds, floods. The entire earth continues to resound with the *orisha's ashé*, for those who have ears by which to hear.

Dr. Comemierda

The distance between Blessed Sacrament and Miguelito's apartment was less than half a block. But when being chased, it might as well have been miles. No matter how fast Miguelito ran, holding on to his 1960s-style kid's briefcase full of schoolbooks for dear life, he knew he would not be able to outrun the taller, skinnier, faster boys. "*Coño*," he thought to himself, "would it have killed me to exercise more? If only I wasn't so heavy, I could run faster." His family, living in poverty, did not understand proper nutrition so he ate whatever he wanted when it came to chocolate and other unhealthy snacks. Rather than calling him by his name, his classmates instead taunted him with "dirty spic," or "smelly belly." He wasn't sure what "spic" meant. Short for Spanish? But "smelly belly," he understood. True, he had a bit of a belly, but smelly? He didn't think so because unlike several of his classmates now chasing him, he took a bath each day and always wore a clean shirt. But because white kids said so,

Miguelito assumed that maybe he did smell, so he would scrub extra hard as if trying to wash off the spic that was forever affixed to his skin and causing this odious odor he couldn't detect. But no amount of soap would ever make him white enough. To be a Latino in the U.S. was to be perpetually soiled, polluted, and diseased. This obsession with cleanliness followed him into adulthood, when he would take two or sometimes three showers a day and apply the most fashionable and expensive men's cologne. He could not control being a spic, but he could try to control how he smelled.

Because all spics are alike in the white imagination, most can't or don't bother to know the difference between a Mexican, a Puerto Rican, a Dominican, or a Cuban. In their minds all pose a threat. They are all dirty. The grandparents of the Irish and Italians boys at Blessed Sacrament chasing Miguelito on this day had also been considered dirty and dangerous during their own youth at the close of the nineteenth century. As immigrants, the Italians and Irish were treated as nonwhite and a threat to national security. But after the second World War, and the passage of the GI bill, many were able to move from the slums of the lower east side of Manhattan to the suburbs of Jackson Heights where they bought whiteness, along with all the perks and privileges whiteness entailed. It didn't matter that blacks and Latinés had also spilled their blood defending a democracy which excluded them upon their return home, there was no GI Bill waiting for them, no avenue to white respectability, nor would there ever be. No manner how much Latinés strived to assimilate, they would always remain alien, and they would always remain dirty spics.

Funny the way those oppressed yesteryear become today's oppressors. When the Irish and Italians became white, they adopted white tastes. The hatred once aimed at them was, to their relief, now directed at people whose skin tone resembled the color of shit. Learning to fear and hate is always easy, especially when it provides access to privileges once denied. Their parents might fear the dirty spic, but these boys were going to prove they were not frightened. And what better way to prove their fearlessness than to gang up and beat the crap out of the slightly overweight Cuban boy who had the nerve to show up and attend their school.

Miguelito was too young to comprehend what was motivating his classmates to have such hatred. It was hopeless to imagine a day when they could become friends. Changing his name to Mike was the only way he knew how to symbolically beg their forgiveness for his dirtiness, to erase that awful and unclean identity, and to try to belong. Unfortunately, it failed to work, leaving him today with just one recourse. Run. He valiantly tried to stay ahead of the seven boys chasing him. But they were gaining. He could feel their presence closing in. Always good at math, he calculated being overrun a few feet before the halfway point to the safety and security of his apartment building. Unable to grasp the psychological motivation of the boys chasing him, he, like so many outsiders before him, internalized feelings of worthlessness and alienation and redirected the anger for the predicament in which he found himself inwardly. What was wrong with him? Miguelito wondered as he ran. What makes the kids instantly hate him? Why was he such a *comemierda?*

Despite changing his name, he knew he could never belong and that he would always be an outsider. "Keep running," he yelled at himself, out-of-breath, "don't slow down." But Miguelito could not run away from a history which brought him to this day on the sidewalks of Jackson Heights, nor could he run from how the infantile minds of his peers were shaped by their parents' fears and hatred. He could only run from the constant beatings he was forced to accept as he kept trying to obtain an education. As painful as the Irish nuns' whacks, slaps, and pinches were, his classmates' poundings were by far worse, leaving lifelong scars on his psyche.

Years earlier, a few weeks into first grade, three classmates had extended their hands in friendship after school. When he took their hands to shake, they instead jumped him, giving him his first vicious schoolyard thrashing worse than those he received at home. The drubbing was so severe that he still carries on his body the physical scar of that day just below his right eyebrow from the bloody gash which became infected. From these early years, he learned never to trust white people again. Not a month would transpire from his first until eighth grade that he did not engage in some type of clash with the other schoolboys, most of which were physical. Once in a while he might win a fight, but more often than not, he ended up bloody. The fights he won, he soon learned, were those when he threw the first punch. He was able to do this with some kind of sixth sense – like Spiderman's tingle – which would activate to warn him of imminent danger.

While his lungs burned for air, the seven boys finally caught up to Miguelito. He felt a hand grab the back of his collar, pulling him in the opposite direction from which he was running. Losing his balance, he fell to the concrete sidewalk, tearing a hole on one of the knees of his pants and scraping his hands which he instinctually extended to break the fall. "*Coño*," he thought to himself, "mami *is* going to give me a beating for tearing up these pants that are not even a month old." The boys were now upon him, bent over, swinging their arms as Miguelito lay on the sidewalk, doing his best to shield his head and balls. Punches and kicks. Kicks and punches. "Spic." "Fag." "Go back to where you came from." "Retard." "Fat ass." "Cry baby." A cacophony of slurs and insults rained down on Miguelito along with the punches and kicks. The poor second grader tried looking around as they kept bashing him, hoping, praying to a silent God that some adult would walk by, take pity on him, and intervene. But no savior materialized. The punishment lasted for less than a minute, but its emotional wounds would last longer. Laughing and giggling the boys soon tired and ran away, leaving Miguelito cowering on the sidewalk with muddy clothes and a bloody face, mustering all his will power not to cry. Tears were reserved for late at night, after everyone else in the apartment was asleep and unable to witness this moment of nonmacho weakness.

Eight years of abuse at the hands of young, slightly built white boys took their toll. Although he was always anxious when in school, he learned to swallow his terror. During those eight years of constant elementary school beatings, Miguelito became motivated to get in shape. He worked out with weights to try to turn his fat into muscle. While not totally successful, he nonetheless developed a better physique. During the summer before his family moved to Miami, he targeted several of his tormentors of the past eight years. Like the wise and calculating *orisha* Orúnla, Miguelito prepared to forcefully respond to his bullies. There is something about being a human punching bag for so long that causes a sensitive boy to snap and embrace violence. This was also true for gods.

The otherwise nonviolent and diplomatic Orúnla, who had grown up buried to his neck in the earth, moved back to his beloved forest after his separation from Yemayá, seeking solitude so that he could lick his emotional wounds and grieve in peace over lost love. But his presence was unwelcomed by the lord of the forest. Osain, who was not conceived by gods or humans, but rather sprung forth from the bowels of the earth like an herb, came to be celebrated as the master of all trees and plants which grow wild in the woodlands. He is also recognized as a great herbalist, knowing the medicinal secrets of every plant. People have come to depend on Osain's knowledge of nature's properties for survival.

When Orúnla relocated to the forest, a contentious relationship between the two *orishas* soon developed. Orúnla's unannounced return became the root cause of their animosity. Osain bristled at the loss of privacy. An antisocial, Osain was incensed by the constant flow of visitors traipsing through his forest in search of Orúnla's skills in divination. "*Comemierda,*" Osain yelled at Orúnla. "Go back to where you belong! Who invited you to my domain? You don't belong here. You're not welcome." Orúnla simply ignored Osain's taunts. But the older *orisha* pestered on; intimidating and hounding poor Orúnla, who only sought peace in a new land. "Let's settle this like men. Name the place and time." But the sensitive Orúnla refused. This only angered Osain more. One day he ambushed the unsuspecting Orúnla, coming from behind and knocking him to the ground. He then rained punches and kicks on the defenseless Orúnla who was trying to shield himself. Badly battered, the *orisha* of divination was left at the steps of his new home half-conscious.

Frustrated and fed up with Osain's provocations, Orúnla approached his brother Changó for assistance in putting an end to Osain's xenophobia and his hatred of the newcomer to the forest. "I have a plan," Orúnla told Changó, "but I need your help with the fire you lord over." Together, they conjured an incantation involving twelve torches with twelve flints. One particular morning, as Osain rifled through the forest looking for herbs by which to inflict more harm upon Orúnla, part of his plan to keep up the bullying to make the youngster leave, the *orisha* of divination struck, throwing the first punch. As

Osain turned around from the force of the blow and tried to cast his own spell, a flash of lighting lit up the sky, setting the entire forest on fire, trapping Osain. Soon he was surrounded by walls of fire closing in on him. The heat and thick black smoke made it hard to breathe. Fear gripped the *orisha* as it dawned on him that he would not survive unscathed.

Barely alive and badly burned, the encounter disfigured Osain. With the loss of an eye, and a badly burned face, he looked like a cyclops, as if his remaining eye was centered on his forehead. He lost an arm and leg, forcing him to now hobble around the forest with the aid of a twisted tree branch. One of his ears uncharacteristically swelled, becoming outsized and deaf, while the other shrunk but yet becoming so hypersensitive to noise, he was able to hear a leaf fall to the ground even though he might be miles away. The disfigured Osain realized that this continuous battle might end worse for him, thus it was wise to put an end to their clashes. Fighting between the *orishas* ceased, as they were forced to learn how to live in peace. With time, the two *orishas* not only made their peace, but they also became inseparable. Peace through strength, cunningness, and violence – this is the lesson Miguelito learned from Orúnla and from life.

Unfortunately, Miguelito was no Orúnla. He never made peace with his white tormentors; mainly because they remained unwilling to welcome or accept him. How can one find peace with those whose burning desire is your demise? As Miguelito prepared to move to Miami that summer, he did plot his revenge. Discreetly, he followed his elementary school classmates, tracking them down one by one, until he could catch them alone. Then, like a depraved lion, he pounced on them, unleashing eight years of fear and fury. One by one he beat the shit out of them. Eight years of abuse were paid back tenfold. He kept hitting them over and over again just to feel more of their sticky blood on his fists. Their whimpering was cathartic as he drank in their sobs of pain. It was a parting gift long overdue. And yet, it was an empty healing. The momentary feeling of satisfaction quickly dissipated, leaving him still scarred. Violence not only changes the perpetrator, but the victim as well. How does one cease from believing that the proper response for being disrespected is a left hook as opposed to words? How does one become a new creature, different from what was taught since childhood? How does a boy taught violence become a violent man seeking to be nonviolent?

Years of living in dread did not dissipate with revenge. Relocating to Miami did not bring an end to violence. The de la Cruz family moved into a neighborhood off Bird Road which at the time was predominately white, causing a new knot in his stomach. Miguelito may have tried assimilating, still, he stayed alert around the other white kids in his new neighborhood, especially those declaring friendship. But as more and more Cubans, like his own family, bought homes, white flight provided more affordable houses for other Cubans. The stress and fear experienced by these homeowners of an alien race moving in next door was again manifested among Miguelito's classmates at Southwest High, home of the

Eagles. His years there were marked by constant tensions and divisions between Anglos and Cubans. He found himself – not out of choice – fighting alongside other Cuban kids. This time he was not alone.

The growing number of Cuban kids just increased tensions at the high school feeling itself under siege by an invasion of dirty spics. Their taunts became a bit more sophisticated. "Swim back to Cuba with a n*gger under each arm," was a phrase often hurled at Miguelito. "Smelly spic!" again with the uncleanliness. It wasn't only his body odor coming into question, but also his intelligence. "You should learn a trade, like mechanic or carpenter," his school's counselor advised. It mattered little that his SAT scores were significantly high, or he dreamt of doing something his parents never had an opportunity to do, go to college. But working with his hands and not his brain was the route his advisor plotted for his future. Obviously, she was no Orúnla. With no guidance on how to further his schooling, no money to pursue higher education, and no knowledge of the concept of grants, scholarships, or student loans, he shrugged and enrolled in the local community college to take classes at night and get ahead of the game next year.

The subtle ethnic discrimination expressed by his counselor was not so subtle among his classmates. At Southwest High, there were Cuban turfs and Anglo turfs. Two segregated high schools coexisted in one building. A quick glance at his 1977 yearbook revealed few Cubans, if any, attended football games or school dances because they were not welcome. While the Anglo teenagers enjoyed the full high school experience, Cubans played sports among themselves on the streets after school and threw house parties. But even in separated spaces, there were times when they were forced to encounter each other. And like Orúnla and Osain, sparks igniting violence would ensue. "Rumble!" someone would yell calling for fights to break out between the two groups. There was always that one kid on each side who served as provocateur, relishing fights, and always willing to throw that first punch. Regardless as to which side the punch came from, or who was at fault, everyone was duty-bound to defend their group. Failure to do so would label one as a *maricón*, the ultimate insult in a hyper-macho Cuban world. One quickly learned to travel in packs for "safety." Never enter a bathroom by yourself was the first rule.

Miguelito played the role of the macho during the day at high school, but at night he attended community college to fulfill the legal requirements to obtain a real estate license. Maybe if his academic counselor would have guided him toward a university, a different life path would have unfolded. Not knowing any better, he followed her advice and learned a trade which would eventually lift him out of poverty. A few weeks after turning eighteen, he took the state exam and became the youngest real estate agent in the State of Florida. A year later, after turning nineteen and graduating from high school, he took his broker's exam, which he passed, and immediately opened his own real estate company –

Championship Realty – becoming the youngest real estate broker in the State of Florida at the time.

Putting away childish things like fist fights, he began to work in the adult world. No more physical encounters for him. From now on he would use words. Fighting became monetized. Now he won with sales instead of fists. Jabs became contracts, punches translated into closings. As a salesman he sold more houses than any other of the fifty agents at the brokerage firm. Always overcompensating, he outsold all his white older and more seasoned colleagues. As a broker, he kept expanding his company until he had over a hundred salespeople working for him. Despite his obvious success in the business world, his feelings of apprehension and fear were not as easily vanquished. The traumas he had buried or dismissed as inconsequential and painful childhood memories would re-emerge from time to time.

Had he studied basic psychology he might have come to realize what he had internalized. Whenever Miguelito found himself around young, slightly built white men, whether working as a Realtor or later in life as a professor, he found those old feelings resurfacing. He stuttered, his ability to speak English diminished, his stress levels shot up, he became nervous, and he had trouble concentrating. He seemed to overcompensate by being extra friendly, hiding his fear and anger behind a mask of upwardly mobile Latin charm. At other times, he became overly competitive as if to prove the accusations of inferiority were lies. Whether fight or flight, he came off self-centered, obnoxious, insecure, scared - he came off like such a *comemierda*. He didn't have these difficulties when verbally jousting with African Americans, Asian-Americans, indigenous people, internationals, or other Latinés – just young, slightly built white men. Not even older white men, nor overweight men. Not white women nor gay white men – just heterosexual young, slightly built white men.

Regardless of whether they were young jerkwads in elementary school, slender and "hip" young businessmen or liberal politically correct professors, Miguelito received the same message from them all: he didn't belong in their business, in their civic club, in their school or on their committee, and they would make sure he knew it and was kept out. Those boys at Blessed Sacrament did their job well, and their punches were no longer needed because he had internalized his own discipline. Punches were no longer necessary; a sideway glance was sufficient. Maybe this is why when he was in social settings with white folk, he came off as such a *comemierda*.

Being a *comemierda*, storming the wrong windmills, seemed to come natural for Miguelito, a characteristic which the two women in his life, his mom, and his wife, could agree upon. When he first told his dear sweet mother Marta that he was awarded a doctorate in philosophy, she responded by affirming that from now on, she would be sure to call him *doctor comemierda*. What had remained hidden from peering eyes into Miguelito's life, but all too obvious to those who knew him best, was that besides being narcissistic, he was also highly opinionated, vengeful, and combative. In every interaction in which he engaged, he must be the best, the winner, the alpha male – a machismo literally beaten into a once sensitive boy. *"Cuidado conmigo,"* he would often boast, *"porque yo como candela."** He always assumed that like a former president, being an asshole was due to him being a Queens' boy. Whatever the reason or excuse for being a *comemierda*, the consequences were damning as he continued to act contrary to how he would have preferred to be – gentle, kind, forgiving, and loving. Try as he may, he always seemed to backslide to a modus operandi which appeared all too second nature. He was curse by constantly being in fight mode. *¡Que comemierda!*

---

* "Be careful with me, because I eat fire."

¡Qué Viva Changó!

When Ayáguna, the violent and aggressive avatar of Obatalá, discovered the incestuous betrayal committed by his beloved son, the first-born swaggering Oggún, his first reaction had been to blame the victim of the rape, his wife Yemmu. Wishing to impose insufferable distress and unbearable heartache, he directed his wrath toward that which she most treasured – her children.

First, he cursed the next child which would come forth from her womb, decreeing that it would be buried alive. Then he banished her beloved toddler Changó from their home. Without even a moment to pack his favorite toy, Changó was instantaneously sent away with only the short red pants and shirt he happened to be wearing the moment the curse was pronounced. The poor child was too young to fully understand the consequences of what was about to befall him. He barely even remembered the journey, sleeping through most of the way. When he arrived at his new home, located high on top of the palm trees, the little boy felt the anguish of being displaced, dislodged, and disoriented. The sorrowful plight of removed and repatriated children is the same for *orishas* as it is for humans. Too young to comprehend why they are cast into exile creates lifelong feelings of abandonment. A yearning to return to a home which cannot be remembered becomes an itch that can never be scratched. Changó was psychologically scarred for life by this experience, just as Miguelito and so many other refugee children would be, growing into adulthood struggling with the anxiety of never belonging, of being casted away. Changó and Miguelito suffer a rejection from both the old culture from whence they came and the new culture in which they find themselves. Loss of support networks - extended families, long-term neighbors, familiar local guides, instructors, and landmarks – all disappeared in an instant.

What is left in the imagination of the refugee is a mythological Eden, an ethereal place where every conceivable item *es mejor* - better, where the sky was bluer, the sugar sweeter, the bugs less pesky, and life richer in every respect. Other immigrant groups mostly leave behind painful memories of the old country, joyfully anticipating a new land where streets were paved with gold (naively unaware they would be expected to do the paving). But for those torn from their place of origins, everything *en el exilio* – in the exile, when contrasted with what was left behind, was found lacking. Changó's new surroundings were not what he would come to loath. His old surroundings were what he missed. He physically ached to once again be in his mother Yemmu's arms, to play with his older brother Elleguá and the rooster Osún on the old yam farm.

With time, unremembered memories would become nostalgic fantasies of an idyllic place only existing in his vivid imagination. And even if he was ever, in the future, to return to the actual place which witnessed the first years of his life, that same land would never live up to the illusion which he had created for himself. Changó often marveled at the blissful innocence of others who took for granted revisiting the house holding their childhood memories or eating mangos from the gardens their grandmothers planted. How can anyone define themselves after being torn from the land which gave them their identity? How could Changó ever find fulfillment *aquí* - here, when *allá* - there, continuously beckoned for his return? How can Changó ever die in peace when his heart is buried in the yam farm of his parents? Since going into *el exilio*, he left his land, his life, his love. Perhaps there can never be a return to one's native land, only fractured memories upon which it is recreated – a new way of remembering which conveniently forgets reality.

Dadá, the goddess of gardens and the deity of the unborn, was given the responsibility to care for her younger brother Changó. Until the birth of Dadá, humans had heads, but no brains; not knowing why they even existed. She is the one who provided them with senses – to see, to hear, to smell, to think, to reason. Considered the *orisha* of enlightenment, she resides in the brains of all humans. She became so close to the child she was tasked to care for that she even adopted his colors, red and white. But while Changó's colors are separated by every other bead of the *eleke* - the beaded necklace worn by his devotees - Dadá's beads are arranged in a two-by-two combination. Still, no manner how loving and attentive she was toward the child, she could never substitute what was taken, what was lost.

Like most refugee children, Changó often cried, struggling with bouts of anxiety and hopelessness, manifested in the form of nightmares, headaches, and stomachaches. As he grew older, he kept the pain of being abandoned by his mother bottled up, leaving in its wake a profound sense of loneliness. He blamed himself for his exile, a common trait among those forced out of their place of origins. Changó's thoughts tormented him: "What wrong act, what evil thing did I do to justify this banishment? Surely, I must have done something to warrant drastically being cast out of my home. Why am I such a *comemierda*?" Regardless as to how successful he may have been in masking his pain later in life through wine and women, such trauma always finds a way of seeping out. In Changó's case, he became more irritable, participating in more aggressive behavior – especially toward women. His cantankerousness led to many physical altercations, bar fights which only developed impressive fighting skills; eventually becoming a mighty warrior in his own right. Alienated boys like Changó and Miguelito, who never are fully accepted or respected in their place of physical refuge, quickly become a target for the cruelties of local boys. An easy mark, unless they learn to fight back. Children who find themselves at the mercy of xenophobes find pacifism only leads to more beatings.

As Changó became a lean muscular man who was easy on the eyes, he held on to one weakness: he continued to blame himself for his exile, struggling to understand or discover what terrible thing caused his perpetual banishment. What mother could deny her instinctive love for the child she birthed? She must have given birth to a monster. Changó's self-image was so bruised and so low that he developed an elaborate mask by which to hide the pain of dismissal and displacement. His enticing smile on his manly face veiled the tears of an unfulfilled little boy always looking for a way back to the home of his imagination, a home which never existed. His scintillating dreamy eyes masked the sadness of having lost his mother's loving touch. His quest for the warm embrace of his homeland, intermingled with his need for motherly doting affection soon manifested itself perversely. He first married the regal, serene and maternal Obba, settling in the town of Oyo, truly hoping to find the love of a woman and the stability of a home cruelly denied to him as a child. Obba had a gentle, trusting soul, one which bordered on naiveté. But poor Obba was unable to meet his unrealistic expectations. Not long after his marriage Changó continued to seek out ways to fill the oceans of emptiness within his heart between the legs of any woman or at the bottom of any bottle. An incurable womanizer, he reveled in bacchanalian festivities.

Much to the chagrin of his wife who suffered in silence, the ultimate carouser was always ready for a good time. Soon, he developed a reputation for unchecked virility, unrestrained passion, and uncontrolled lust. He also had a hot temper. Whenever he was angry, thunder in the sky would roll out from his furrowed brow and fire would literally shoot out from his nostrils. People would come to sing: "fire in his eyes, fire in his mouth, fire on his roof, you ride fire like a horse." He came to represent the extreme behaviors of hyper-toxic masculinity. He was either making passionate love or passionate war, and there was little difference between the two in Changó's eyes.

One night while partying, he noticed the *orisha* Orúnla, his younger brother, sullenly sitting in a corner. What a waste, Changó thought to himself. Everybody knew Orúnla was given the gift of dance, but his brother could care less. In a way, Changó understood his predicament, for he himself had been given the gift of divination which served him no good when all he cared about was frolicking and fucking. That's when it occurred to him, why don't they just exchange gifts? He hurried over to Orúnla with his proposition. As Changó spoke Orúnla's countenance lifted, since he, like most, had always wished for the ability to discern the future. That very night the two *orishas* exchanged gifts, and neither ever regretted the transaction. From that date forward, Changó, to the delight of all the goddesses, could out-dance anyone. Whenever he would dance, he would do death-defying somersaults, spit fire through pursed lips, and stomp about wildly while grabbing his *cojones*. At one of these dances, he met the seductive Ochún who was quick to dip her index figure into her honey gourd and brush it across his full lips. The two quickly became passionate lovers.

Ayáguna, may have sent his baby son Changó away lest another case of incest would occur under his roof, but he made it a point as Obatalá, the fatherly *orisha* of peace, tranquility, and harmony, to visit his son regularly, watching the boy mature in stature even though not necessarily in wisdom. Obatalá loved his son deeply and would have been shocked if he knew that Changó was not, as he believed, the fruit of his own loins. If truth be known, Changó had been conceived when his mother Yemmu was away from their farm on a long-extended trip. Unfortunately, she did not plan her excursion well, failing to bring enough money to pay for the expenses of the journey. She had not been too worried because the way home was a straight road and should have only taken a few days. The only obstacle was a river needing to be crossed, but fortunately for her, Aganyú, the god of volcanoes and their rivers of molten lava, would ferry people across the waterway in his small boat for a fee. This giant from the city of Oyo was also the patron *orisha* of wanderers and travelers.

Even though Yemmu had no money with which to pay him, she was sure they could come to some mutual arrangement. Looking up at his enormous frame, towering far above her, she pleaded "please ferry me across the river." But Aganyú, a shrewd businessman, demanded payment up front. Having no money and beginning to realize that Aganyú might refuse, she assured him he would get paid handsomely once they reach the other side. With some hesitation, Aganyú complied nonetheless, safely bringing the beautiful Yemmu to the river's opposite banks. Once docked, Aganyú requested his fee. "But I have no money to give you." Yemmu alluringly whispered, "Surely there must be something else you desire that I can offer?"

The lonely Aganyú thought for a while about Yemmu's obvious proposition. He didn't want to anger her husband, the elder Ayáguna, for even though this incident occurred before he became the mighty Obatalá after the discovery of Yemmu's rape by Oggún, he was stilled feared by all the other gods and goddesses. After a few reluctant moments, the giant grinned and roughly grabbed Yemmu, dragged her behind the bushes, and found satisfaction on top of her in less than a minute. Aganyú rolled off Yemmu and lay content next to her. Yemmu's waters may cool the molting lava, but they only increase her own heat. Once Aganyú's lust was quenched, fear reemerged. Before he could express his concerns, Yemmu, annoyed, unsatisfied but not having expected much more, kissed the giant on the forehead, splashed quickly into the river to wash herself off, smoothed and rearranged her skirt, and hurried to continue her journey home, leaving Aganyú to deal with his fears and anxieties by himself.

The next day, while she was still some distance away from the farm, Ayáguna, who was working alone in the fields, caught a glimpse of her silhouette. Being apart for over two weeks, and deeply missing his wife, he ran to greet her. Once he came upon her, caught in a moment of hunger, he tore off her clothes, and took his wife in the open field beneath the shining sun and bright blue sky. This time Yemmu found satisfaction because she loved him just as he loved her. Nine months later, Changó was born.

Since his indiscretion with Yemmu, Aganyú the giant did his best to avoid everyone involved: the mother, the child, and especially Ayáguna. The child's fiery personality was evidence of his true father's character, as the lord over volcanoes, and whose lava provides the hot seed to germinate life within the depths of the ocean's steamy waters. But naturally, Ayáguna continued assuming that the baby was his, even though he would feel, once in a while, that something was not quite right. A fleeting moment of doubt which he could not quite explain would occasionally trouble and puzzle him. Perhaps it was due to this nagging suspicion, held to himself for so long, that Ayáguna's wrath was so quick to ignite on that fateful day when he caught his wife being raped by their son Oggún.

Ironically, the real reason the boy had been cast out was due to Ayáguna's fear that when Changó grew older, he would repeat his brother's disgraceful act of taking his wife. And yet this almost inadvertently happened. At one particular all-night party Changó met Yemayá, the goddess of the oceans, for the first time since he was a toddler. He did not recognize that before her transformation, she had been Yemmu his mother. Changó was smitten by her mature and majestic beauty. "What a prize," he thought to himself, and immediately set out to seduce the woman dressed in royal blue with white accents. Yemayá, of course, immediately recognized her son, disappointed by the life he had chosen for himself of constantly chasing skirts, heavy drinking, and unceasing brawling. Noticing his attentions, she cozied up to him and cooed into his ear, "let's leave this boring party for someplace more private and intimate." Impressed with himself over such an easy conquest, he submissively followed her away from the crowded festivities toward the edge of the ocean. She ordered Changó into the boat so they could row to a small island where her home was located, not far from there. But the mighty god of thunder hesitated, for fire, after all, is always afraid of water.

Lust exceeded his cautiousness. Carefully, Changó boarded the dinghy, but first he gave Yemayá a gentle spank on her behind, maybe as a reminder, more to himself, of his strength, manhood and dominance. She responded in kind with a playful yelp, masking her fury over Changó's impudence. Once they were together in the boat, Yemayá guided them toward open sea, moving farther and farther from the shore. Suddenly, she stood up and dove overboard into the ocean, disappearing beneath the waves, abandoning the startled Changó who was quite ignorant on the matters of sailing or swimming. Huge waves began to heave the little boat, lurching it up and suddenly down, while walls of water came crashing down upon his head. As the boat overturned, the waters engulfed him, and he began to sink. Time slowed to a stop as the quiet deep slowly surrounded him in a freezing and tender embrace. As the waters found their way into every orifice of his body, and as the darkness blocked out his thoughts so that he could no longer see his memories, he found he was unable to inhale as the spark of life became consumed. "Aarrrggghh" he gurgled, as the air bubbles emerged from his freezing lips.

Aroused, the seaweed reached up from its warm depths between two leg-shaped coral rock formations, reaching upward, in a seductive slow-motion dance of curvy undulations, coiling caressingly around his ankles, rubbing and wrapping itself around his legs, around his throbbing groin, around his waist and into his hot and panicked armpits. The fronds of the plant coiled around his neck muscles, which were bulging and throbbing from lack of oxygen, as his internal fire smoldered out. He continued to be pulled down, down and further down into the depths of the cold sea. Soon he would become another offering for Olokun. With his last ounce of strength, he forced himself to break free of the seaweed and shot upward to break his head up out of the waters, fighting the thought of spending his future in a watery tomb.

"Aarrrggghh!" He shouted with his one last gasp of air as he splashed on the surface, wasting too much energy because he could not swim. He saw Yemayá approaching him, riding on top of a wave, glorious in her blue gown, with sprays of sun-kissed ocean mist shining around her in the rising sun. "Have mercy on me," Changó managed to spit out, through gulps of seawater. "I will save you my son," Yemayá responded, "under one condition: that you learn how to respect your mother." At that moment Changó recognized Yemmu as Yemayá and he burst into tears, which comingled with the salty ocean waters. He begged Yemmu as Yemayá to forgive how he mistreated her at the party.

Instantly the sea quieted, and his mother helped the quivering Changó to scurry onto the boat. They silently made their way back to the stability of land. The resentment he had held all these years over Yemmu's abandonment did not instantly dissipate, but a crack on the wall of bitterness he erected began to develop. Decades would pass as healing slowly began to take hold. One immediate result of his encounter with his mother did lead him to become more attentive to the women he continued to entice, as he labored to become less self-centered in their lovemaking and ensuring that the women would conclude with their needs also being satisfied. And while he learned to respect Yemayá, still, he remained disgruntled, not understanding why he was sent away, unsatisfied until the day his brother Elleguá divulged the truth. Secrets always have a way of seeing the light of day; especially when Elleguá the trickster is involved, who always seemed to know the latest gossip among the *orishas*.

On one particular night of strong drinking and exhaustive dancing, Elleguá left the party and went outside to cool off. He noticed Changó was on the porch as well, sitting on a wooden bench that began to smolder with the heat he was generating while watching a beautiful woman's backside through the window. Elleguá nodded with a knowing smile and started a conversation while they both continue to sip *cheketé*, a drink made from honey and sour oranges. They were not merely brothers, but also good friends. "*Oluki mi* my friend, how I have missed you. I always regretted that we haven't spent more time together. What a shame father sent you away when you were a child, all because of Oggún."

"Oggún?" Changó was puzzled, "What does Oggún have to do with my banishment?"

"Oh, forgive me brother, I thought you knew. Please, forget what I just said."

"Thought I knew what?" the confused Changó asked as he quickly sobered up. "Tell me what you know."

"Dear brother, I am all too aware of your volcanic temper and am afraid to tell you, afraid of what you might do. But then again, you do have a right to know."

"Know what?" Changó asked with irritation, frustrated with Elleguá's constant game playing. Elleguá picked up on the tone of his brother's voice which rolled as not-quite-so-distant thunder and decided it was prudent to finally let Changó have the details. He told Changó of how his brother Oggún had violated their mother, how Ayáguna, before becoming Obatalá had caught them in the act, and how in an attempt to punish their mother, and avoid any future incestuous acts from occurring, their father had banished her future and favorite child. After Changó sat there stunned, he became literally thunderstruck, which was heard as a loud crack in the sky, right above their heads. Then Elleguá let the second shoe drop. "The funny thing is that while our father thought he was banishing his son, unbeknown to him, he was really banishing his step-son."

"Step-son!!" Changó choked. "What do you mean step-son!?!"

"But surely you know that you are not Ayáguna's son? That you were fathered by Aganyú?" Of course Elleguá knew damn well Changó had been unaware of any of this. Without responding, nor saying a word, Changó stood up and left. He wanted to cry, he wanted to punch someone, and his crazy emotions caused the sky to flash with lightning and the clouds to billow suddenly with roiled thunder. Calming himself, he decided that what he needed now was to think. And think he did. For over a week he neither partied, danced, caroused, brawled, nor ate. He just sat where he mainly dwells, on top of the royal palm tree. Thinking. There, above the tallest and most regal tree, where the tops are often lopped off by lightening, Changó sat, day in and day out, thinking. By the time he climbed down he knew what had to be done. While it may be true that he consistently displayed a reckless and destructive use of power, he was still the *orisha* of justice, and justice is what he sought – if justice could be defined as revenge. He wanted to avenge his mother by destroying Oggún, and by confronting his true father. Neither task would prove easy to accomplish.

He first tracked down Aganyú, all the way to the river where the giant continued to work in his daily task of ferrying people across. Not since the night he almost drowned did Changó experienced fear. Nevertheless, he swallowed hard and forcefully demanded, "Aganyú, recognize the wrong you have committed against my mother. Be a man and take responsibility for your actions!" Aganyú kept sitting in his boat, his face turned toward the water, ignoring Changó's pleas. Incensed, Changó angrily stomped right up to the edge of the little dock and shouted: "Give me justice, damn you!" Finally, Aganyú turned toward the young Changó and roared. "Get away from me boy! I don't know what you are talking about. I am not your father. Your *puta madre* is a fuckin' liar!" Aganyú's denial only made Changó angrier and more persistent since he has always despised lies and deceptions.

"I am Changó, son of Yemmu – now Yemayá, the wife of Ayáguna – now Obatalá; and you are my father!" he bellowed at the top of his lungs, as lighting crashed all around them and thunder could be heard from miles away. Yes, Aganyú could see much of himself in Changó, especially that burning temper. But he could never admit to the affair lest the powerful Obatalá would seek vengeance for trespassing upon his property. And although he still feared Obatalá, he was enraged by the insolence of the young man standing before him, so once again he turned his back. But Changó dogged him like a pit bull chomping away on a meaty bone. It wasn't long before the volatile Aganyú turned around and spewed hot molten lava from his mouth, hurling Changó into the skies. Changó was shaken, his clothes were singed, but he was not hurt since any true child of Aganyú, would be impervious to fire. Changó left that first encounter defeated. With the passage of time, he continued to persist - day-in and day-out - wearing down the mighty Aganyú's resoluteness. As Aganyú's heart softened, the two *orishas* began the long arduous process of reconciling as father and son. Unfortunately, such a happy ending was not to occur between Changó and his brother Oggún.

Unlike his encounter with Aganyú, where Changó sought satisfaction through recognition, he sought satisfaction from Oggún through revenge. Once he and Aganyú made peace, and after a long rest, he mounted his white stallion Echinlá, and rode as quickly as lightening to the land of Takúa to confront Oggún. Oggún, after being seduced from a life in the forest as a hermit by the enchanting Ochún who had led him back to civilization like a lamb after her tantalizing honey-covered fingers had touched his lips, ended up marrying her. But alas, the marriage was short-lived. With time he met the tempestuous Oyá, goddess of the wind and storms and ruler of the cemetery gates. A ferocious beauty, she, like Oggún, was a warrior in her own right. Oggún left the petite and lovely Ochún and married his stormy new love, making their home in the land of Takúa, where they both jointly ruled. At first, they lived an idyllic life, but with the passage of time, Oggún, the incurable workaholic, spend most of his waking hours divided between his forger and hunting in the forest. It wasn't long before Oyá felt neglected. Maybe if Oggún would have paid his wife more attention and stayed home, the many battles with his brother could have been avoided. But then again, maybe their feud was inevitable since both of these *orishas* flourish the most when they are engaged in physical conflict.

When Changó arrived, his brother was at the forge beating metals into swords on his anvil. Changó did not confront Oggún at his workplace but headed instead to his brother's house. There, behind the house, he spotted Oyá working in her garden, wearing a red cropped top and a multicolored skirt that created billowing whirlwinds as she moved. She was more attractive than he expected: an exciting woman with wild and big dark hair, who was also temperamental and powerful in a raw and earthy way. He strutted toward her as she was busy planting, allowing his shadow to fall upon her. Oyá looked up, brushing some of that enormous enticing hair away from her face to gaze upon the posturing Changó, who knew just how handsome he truly was. He wore clean white knee-length breeches and a red vest laden with gold braid and cowrie shells. The sight actually took her breath away, strangely arousing her, even though she fought to maintain a certain aloofness.

"Who the hell are you," she asked, "and what the fuck do you want?" "You," he responded. Without saying a word, he grabbed her by the hand and led her into the house. Although Oyá found the dazzling Changó more desirable than the homely Oggún, she tried nonetheless to pretend resistance for the sake of propriety, but if truth be told, she was too fed-up from being ignored by a husband who would rather make war than love. She eagerly followed Changó to Oggún's bed. Few women could resist his piercing eyes and sensuous full lips. He had always been able to seduce any woman he wanted, known for keeping forty-four wives in his stable sexually satisfied. Soon her knees weakened, and her body responded to his surprisingly gentle touch. And while Oggún pounded at his metals a few yards away, Changó pounded away at Oggún's wife. His gift in lovemaking was the surprising softness of his caresses, always leading the women to ecstasy before himself. Their love making was passionate as the lord of thunder and the goddess of the storms merged into one. For Oyá, it was as if fire was burning into her life force as she trembled in pain and pleasure. By far it was the most fulfilling sexual experience either had ever engaged in.

Changó's initial purpose had been to shame his brother by seducing his wife, leaving both humiliated, but now everything had changed. The two new lovers found themselves eternally linked; just as strong winds always announce the coming of the lighting storm. As everyone knows, whenever the wind picks up, thunder is not far away, chasing after it. As they lay perspiring together in Oggún's bed, Changó was amazed at how quickly he had fallen in love. He talked Oyá into leaving with him, and the neglected wife did not need much convincing. Mounting the faithful steed Echinlá, they both rode off to his homestead in Oyo. She didn't even bother to leave a note for the unsuspecting Oggún.

Late that night when Oggún returned to his home, he first noticed how quiet it was, and how there was no sound of a whirlwind skirt moving from room to room. He searched the house, but there was no Oyá. He searched throughout his realm, but no one in Takúa knew where Oyá was, although a few said that they had seen her ride off with Changó.

"Changó?" wondered Oggún, completely baffled, "what could that mean?" Wasting no time, he headed toward Oyo to fetch his woman, thinking the worst and ready for a fight. When Oggún arrived at Changó's palace, he demanded the return of his wife. This was the moment Changó had been waiting for. "You motherfucker," Changó bellowed, reminding his brother of the reprehensible act he committed. Oggún realized immediately that the seduction of his wife had been to satisfy the hunger for revenge. Oggún still felt sorrow and guilt, but it had subsided over the years and he had begun to find healing in his spirit. But this reminder revived the pain and ripped open the deep wound he had committed upon himself, becoming angry once again with this very old rage from what seemed to be the beginning of time.

Soon, the two brothers were locked in combat, as thunderbolt struck iron. The start of all earthly warfare can be traced to this one moment. Although Oggún is the Lord of wars, it soon appeared as if he would be defeated. Oyá, either out of pity or a remembrance of a once-felt endearment, stepped in between the two brothers and brought an end to the fight. But this was a temporary reprieve, as many future battles lay ahead, and since that day, the two *orishas*, Changó and Oggún, remain mortal enemies.

From this first battle, Changó no longer would use tools made of iron. Even his emblem the *oshe*, the double-edge thunder ax, is made of wood. Soon after, Oggún left the town of Oyo while Oyá remained as one of Changó's mistresses, his favorite concubine. She may not be as sensual or alluring as

Ochún, but she was a mighty warrior – both in the battlefield and in the bedchamber. This passionate jousting was not limited to lovemaking. Whenever the couple fought, usually because of Changó's womanizing, their confrontations were fierce and the elements – the thunder, lightning, rainstorms, and wind – all bore down upon the world of humans with ferocity. Yet, whenever she battles by Changó's side against a common enemy, they are unstoppable, able to accomplish anything.

There was a time when Changó was engaged in a losing battle. Surrounded, hungry, tired, and wounded, it seemed inevitable that he would soon be captured and killed. He struggled to crawl his way to Oyá's house, seeking succor. If he could only rest, he could regain his strength to fight another day, able to triumph over his enemies. But first he had to somehow find a path through enemy lines. Oyá had an idea. Cutting off her giant and wild hair, she made a wig for Changó to wear after she shaved off all his own hair. Then, she clothed him in one of her dresses, hence the origins of Changó's sexual duality. It is as if all braggadocious machos have a hidden gay side. Disguised, Changó was able to walk through the enemy camp undetected and once safe, he rested and regained his vigor. Soon, he was ready for battle. He rode into the enemy's camp, at full force. At that exact moment, Oyá appeared swinging a sword in each hand, proving that she is a woman fiercer than her lover. Together they routed Changó's foes. Since then, she has been his inseparable love and war companion. Together - invincible.

Macho, Macho, Macho Man

"*¡Coño, tu sí eres macho!*"* Miguelito was stunned. This was probably the first time his father had ever given him a compliment. Usually, the old man referred to him, ever since he was a boy, as *inútil* – useless, worthless. Or worse, as *un pedo atravesado*, a term difficult to translate, but meaning something like an obstructed fart. So, to hear his father out of nowhere call him *truly macho* swelled up the young man's ego. At that time, shortly after turning twenty, Miguelito found himself penniless after pouring all his financial resources into founding a real estate company. The business was still in its infancy and had yet to turn a profit. In order to save money, the young entrepreneur moved back into his old bedroom. His father, on this particular day, walked in on him while Miguelito was shaving. Unable to afford the forty-nine cent can of Barasol, Miguelito took to shaving with just soap and

---

* "Damn, you truly are a macho!"

water. For some inexplicable reason, this impressed his father, shaving *á lo macho*. The young man, normally starving for his father's approval, was so moved he never again used shaving cream, even when he was able to afford to buy the cheap red, white and blue can by the case. But becoming macho in his father's eyes proved more painful than the razor burns acquired for shaving without soothing lotion. No one is born a macho. They are forged and made into one through the painful process of years of beating out any traces of sensitivity or gentleness.

As it so happened, despite the financial deprivations he had experienced as a child, or maybe because of these scarcities, Miguelito developed into an extremely sensitive boy. He was quick to weep whenever he witnessed pain, even when the one aching was a Saturday morning television cartoon character. Such tenderness infuriated his parents who were afraid their only child would grow up to become a *maricón*. The boy was simply too soft, too gentle. They believed he needed to be toughened up. For them, **to be a real man, a macho, implied domination over, and the protection of those who fall short of the braggadocious toxic masculine ideal. Machos, by definition, bear the responsibility of educating and caring for those who lack the aggressive virility measured by the size of their *cojones*.** If Miguelito was to become a macho, he needed to be hardened. Going beyond the mantra of "boys don't cry" which was beaten into him, they found a so-called doctor, who allegedly was once licensed to practice medicine in Cuba, to begin a treatment of eleven testosterone injections prior to the boy reaching puberty. Every two weeks this "doctor" would come to their apartment to give their son his shot of manhood.

Marta and Manuel were determined that no son of theirs would grow up to be a *maricón*. That simply would have been *el colmo*, the last straw, the very worst thing that could happen to any decent Cuban family. In their minds, death of their beloved child was preferable than him becoming queer. They would do whatever was necessary to prevent such shame from befalling the de la Cruz name. For now, bimonthly shots. Some time later, his real initiation into manhood.

The testosterone treatment was not what was responsible for Miguelito's increased interest in the shape of women's bodies. Years before the start of his medical regiment, he was quite aware of his emerging sexuality. When he was **about seven years old, living in the low-income Irish and Italian neighborhood in Queens, the once-ruthless Cuban cop obtained employment as the passive stereotypical superintendent of a six-story colonial revival building constructed in 1934, located a few blocks northwest of Roosevelt Avenue and Junction Boulevard. In 1909, with the completion of the Queensboro Bridge, on about 300 acres of marsh spotting the occasional small farm, a village named Jackson Heights began to emerge. As the transit lines from Manhattan snaked their way into Queens around 1917, garden apartments were built for the white middle- and upper-class Anglo-Saxon Protestants. These buildings were kept for white tenants through deed restrictions and city ordinances. The** neighborhood became an oasis for those wishing to escape Gotham's urbanization with its commercial cluster, housing shortages, crime and grime. Jews began to move into the neighborhood during the 1940s. It would take another decade before the first middle-class Spanish-speaking family, immigrants from Colombia, also made Jackson Heights their home. The de la Cruz family joined the influx of new tenants from India and Latin America in the mid-sixties, while white Protestants with enough economic means were able to move out, leaving behind mostly Italians and Irish Catholics from the lower working class. Middle-class African Americans also started moving into the neighborhood during this time, but they were kept segregated east of Junction Boulevard.

The de la Cruz family were the first Hispanics on the block, making Miguelito the first Latino ever to enroll in Blessed Sacrament elementary school. By the time the school closed in 2009 to become PS 280, the student enrollment was almost 90% Latiné. But back then, during the mid-sixties, when Miguelito first attended class, the parochial school was primarily responsible for teaching the neighborhood Irish and Italians kids who regularly rumbled among themselves, but now with Miguelito's arrival, occasionally joined forces to pick on him. Whenever he found himself in a scuffle, he had to do whatever it took to be victorious, because if he ever came home bloody and defeated, or worse, ran away in fear, Marta would give him a worse thrashing for not being man enough to handle the fight. Her beatings usually involved the stick of a broom. *"No seas maricón,"*[*] Marta constantly yelled at her boy, which was her way of impressing upon him the importance of not being a coward. By the time he was ten, thanks to the Greek actors portraying Puerto Ricans in the film *West Side Story*, he began to learn what a Latino man was supposed to be, and how he was supposed to act. A wannabe gangbanger, he started carrying a switchblade.

Blessed Sacrament Church and its adjacent elementary school where Miguelito spent the first eight years of his education was half a block from his family's apartment. There he was confirmed into the Holy Mother Church, picking St. Francis as his confirmation saint. He came from a long line of devoted Catholics. His paternal grandfather was a Catholic priest, who lucky for the young boy, met his wife – and Miguelito's grandmother - while serving her communion, among other things. Thanks to an early nineteenth century tradition, a seat at the Catholic seminary in Camagüey Cuba would always be reserved for all future first-born de la Cruz men, Miguelito's grandfather and his first-born son, Miguelito's uncle, had enjoyed their guaranteed attendance there. The uncle, however, would later abandon seminary when he discovered too many Marxist books in the school library. No doubt, if the de la Cruz family would have stayed in Cuba, Miguelito too would have gone to the Catholic seminary and become a Roman Catholic priest.

---

[*] "Don't be a fag,"

Not only was Miguelito confirmed into the faith at Blessed Sacrament, but it was also there, years before his testosterone treatments ever began, that his first sexual awakening occurred as he became spellbound by nuns' legs. He was in second grade when Vatican II concluded, which was the Catholic conference radically liberalizing the worldwide church. But for an eight-year-old boy, the only radical change he noticed was that nuns could now display the hair on their heads as well as their legs previously hidden under their ankle-length skirts. Pre-Vatican II, the Grey Nuns of the Sacred Heart who taught at Blessed Sacrament wore skirts low enough to cover their boots and tucked all their hair under their Catholic hijab. After Vatican II, what was impressed upon the small boy was how the new veils exposed a portion of the nun's previously covered heads. They were blonds, brunets, and redheads. Some of the nuns had long flowing hair while others had graying or totally white hair. More important than nun's hairstyles were the length of their skirts, now raised to just below their knees, exposing their legs for all the world to see. He was too young and too immature to appreciate the radical changes taking place in the parish but was really captivated by the nun's long – and he imagined - silky legs.

This was also around the time Miguelito experienced his first encounter with sexual abuse. One of the Irish teenage girls from the school, probably around fifteen, lived in his apartment building and was paid a few dollars a week to watch over him after school and supervise his homework while his parents worked. Once in a while the bored teenager would force Miguelito to touch her and her friend. "Here, give me your hand," she would say, guiding it between her and her friend's legs as they squeezed hard. "Tell us, which is warmer?" This left poor Miguelito confused. They were older and he had to obey them. He knew something was wrong. No, he shouldn't be engaged in their games. And yet he felt aroused. Repulsed. This was what his parents meant by becoming a man. Right? To be a macho, in their eyes, always meant to be sexually ready for anybody, anywhere, anytime. This is why they had no qualms giving him Playboy magazines since he started elementary school, a collection he kept under his bed mattress and every so often brought to school to share with the other boys in his class. Maybe if they were too busy ogling centerfolds, they might be less inclined to beat him up. Still, he didn't want to touch these older girls, and yet a part of him did. Was he wrong to struggle with the emerging expectations of exhibiting some type of supercharged sexual persona, always at the brink of sexual desire and release? At eight years old? Couldn't he first just be a kid, free from these confusing and shameful feelings? The poor boy went from playing with miniature fire engines to a having a burning desire to play with women's bodies.

By the time Miguelito turned twelve he had his first puppy love crush on a girl his own age, Silvia, with dark black hair and Moroccan eyes. Both were more enamored with the idea of being sweethearts than with actually having any type of relationship. They would exchange love notes – well, at least notes that said they liked each other "very, very, very much," so this made them feel as if they were courting. So cute, so innocent, so different than what those older girls made him do when he was younger. But whenever he was alone with Silvia, the shy, timid Miguelito simply did not know what to say or how to behave. Was he supposed to grab her pussy like the older girls had taught him to do? Or was he supposed to just hold her hand? Was he supposed to kiss her? On the cheek? On the lips? Totally confused, Miguelito turned to Guillermo, a friend of the family with whom he always found it easy to speak about such things. Ironically, Guillermo was everything his parents feared their boy would grow up to become, a *maricón*. And yet, Guillermo was no coward. In fact, if being a macho meant fearlessness, boldness, courage and possessing humongous *cojones*, then Guillermo was probably the most macho man the young Miguelito had ever met. And so Miguelito's first lessons about love were taught to him by this gay man. How sad that these lessons about gentleness and good manners would soon be undone by his macho father.

As a practitioner of Santería, Guillermo was a devotee of the *orisha* Inle, a beautiful teenager with chiseled cinnamon abs who made his living healing others through the herbs he gathered in the forest. Inle was impeccable in his sense of fashion, especially when sporting his favorite calf-length harem pants which were a pinkish coral blue. He enjoyed going shirtless, allowing the sun's rays to gently caress his bare and naked chest. His long silky hair worn in seven braids was typically wrapped in a green turban, highlighting his smooth babyface and giving him a feminine appearance. One day, while sitting upon the rocks where the forest meets the ocean, he heard a splash which interrupted his examination of certain curious herbs he had recently gathered. Looking up he caught the eye of Yemayá who had emerged from the sea and for some time had been admiring the beautiful boyish herbalist from afar. Appreciation for his good looks soon turned to thirsty obsession. Playing coy at first, she splashed around the seashore trying to further engage him. When the pansexual Inle did finally notice her, he immediately was hooked, falling in love, or was it in lust, with the much older ebony goddess of the sea. She wore a blue skirt and her now soaked see-through top outlined the voluptuous breasts with which she nourished all of creation. Upon her kinky curly hair, she wore a majestic crown made of seashells and living starfish.

"Marry me!" demanded the impulsive Inle. But Yemayá refused, being that her home was in the sea. "Live with me instead," she softly purred. "But how could I," he responded, "for I am limited by lungs needing their constant fill of oxygen." As Inle pondered his limitations, Yemayá, without any prior indication, grabbed the young man and passionately kissed him, wiggling her tongue quite pleasantly down his throat like a raw oyster. They slowly submerged into the cold embrace of the ocean waters, where he soon realized that this kiss revealed the secret of breathing underwater. Inle was thus able to join her at the bottom of the ocean, where they spent months engaged in passionate lovemaking. Days were spent without ever leaving their bedchamber. There is something, Yemayá thought, about a young man whose endurance and raw potency makes up for a lack of experience. He was, after all, always at the ready. The longer they remained intertwined, the more she took it upon herself to tutor the undisciplined lad on how to bring a mature experienced woman to full climax. He learned that by controlling and delaying his own quavering eruptions, she would be fully satisfied, and his own release would be more enjoyable than expected.

As their intimacy grew more creative and experimental, Yemayá began to let her guard down. Soon she was teaching him more than just multiple coitus positions. Unwisely, she revealed her enormous treasures, teaching him many mysteries including the art of divination which she previously stole from Orúnla. The young Inle was a fast learner. Sadly, such pleasure-only based relationships quickly lose their appeal. He adored her but began to tire of his watery existence, getting a little bored and missing the feel of dry green grass crushed under his feet, the musky smell of the forest, the beating heat of the sun which penetrated his bones, the chirping of birds, and the gentle morning mist fondling his face. Yemayá, even less devoted than him, was nearly done with her fill of his youthful stamina. She was ready to dismiss the boy and turn toward the pursuit of more mature and seasoned coupling. However, she feared to send him packing, since, after all, he was acquainted with the secrets of her domain. Could she trust him? Would he reveal what he knew to the other *orishas*? Would his acquired knowledge in divination diminish her own powers? She eventually banished him to live at the intersection of rivers and ocean, but first she cut off his tongue, so that if he ever wanted to talk again, it could only be through her.

Guillermo, an Errol Flynn look-alike except for the orangey hair which came from a bottle, was much like the *orisha* Inle. Both had paid a heavy price due to their sexuality. But unlike Inle who could never again speak, Guillermo, comfortable in his own skin, chose instead to be vocal. During the early 1960s, men who embraced same gender-loving relationships ran the risk, like Inle, of being tortuously silenced. But Guillermo refused to live a lie. He was very candid about his sexuality. He held no trepidation with putting on makeup or wearing clothes which could at the time best be described as flamboyant. A tremendous bravery was required to be openly gay during this time when harassment and arrest was quite common at the hands of New York's finest.

Solicitation for same-gender loving relationships was illegal in the Big Apple. Violation of the law included holding hands, kissing, cross-dressing, or dancing with someone sharing your gender. Every so often the de la Cruz family would pile into their Buick Skylark and drive to the police station to bail Guillermo out after one of his arrests for one of these infractions. Years later, during the early morning hours of a 1969 summer's day, he would be among the gay men of color who participated in the Stonewall riots over in the Village. Stonewall Inn, which catered to queer Latinés, was rumored to be run by the Genovese family. The spark which launched the Gay Liberation Movement has been so whitewashed many forget the protest that summer night was ignited by queer people of color.

Manuel wasn't interested in any such liberation movements. Instead, he found queers had a utile purpose in saving his former compatriots. Fearful of the plight of former colleagues left behind, he worked hard to help get them out of Cuba. The tightening of immigration policies meant those who were married to U.S. citizens had a greater likelihood to migrate. Thus, Marta and Manuel helped to arrange marriages of convenience. They would recruit Latiné gays and lesbians in the States to marry single Cubans on the island seeking asylum. In return, the queer person was provided with the cover of marriage during a time when whom they loved was considered a violation of the law. Later, after migration, the couple would wait a respectable period of time and then simply divorce or maintained a plutonic marriage if it suited both parties. Miguelito's parents had many queer friends because, like so many other Latinos, they were not homophobic in the way *yanquis* were. They did not fear the gay man, but just held him in contempt for choosing not to demonstrate manhood through acceptable norms. So much of Cuba's social norms revolved around a dance among machos.

One could even argue that the entire Cuban Revolution could be understood as a virile contest to see which side – the batistanos or fidelistas - were the most macho. On one side of the dancefloor were the generals and police officials in the cities defending the dictatorship of Batista and on the other side were the rebels and revolutionaries in the mountains supporting Fidel. Manhood and nationhood merged, best demonstrated by which side was more macho with the largest *cojones*. In this Cuban dance, both the fascist and the Marxist have much in common, different sides of the same macho coin. Both crave to lead in the dance, to dominate and domesticate their partner, seeking to make the other their bitch. Both sides abhorred the feminine. This culturally accepted form of homophobia suggested a shared fear of betraying one's own hidden queer inclinations. In reality, no one really had *cojones*. The macho always lives threatened by their possible loss, while the one domesticated to the passive role is forcefully deprived.

Guillermo, loved by Miguelito's parents as if he were a younger brother, even as they pitied him for not truly being a man, became a willing queer ear for a straight twelve-year old boy who was baffled about girls. "How do I ask Silvia out? Do I pay for her movie ticket? Do I hold her hand? Kiss her?" Before Miguelito gained the courage to ask Silvia to the matinee show at the Polk movie theater down the street from their apartment building, Guillermo had already spoken with Silvia's parents, offering to serve as chaperone. Guillermo patiently answered Miguelito's unending questions, always with the goal of teaching the young man how to respect a young lady. Moving away from binary gender constructs, he tried as best he could for the 1960s to teach the importance of establishing a relationship not based on macho illusions. For about a week before his big date the boy learned how to treat women with respect and preference. Unlike what he witnessed at home, a man never hits a woman, and before kissing or even holding hands, the couple should first become friends. "Relationships were to be based on talking, not grabbing" Guillermo insisted. For the first time, Miguelito learned concepts like soulmate and life partner, reinforcing but for a moment, his gentler sensitivities. "Going to the movies is just that, a chance to talk after the flick," Guillermo impressed upon the boy. "Don't rush things. You have a whole life ahead of you. Learn now what it means to develop deep trusting bonds." This healthy perspective could have carried the young boy to more fulfilling and wholesome interactions with women for when he entered teenage and early adult years. Unfortunately, his **father was very much worried that** Miguelito, at age twelve, was still a virgin. He would mockingly call the boy a *señorito*.*

"No son of mine is going to be a *maricón*," Manuel bellowed at Marta. "I'll call Montenegro," he decided. Montenegro was also a former cop in Cuba who they helped leave the island. In *el exilio*, the man became a pimp and hustler, always looking for an angle by which to make money, mostly on the wrong side of the law. The betrayal of the child's trust came to pass once his parents convinced themselves they were helping their son become an adult, specifically helping a soft sensitive boy become a tough man who could survive in a world out to screw him. "This is my responsibility as a father,"

---

* Señorito in an insulting term equivalent to the honorific title 'Miss'.

Manuel thought, "my duty, to make a man out of this boy." Marta remained uncharacteristically silent. Based on her own tragic experiences, she has been taught to see through the eyes of the macho culture which had inflicted its own abuses upon her. Although such things concerning the deflowering of future machos was best left to older men, she nevertheless convinced herself it was a necessity to ensure her son's ability to flourish in a man's world. Accepting the legitimation of what men must do, robbed her of her voice and suppressed her motherly instinct to protect her child.

One night the former cop set out to fix this shameful problem of having a virgin son by hiring a sex worker through his friend Montenegro. Some would call this child abuse. But could it really be called that? Ridiculous. It was tradition, the father's responsibility to make a man out of his son. But at twelve? It was a gift, something to brag about, not complain. Right? Only a *maricón* would complain, and Miguelito was no *maricón*. For Miguelito to object would only prove he was a *maricón* and incur the eternal disappointment of his parents. He cannot continue disappointing his father. He had to man-up. And yet, there was feelings of embarrassment, of shame. But he can brag about it at school, showing off he was now a man. But how exactly do you talk about something which was by law illegal? And who in his elementary class would have believed him? And if he would have shared his dirty little secret, more than likely it would have been met with incredulity rather than winks, sly smiles, or high-fives.

All this was normal. Every boy goes through this ritual. Right? But he never heard anyone his age speak about such things. So confusing. He just had to play his part. He just had to be a dutiful and obedient son. He trusted his parents so it would all turn out for the better. Right? There is nothing wrong with what was about to happen because his parents orchestrated it. Besides, who ever heard of a man being raped by a woman? Laughable to even consider such a question. Right? Is twelve too young to know you do not want to, even if you think you do? Besides, isn't this the stuff of fantasies? Scenes of older females seducing and sleeping with teenage boys have been the erotic substance for countless novels and coming-of-age movies. Coo coo ca choo Mrs. Robinson. So, it really can't be wrong. Or can it? So confusing.

Miguelito felt nauseated but knew this is what real men bragged about, and which had to be kept secret. On the other hand, *not* bragging about it would mean he didn't enjoy it and would be branded a *maricón*. He should feel lucky for "having conquered a vagina" even while he felt it had been the other way around. He remained scared shitless throughout the encounter, not knowing what to do, what to touch, or how to act; still, this humiliation was supposed to be the moment Miguelito became a man. That was what his parents wanted. That was what he wanted? But all he felt was embarrassment blended with arousal, disgraced, pleasure and dirtiness, an erect self-disgust panged by a throbbing libido. The remaining embers of innocence were fully extinguished that fateful night and he developed, in order to survive from it all, a very obnoxious attitude toward women who, in his mind, came to believe they existed solely to please men.

The sex worker was beautiful, no doubt about that. A Latina with bronze skin and long, straight black hair that wisped across her hips, thin and quite buxom. Renting out her body to strangers is what put food on the table for her and her young daughter. Single mothers would do anything to feed their children, even perpetuate the cycle of their own oppression for the sake of their child. And there were always men like Montenegro available to abuse her financial plight. As a mother-surrogate, she tried to accept the role of teaching Miguelito about life and sex, but such a misogynistic lie falls short, leading her - all too often – to dull her senses by drinking more than she should. How tragic, that this motherly teacher is forced to perpetuate into the next generation the abuses she and other women suffer at the hands of men and women like Miguelito's parents who believed this is what it took to make a man out of him. Becoming a man meant becoming a bastard like his father, assuming power to control the important decisions of life. Abusiveness toward women symbolized the intoxicating dominance over all who fell short of the definition of a *macho*. For a while, Miguelito did become his father's son through scars carved into his psyche which would never fully heal. The first casualty of becoming a *macho* was the end of his tender emerging friendship with Silvia.

A few nights later, when he was supposed to pick her up and take her to the movies, Miguelito failed to show up. No call, no cancellation. He simply did not show up at the appointed hour. Knowledge had made puppy-love too infantile. Poor Silvia. She went shopping with her mom a few days earlier, purchasing a mod outfit. She sat waiting in her living room that night for the knock on her door which never came. After a few hours, it became obvious she was stood-up, and at such an early age. "Por que mami," she sobbed, not really wanting an answer. Refusing comforting words from her parents, she cried herself to sleep that night, never knowing why the boy who obviously had a crush on her a few days ago, lost interest so quickly. "What is wrong with me?" she mused. She racked her brains trying to figure out what she did wrong. Guillermo, embarrassed over Miguelito's brutish behavior after vouching for the boy to Silvia's parents, seldom talked to him again. So many lives damaged and betrayed for the sake of propping up and perpetuating *machismo*.

As Miguelito entered his teenage years he was no longer interested in other women his own age. He sought to use older women just as they, like Yemayá, were eager to use him. Few were able to resist Miguelito's bedroom eyes. Like Inle, there was much he could learn from more mature women who knew exactly what they wanted in the bedroom and enjoyed breaking in young studs. As he matured, he continued to seek these older, more experienced women, specifically white women, who were ten, twenty, and even thirty years his senior, who took great pleasure in introducing him to their friends as their "hot-blooded Latin-Lover." To be taken by Latin Lovers, these white women could go slumming, losing themselves to their secret primitive urges, like a male version of the *femme fatale* characters they had seen in the movies. But great loneliness exists when relationships are nothing but physical.

Banished to the in-between place, where the fresh waters of rivers converge upon the salty waters of the sea, Inle experienced unbearable loneliness. He was back on the firm land he missed, harvesting herbs and providing tonics for the infirm. But his heart ached when he thought of Yemayá and reminisced on the hours spent laying in her bed, the sweet aroma of the sheets and pillowcases that had been drenched in their sweaty lovemaking. He lived in silent solitude, without a tongue, feeling the weight of crushing emptiness. With time, he was joined by Abata, who had also been seduced and then rejected by the queen of the sea. The *orisha* of swamps and marshes had been made deaf and also expelled to live with Inle. Over the years they developed a deep companionship and the ability to communicate telepathically, the way married couples do after years of cohabitating. Soon the two young men became inseparable and passionate lovers. From then forward, Inle would always be spotted with two intertwined snakes wrapped around his body, snakes being the symbol of Abata. Not surprisingly, Inle became the patron *orisha* of the queer community, a people silenced by society due to their sexuality. Occupying a space which is neither salty nor fresh, neither ocean nor river, neither masculine nor feminine, Inle in the spirt world and Guillermo in the world of humans provided comfort and support against the corrosive and destructive powers of machismo. For Miguelito though, it was too late to hold on to his innocence, his sensitivity, or his gentleness, as he learned to be an uncaring misogynist like his father.

And what about Guillermo? He remained in Jackson Heights for the rest of his days and saw a hostile community become more welcoming. Well into his sixties, forgotten for his role at Stonewall, he was shaken by the murder of Julio Rivera, a twenty-nine-year-old gay bartender. Three white skinheads, wishing to reclaim Jackson Heights from the gays, bashed in his skull with a hammer not far from where he was living on 37th Avenue. This heinous crime was another transformative moment, sparking a movement for equal rights in Queens, a movement in which Guillermo participated. Three years later, Jackson Heights held its first pride parade in 1993 and Guillermo was there waving his rainbow flag.

Call Me Mike

"Aaaaaaaaaaaa." Piercing shrieks from a scrawny twelve-year-old girl with sorrowful grey eyes and golden hair pulled back in a ponytail filled the air, momentarily paralyzing her companions. Miguelito, by then a fourteen-year-old, would remember this high-pitched shrieking sound for a very long time afterward. Just a moment ago, before Sally Kolbert had seen the gruesome site causing her shock, the kids had been singing the Dolphin's fight song at the top of their lungs: "Miami has the Dolphins, the greatest football team, we take the ball from goal to goal, like no one's ever seen, *something*, *something*, *something*, Miami Dolphins, Miami Dolphins, Miami Dolphins number one." They were headed south along the train tracks next to 72nd avenue toward an open field of dirt and vegetation on Bird Road. Four years later these sixty-five acres would be developed into the Barnes Park, named for Miami's first Director of the Parks and Recreation Department. But for now, as the kids made their way toward the untamed neighborhood's open space which spotted overgrowth so thick that it could only be penetrated with the hacking of a machete, they hoped to amuse themselves with all kinds of afterschool games. An hour ago, they had dropped their schoolbooks off at their respective homes and gathered at Sally's house because her mom could be relied upon to provide tasty home cooked snacks.

Mrs. Kolbert, as wide as she was short, liked to brag about how she had ignored the Hippie fashions and wild and free hairdos of the 1960s, insisting instead on stubbornly maintaining her beehive hairstyle. She had her nails and hair done every Thursday at 10 am and dressed "appropriately" with her neatly ironed outdated dress and imitation pearl necklace which matched her short-sleeved, pearl-button cardigan. She ruled over her domain, a three-bedroom, one bath stucco house – more so than a home – filled with hand-me-down Eisenhower-era furniture. From her natural habitat, the kitchen, she made sure to prepare a fresh batch of cookies for the neighborhood kids to devour, baked from scratch, not from cheap box mixes, so that the neighborhood kids could inform their parents that Sally came from a good home. Maybe if women spent more time in the kitchen rather than the workplace, the God-ordained social order wouldn't be going to hell in a handbasket, she regularly thought to herself.

Middle-schoolers usually gathered at Sally's, although it often felt just a tad bit too perfect with nothing ever out of place. On this lazy Wednesday afternoon, only boys showed up at her door. Every so often some girls would participate, but on this particular day, it was just boys, meaning more than likely they would end up playing touch football. Miami's football fever was still on everyone's mind since just a few weeks earlier, during Super Bowl VII, the Dolphins trounced the Washington Redskins, becoming the first NFL team to go undefeated for an entire season. Don Shula could surely do no wrong. Sally didn't really mind playing football with the boys. She knew she could throw the pigskin better than any of them but would have preferred to play hide-and-seek, especially if she could find a place to hide with the new Cuban boy she had a crush on.

Miguelito's family had moved into the neighborhood a few months ago from New York. Although motivated by a possible role for his father in some Cuban counterrevolutionary plot, the move provided the opportunity to escape the cold winters and the skyrocketing violence found on the streets of the Big Apple. The PR advertising campaign to promote tourism which would be released a few years later – "I ♥ NY" – could not mask how crime and neglect finally took its toll. Besides, Miami's climate reminded his parents of the country they left behind, and a safer environment, or so it seemed a decade before the rise of the cocaine cowboys.

Sally was smitten from the first moment she saw Miguelito helping his dad unload the tin looking moving truck with the orange cab. Unfortunately, her family did not feel the same way. "Damn Cubans," her balding father with mutton chop sideburns bellowed when he first noticed them moving into the house next door. "You can be sure home prices will be dropping soon," he predicted. "Happens every time those goddamn people move into a neighborhood. At least they're better than the n*ggers, even if they're still a whiter mongrel race. Maybe it's time to sell and move to Fort Lauderdale?" Sally frowned, not quite understanding her father's anger, but instantly absorbed his racist tirade as true and factual.

On this particular humid February day, Sally's father, with his white button-down collar short-sleeve dress shirt and black polyester clip-on tie, was off working as a comptroller in the City Manager's office, blissfully unaware that his daughter was spending her afternoons with a property-depressor. Even her mother believed Sally's lie, when all the kids left after snacks, that she was going over to a girlfriend's house. If Mrs. Kolbert knew the truth, she never would have allowed her daughter to leave. And if Sally's father found out, he would have immediately put their house up for sale and moved them to the next county. But Sally's secret would remain safe today.

Greg was the oldest and skinniest of the four boys, although his grubby face was often puffy from constant sniffling due to allergies. Stan was the moody one, probably due to his older brother recently dying in Vietnam, a fate all four boys believed awaited them once they turned eighteen. Billy was Sally's age and sat next to her in English class, and Miguelito was literally the new kid on the block. Greg was wearing a Miami Dolphin t-shirt whose short sleeves he often used as a handkerchief for his running nose. He brought along the football hoping everyone would agree to play a few games. Mrs. Kolbert graciously served the warm oatmeal cookies, although she had recently stopped offering cold milk. She didn't want to throw away whatever glass Miguelito might use. It would eventually just be too expensive to keep replacing them. True, it would have been easier to tell her daughter not to invite him, but as a devout born-again Christian, she did not want to appear unwelcoming. She was no racist, she constantly told herself, but you just never know what kind of germs those kinds of people carry. While some of her best friends were Cuban, she still made a mental note to have *the talk* with her daughter. As the Bible teaches: birds of a feather should flock together.

Miguelito seemed like a polite enough kid. Still, Mrs. Kolbert felt uncomfortable with a Latin boy around her daughter. Visiting after school with other kids was fine for now, but Mrs. Kolbert noticed Sally's body starting to change. She was developing underarm hair, and it was only a matter of time before Aunt Flo would start making her regular visits. The last thing her daughter needed now as she moved into her teenage years was any type of malicious gossip. Hmmmm, Mrs. Kolbert thought to herself, maybe it's time to enroll her in the church's new private school, where her daughter could mingle with a better and more spiritual class of people. Ever since public schools started to desegregate, some churches responded by opening Christian schools, advocating the importance of providing their children salvation from the predominate anti-Christian secular educational curriculum. Mrs. Kolbert continued to insist on being fooled by such a righteous-sounding defense. In her mind, God needs to be central in the lives of children and only Jesus can save. All this unrest in our streets can be traced to the day when the government started prohibiting prayers in school. Kids need prayer. What would end all this unrest is a Christ-centered education provided right from the start; a place where false teachings like evolution would not be tolerated. Mrs. Kolbert sighed. This was what parents would constantly tell themselves, an excuse they repeated so often they actually came to believe it, even though it was common knowledge that the real purpose was to provide a loophole to the Supreme Court's mandate to desegregate.

Miguelito, at the time, was oblivious to these deep concerns buried within the hearts and minds of his adult Anglo neighbors. He was just happy he could quickly make friends after having moved from New York. By the time the de la Cruz family arrived in Miami, Miguelito really wanted nothing to do with his parent's reminiscences, wishing, more than anything, to be as white as his racist neighbors. He tired of hearing how everything was so much better in Cuba. If Cuba was such a great prize, why didn't his parents stay and fight for it? Of course, he would never betray his parents by voicing these thoughts out loud since it would break their hearts. So, he found other ways to rebel which even he couldn't really explain. Late at night, he would watch Walter Cronkite on the 11 o'clock news on CBS, imitating his pronunciation, repeating the opening top stories while trying to match the pitch, tone, and inflection so that he could sound like a real American, in this case an American from St. Joseph,

Missouri. And yet despite all this practice and sessions with the school speech therapist, anyone who has ever heard Miguelito speak knows that he failed miserably.

He would tell all his new white friends to just call him Mike. A few times he even introduced himself as Michael Cross. He wanted so much to be accepted as white, to be just like them, that he stayed out of the sun as much as possible and when outdoors used large quantities of sunblock in a vain attempt to not appear too brown. If he wanted to belong, he would have to circumcise his Cubanness. Miguelito must die for Mike to be resurrected. This is not the first-time violence was imposed upon his very name. As a first grader learning to spell his surname, the Irish nuns at Blessed Sacrament wrote "De La Cruz" on a piece of folded carboard and placed it on his wooden desk so he could practice. When he tried to explain that the "d" and the "l" should be written in lowercase, they insisted all last names had to be written in uppercase. When he refused, he had his knuckles wacked with a ruler. To this day, as evident on the front cover of all the academic books he would eventually write, his name, in print form, always appears with capital "D" and "L," a legacy which continues with his offspring. Assimilation is not so much a choice, regardless of what one believes. It is mostly painfully reinforced.

When his family left New York and moved to Miami, he avoided the other Cuban kids, preferring to make friends among the Anglo ones, hoping to eventually fully assimilate, somehow washing off the Cuban stench which clearly caused so much disgust and anxiety among white people. And why shouldn't he try? When given a choice between the privileges which comes with whiteness and the repression associated with darker hues, even as a child he knew the former was the better deal – or so he thought. He now lived in the greatest country in the world with every intention of making it big. He would succeed where his parents fell short. Who knows, he could even grow up to one day be a congressman or even a governor! And why not? What could stand in his way? Who cared if the other Cuban kids called him *un cubano arrepentido* – a repentant Cuban. With all his heart he believed the mythology that if he worked hard, if he kept his nose to the grindstone, he could become successful. Those begging for money on the street corners were there because they were just lazy and unwilling to apply themselves. There was no way in Hell he was going to join them, so he planned out his steps carefully. Eventually, he opened a real estate company and even had a brief political career as a candidate for the Florida House of Representatives. But that was still a few years away. For now, all he wanted was to play games with his new Anglo friends and have some fun.

He was glad to make friends quickly, but he was somewhat annoyed that Sally was always hanging around. Couldn't she go play with the other girls? At least her mom made great cookies. How he wished his own mother would be more like her - so proper, so immaculate, so white. He could never bring his friends over to his house because he just knew his mom would embarrass him in her *bata de casa* – her housecoat - serving Cuban desserts like *pastelitos de guayaba*. Although he was somewhat conflicted about this. After all, he loved guava pastries, especially the ones with cream cheese, but surely his friends would hate them because they were weird and foreign. He recalled sharing a pastry with Greg once who, after taking a bite, promptly spat it out. After that embarrassing episode, Miguelito also stopped eating them.

The boys wolfed down the oatmeal cookies at Sally's house and then headed out to the opposite end of the block. They waited for about fifteen minutes for Sally to join them after she convinced her mom she was going over to the house of a girlfriend. Once reunited, they headed for the open field. At the time the de la Cruz family was living south of 40th Street, also known as Bird Road. To get to the open field they would have to walk east for about half a mile along the canal and then cross over the railroad tracks. Miguelito hadn't yet become used to playing outdoors in February wearing shorts and a t-shirt. Temperatures in his former New York were barely hitting the 50s, but today Miami sported a gorgeous sunny day in the mid-70s. He really loved Miami! Sally was wearing red "short shorts," the kind where the tips of her bottom cheeks sought freedom. *Cubanitas* would never be allowed to walk around not fully covered, Miguelito thought, regardless as to how hot she or the day was. "Date the *americanitas* and have fun," his mother would constantly remind him, "just be sure to marry a *cubanita*."

Because Sally was walking in front, leading the boys in the Dolphin fight song, she was the first to see what appeared to be the grisly remains of some sort of animal next to the train tracks. With the wind at their backs, they hadn't smelled it yet, but Sally knew immediately it had been a dog. Finding a dead animal by the railroad tracks was not necessarily an unusual site. They did occasionally get hit by passing trains, especially at night. What was disturbing in this case was that the dead animal seemed staged, like some kind of ritualized sacrifice.

"Aaaaaaaaaaa," Sally shrieked, frightening the boys. None of them understood the meaning of what they were seeing, although for some strange reason, Miguelito had not reacted like the others. He instantly recognized it for what it was, a sacrifice made to one of the deities of his parent's primitive religion. At the time, there was no way he could have known that it was his own father who had left the carcass of the black dog by the tracks the previous night, smeared with *corojo* butter and wrapped in a green silk cloth, an offering to Oggún. The sacrifice had been dropped off before midnight Tuesday, still within Oggún's holiest day of the week. Because Oggún is the god of metals, he lords over all forms of transportation which involves cars, planes, and trains. One of Oggún's favorite places to eat is by the railroad tracks, hence the ideal local to leave the remains of a sacrifice. It is important that he is fed often, for it is said that whenever people die due to cars colliding, planes crashing, or trains derailing, Oggún was simply hungry for lack of offerings, so he caused the accident to feed on the blood of the fatalities.

Also, with the Vietnam War coming to a close, the god of war would no doubt lose a major source of obtaining the sacred energy *ashé*. Thanks to the spilled blood of soldiers, both American and Vietnamese, Oggún was kept well fed. But with the war's end in sight, and less blood being shed, Miguelito's father felt Oggún would be especially pleased with the *ebbó* - the sacrifice - he was offering. He knew his requisitions would go unanswered by the *orishas* unless they were first fed. He wasn't solely interested in placating the belligerent *orisha*. He wanted, if not needed, the militant god to reciprocate *ashé* for the fearsome task which lay before Manuel.

Much work went into preparing the sacrifice before it would appear by the tracks to be discovered by Miguelito and his newfound friends. A few days prior to the teenagers' discovery, Manuel would call Changó Botanica located on *calle Ocho* and order a black dog. Most *botanicas* procured animals for ritual sacrifices, but mainly hens and doves. Dogs were harder to obtain. Fortunately, the folks at Changó Botanica never disappoint. A mutt was found. How? Manuel neither asked nor cared. He just picked up the dog and took him home. There, he threw the cowrie shells to see if the animal was an acceptable sacrifice for Oggún. It was. Any ordained santero or santera can offer up fowl as sacrifices, but only a few, like Manuel, were initiated into the "Knife of Oggún" a secret ordination allowing them to sacrifice four-legged animals. Once the dog was ready, Manuel picked up the eleven-inch steel dagger whose wooden handle was decorated with green and black beads. Holding down the dog, pressing her head hard against the floor, Manuel sliced her jugular vein, catching the flowing blood in Oggún's green tureen.

Usually, when sacrifices are either pigs or chickens, they are eaten, but not this one. The entire carcass would be left in the open, where Oggún usually resides, so it could decay and return to the earth from which it came. Placing the dead dog in the trunk of his silver '71 Skylark, he drove a few blocks toward the railway tracks. Night has fallen, providing sufficient cover to drop off the carcass. First, he drove toward Woodlawn Cemetery for another ritual, but on the way, he stopped at Versailles, a Miami institution in *la sagüesera* – the southwestern Cuban neighborhood. Walking up to the side street cafeteria adjacent to the restaurant, Manuel gave his order to the buxom middle-aged waitress with blond hair and two-inch black roots. In a smooth sugary voice, he addressed her cleavage, *"Mi amor, dos croquetas de jamón y un cafecito, por favor."** Only when his gaze started to move upward did he notice the *elekes* she was wearing around her neck. All devotees of *los santos* wore these beaded necklaces, *collares*, which symbolizes the *orishas* she venerated. Among the five *elekes* was one consisting of seven green beads alternated with seven black beads in seven patterns signifying Oggún and another comprised of nine white beads alternated with nine black beads symbolizing Oyá. Manuel took this as a sign that his sacrifices would be acceptable and his task successful.

---

* "My love, two ham croquettes and Cuban coffee please."

After finishing his late-night snack, he left a generous tip, grateful not just for the heavenly sign, but for the extra undone button on her white blouse. With a jolt of caffeine, Manuel continued his trek to Woodlawn Cemetery, also located on *calle Ocho*, one of the oldest memorial parks in Miami. Former Cuban presidents Machado and Prío Socarrás, who found themselves living in exile, resided here, interned so far from a home where they were no longer welcomed. After leaving Versailles around midnight, he drove eastward intending to sneak into the cemetery. Along 32nd Avenue, the eastern border of the graveyard, he parked his vehicle and approached the five-foot chain fence, erected to serve as a barrier, which Manuel, along with his knapsack, easily jumped. Besides enlisting the assistance of Oggún by offering up the dog, Manuel would also require assistance from Oyá if he wanted to succeed in defending his family's honor by adding to her realm. The *orisha* Oyá, the only female warrior in the Yoruba pantheon, has dominion over the cemeteries. While she does not make her home there, she does have ownership of its gates and guides the spirit of the dead to their graves.

Once in marble town, Manuel removed from his knapsack nine homemade earthenware lamps to invoke the help of the souls of the dead. To prepare this ritual, he had purchased nine small cheap clay pots at Zayres Department Store located on 87th Avenue and Coral Way. Once home he wrote the name of his brother-in-law, Antonio, on nine slips of paper and placed these at the bottom inside of each pot. Each pot was then filled with some dirt collected from nine different graves which Manuel obtained from the same cemetery the night before, using a small seven-inch garden spade to dig up the soil. He paid for the dirt by leaving at each disturbed grave a copper penny. Back home, he mixed into the pots the grave soil and three types of pepper corns: Guinea, Chinese, and black. On top of the pepper corns went nine spoonsful of *aguardiente*, a type of factory-made "moonshine." Last, a cotton wick was inserted, and cooking oil was poured over the entire mixture. He would light the nine wicks to solicit the dead in assisting in having his brother-in-law join them. Between this and the offering to Oggún, Manuel was sure his plan to punish his sister's husband for the shame he brought upon the de la Cruz good name would be successful.

Only decades later, as the old man's brain began to be eaten away by dementia, did he confess the purpose of the sacrifice he had made so many years earlier to Miguelito. Antonio had been unfaithful to his sister Adela - not that infidelity was ever a problem among fellow machos. In Manuel's mind, all men who did not take advantage of such opportunities were *comemierdas*. As he often said: *"yo suelto mi gallo, los demás que recojan sus gallinas."** No, it was not his brother-in-law's flings that had brought shame upon the de la Cruz name, it was the fact that he had given Adela a venereal disease. This was unforgiveable, sullying the purity of a proper Cuban woman. So, Manuel did what was expected

---

* "I let my cock loose, and it is up to others to secure their chickens."

from all men of honor – he put a bullet in his brother-in-law's head. As far as anyone was concerned, his sister's husband abandoned her, walked away, left for good, he just disappeared. Nobody was ever identified, and no one, especially the police in the 1970s, really cared that another spic had showed up dead by the river. "But *papi*, how can you take human life?" Miguelito asked. "*De la cárcel de sale,*" he responded, "*del cementerio no.*"*

Oggún didn't notice the approaching children, nor did he hear the shrieking of the little girl. He was lost in the moment, indulging his appetites. Of course, if the children would have had eyes with which to see beyond the material, they would all have been shrieking at the sight of a mighty African warrior lapping up the remaining *ashé* from the dead animal's blood. He hovered over the railroad tracks, relishing the strength he gained from the spilled blood. But the total physical and spiritual rapture of the moment was suddenly and rudely disrupted. The *ashé* Oggún was blissfully enjoying was literally torn from his lips. As soon as Greg had recovered from the initial shock of Sally's shrill screech, he felt embarrassed. Being the oldest in the group and just having reached that awkward age of fifteen where he still liked playing with model cars but also imagining himself soon driving real ones, he recognized this was the ideal opportunity to show his companions he was now a man, fearless of death – even if death came in the form of a dog's carcass. While the boys were

---

* "You get out of jail, not from the cemetery."

still frozen in their place, Greg ran up to the carcass, picked it up by its leg, and swung it towards his friends. The dog was not large, but rigor mortis had set in, making the dead animal heavier than what Greg expected. The carcass, stiff as a board, didn't land far, plopping down a few feet before the other kids. Not to be outdone, Stan and Billy ran to the dead dog, each grabbing an unbending leg, and tossed it back in Greg's direction.

Oggún's meal went flying down the track. The two pieces of iron that Manuel placed on top of the carcass, which he respectfully drenched in oil, also scattered. That is when he first noticed the children, especially Greg who was now standing where his meal once lay. Oggún fumed at the insult. He reached for his machete, his eyes blazing red as he towered over this child who dared to cross the mighty warrior. One should never raise the dreadful ire of Oggún because he always extracts his revenge in the form of a bloody accident.

Sally and Miguelito stayed back a bit, not joining in the roughhousing. She was disgusted by the sight and could smell it each time it sailed through the air. Miguelito knew better than to disrupt an offering, even if he dismissed his parent's spirituality as mumbo-jumbo. The boys were laughing and posturing with bravado, taunting him for being a scaredy-cat, afraid of a dead dog. Finally, Sally was done with this tomfoolery. "Enough," she yelled, using the best schoolmarm voice she could muster. "Leave that thing alone. You guys are so gross. Let's just go to the park like we planned." The three boys, outwardly protesting but secretly glad their disgusting display was over, fell in line and continued walking to the open field, but not before Oggún lashed out at them.

Lifting his machete behind and above his head, he brought it down with all his might at the three boys who were conveniently standing together. His machete cut through the three of them, but none of them felt a thing, not even noticing the breeze which swooshed by them. Because Sally and Miguelito did not participate in this insult to Oggún's honor, the machete did not touch them. Years would go by, and decades would pass before those who had been sliced through their bodies and souls would feel the blow. The *orishas* are never in a hurry.

Billy, the youngest of the three would be the first to experience the consequences of Oggún's machete. Some eight years later he would be accepted to Florida State University, located in Tallahassee, the state's capital, where he hoped to major in political science. A liberal, he dreamed of entering politics and fighting for the rights of the disenfranchised. As he drove north with all his earthly possessions stuffed into his '75 brown Camaro, he got sleepy on the long boring drive from Miami, veered off the road, flipped the car into the adjacent canal and died instantly.

Stan would be the next to suffer the consequences of Oggún's wrath. Around the same time Billy died, Stan, who was financially strapped, joined the military to obtain cash for college. Soon he was deployed to a small island one hundred miles north of Venezuela as part of Operation Urgent Fury. After storming the beaches, Stan's unit made its way to the airstrip being built by the Cubans when they met some resistance. During the skirmish, a bullet fired from a rifle by a Cuban soldier who was a devotee of Oggún ripped through Stan's stomach. Pinned down by enemy fire, medics were unable to get to him in time. On that stunning Sunday afternoon in October 1983 on the beautiful island of Grenada, Stan's dwindling life energy lingered painfully under the bright sun until he finally bled to death.

Greg, the oldest, would be the last to taste Oggún's revenge. A fifty-three-year-old successful insurance executive living in Boston and a father of two teens and a toddler, he felt he spent way too much time separated from his loving family. On this particular day he needed to fly to Los Angeles to renegotiate an important contract and woke up early to catch his morning flight while it was still dark outside. He quietly dressed and gently kissed his wife on the forehead so as not to wake her. After fifteen years of marriage, he was still smitten, loving her more now than on their wedding night. He drove himself to Logan on this unusually warm September 11th day to board American Airlines flight 11, a flight which would make an unexpected detour to New York City. *Oggún choro choro* - Oggún devours his offering.

Choosing Brownness

"You don't look brown," the Latina exclaimed, "You look pretty white to me. Why do you call yourself a person of color?" Her question sliced through Miguelito. All too often, rejection from one's own community hurts more than the violence inflicted by schoolboy racists and bigots. As a scholar Miguelito would use the term "people of color" as a way to describe himself. True, he was white enough to pass. Still, he would never be embraced nor accepted by the dominant Anglo culture. A lifetime of experiences assured him that regardless as to how light his skin was, he would never belong among whites. And if truth be known, because of colorism, he would never be fully accepted among people of color with darker hues. "What does it mean," he often wondered, "to be dismissed by your own people for not being Latino enough? He felt like an imposer, as not belonging. No place to call home. Neither in Cuba nor the States. No people with whom

185

to belong - whites or brown. Truly suffering from a schizophrenia disorder of being of two minds.

As soon as Miguelito could, he obtained employment at a Burger King when he turned fifteen. After years of feeding frozen patties to a never satisfied broiler through its feeder belt, he was able to save enough money to buy his first car, a 1960 baby blue, four-door Ford Falcon sedan. Five hundred bucks procured a vehicle nearly as old as himself. So much rust had eaten away at the chassis that a hole began to grow under the driver's feet, providing visibility to the concrete road as it zoomed by. Not only did the vehicle lack power steering and power brakes, but also, none of the gauges worked. Every week he would carefully pump $5 worth of gas and hoped this would be enough. And when driving, he did his best to guesstimate his speed, at times getting it wrong as proven by multiple speeding tickets. No matter how much Miguelito waxed his prized possession to make it look cool, it never came close to the newer models that other parents bought for his classmates at Southwest High as graduation gifts. So, he drove to school and parked at the far end of the lot to hide the bucket of bolts he mistook for a car.

As a boy helping his father - the superintendent - mop the building floors every Saturday, Manuel would occasionally snarl "You see *my* hands Miguelito? Take a good look at them, *coño!*" As Miguelito's chubby hands struggled to grip the mop, his father would hammer in, "you can either work with your mind, or you can work with your hands. *Carajo*, don't you get it? You're so *inútil*." Miguelito was haunted by his father's words while driving to his day job at Burger King or his real estate classes at night. When he passed his real estate exam at eighteen years of age, he thought about the filthy front steps of the tenement buildings he had lived in, and the bent rusted shovel his dad gave him to make a path in the snow for the building residents. When he started hustling houses as his classmates left town for college, he thought about the kids from the rumbles getting an education while he stayed behind making money to help support his parents.

Miguelito became moderately financially successful in his new venture – selling more houses than any of the other fifty sales agents at the Red Carpet real estate office. "A boy wonder," the broker of the firm called him while the mostly Anglo staff fumed in jealousy. And with success came a new car. Surely, he could not be expected to drive potential clients around town in a clunker prone to breakdowns. With the commission of his first transaction, he went to a Mercury dealership and purchased his first, brand new 1979 vehicle - the sport-compact three-door Capri hatchback. The gauges worked, and there were no holes on the floor. Fiery red with a raised central car hood vent and vertically mounted grille was all it took to give the young lad the illusion of having arrived.

Sadly, his attempt at being a coconut – brown on the outside, white on the inside - proved mentally and spiritually damaging. His parents, proud Cubans, gave off very mix messages. Hoping their child would have a better, more secure future, advised him to be as American as possible and to assimilate. But as immigrants themselves, with almost no

English-speaking abilities, they could not provide examples on how to accomplish this. By the time Miguelito was in his twenties, he mimicked being Anglo, trying to "act whiter" than actual whites, waving the 'stars and stripes' at every possible opportunity. He changed his name to Mike, sported no facial hair, parted his hair to the side (the right-side of course), stayed out of the sun, and tried speaking slowly to obscure his heavy accent. Regardless of his best efforts, he continued to be seen and treated as a spic. His exaggerated patriotism and involvement in businessmen's clubs and charity events may have eventually facilitated his escape from poverty, but the cost was the circumcision of his culture; a painful self-mutilation which has yet to heal.

During the early 1980s, "Mike" decided to take a holiday and drive to the old New York neighborhood not just to reminisce over the twelve years he lived there, but to do those touristy things he never got to do while living there. Twelve years and he never went to the top of the Empire State Building, nor visited the Statue of Liberty, nor went to the Museum of Modern Art, affectionally known as the MoMA. He drove up I-95 in his fiery red sports car; the windows rolled down, the wind was blowing through his slightly long dark hair, an eight-track tape of *El Gran Combo* blasting through the speakers. Close to his destination, while on the New Jersey Turnpike somewhere south of Elizabeth City, before exit 13, he was pulled over by state troopers.

"Morning son," the square jawed trooper sporting a military crew cut and hiding behind reflecting sunglasses politely began the encounter.

"Morning," Miguelito responded. Cognizant he was not speeding, naively asked, "what seems to be the problem officer?"

"Well, I'm afraid you were traveling five miles above the speed limit." And without missing a beat, he asked for permission to search the vehicle. Strange, thought Miguelito. Shouldn't he just be given a ticket and sent on his merry way?

Mustering all his courage, Miguelito ask the trooper who was at least a foot taller than him, "what exactly are you looking for?"

The young trooper, maintaining an impeccable polite professional demeanor responded, "You see son, sports cars driven by Latino men with Dade County license plates are suspected of transporting cocaine to New York." This was, after all, the 80s, a time when Miami held the infamous title of being the nation's cocaine capital and the main distribution center for the rest of the country. "So," the law enforcer continued, "If you provide consent, I can do a quick search and then you can be on your way."

Not wanting to create more trouble for himself, Miguelito acquiesced. After a thorough search, and finding nothing incriminating, Miguelito was given a speeding ticket and dismissed. It did not matter what he called himself, in an age where racial profiling is the norm, Miguelito – pretending to be Mike - was a suspect simply for driving while under the influence of being a Latino. It didn't matter how much Miguelito sought assimilation. In the eyes of law enforcement, he was still, and would always be part of the cockroach people. One would imagine that he would have found such police treatment troublesome, an abuse of power, a blatant act of ethnic profiling. But if Mike or Miguelito was honest with himself, it was his reaction afterward that was truly problematic. Continuing his drive to New York City, one thought went through his mind: "Thank God the police are being vigilant in protecting society from potential criminals."

He was not angered about being ethnically profiled but thankful the police were keeping the public safe from perceived dangers. Miguelito's mind was so colonized he did not, he could not understand, how his identity was being shaped and formed by such experiences. He was indoctrinated to see himself through the eyes of whites, accepting the notion that he had a so-called suspicious nature. He wanted nothing to do with the deficiency of being Latiné, a people accustomed to living among rats and roaches. With all his strength, mind, and spirit, he craved white middle-class respectability. The dream of this kid from the latte urban center was to learn how to live at ease in the vanilla suburbs.

Cubans like Miguelito became the WASPiest Latinés. They embraced a whiteness learned from a community which raised them to believe they were still in Cuba and therefore white; refusing to accept that ninety miles is enough to change how one is seen. Gazing into a mirror, Miguelito saw himself the way his parents and community taught him to see himself

– white. But mirrors do eventually shatter. For him the fragile hall of mirrors was smashed when he left Miami in his early thirties with his wife and newborn babies and moved to Louisville, Kentucky for advance schooling. Unable to find employment anywhere, because few wanted to hire a Latiné to any type of job which did not involve a broom or mop, he was finally offered a slight stipend to teach theological Spanish at Boyce Bible College. One day he decided to test his students' ability to pronounce colors in Spanish by pointing at an item in the classroom and asking "*¿Qué color es esto? - What color is this?*" After pointing to several objects throughout the room and soliciting numerous different responses, he realized he had yet to ask a question where the answer would be *blanco*, white. Not finding anything white in the room he pointed to his skin and asked, "What color is this?" To his shock and surprise, the class did not respond with *blanco*, but instead, in unison replied, "*moreno*" - brown.

Regardless as to how he was taught by his community to see his reflection in the mirror, the white Anglo folk saw him as brown and foreign, while the Latiné culture saw him as white and privileged. To North Americans, regardless of his actual skin pigmentation, he was not white because he was not Anglo. To the Latiné culture, he simply was not brown enough. Miguelito, like the cross-dressing Changó seeking escape, was also a cross-dresser, but in his case, an ethnic cross-dresser. In Miami, because most light skin Cubans see themselves as white, they have the power to be white. But once they leave Miami, as transethnic people, they cross-dress to brownness. The colorism of many black and brown folk dismissed Miguelito as belonging, even though he continues to carry on his body the stigmata of white racial violence. Illusions that his business acumen or his academic publications would be sufficient for acceptability among the white academy burned and crashed. He was and would always be just another "smelly spic," regardless as to how nice and politically correct were those ensuring his exclusion.

But if he was a spic *aquí* - here, then he was a maggot *gusano allá*, there. Living in the shadows of his parent's dismembered remembrance, he tried to forget the fantasy island of his origins believing it was the means of succeeding in this new adopted country. After all, separation from his parent's island would last five times longer than that of Odysseus to his. But unlike Odysseus, who was returning to a place he was familiar with, Miguelito failed to piece together some type of rootedness upon the shifting sands of his parents' false memories. Every exilic Cuban over a certain age lives with a particular trauma caused by the hardships of being a refugee. Homesickness for a place that was never his home, mixed with a mythological nostalgia, romanticization and an unnaturally taught hatred toward various actors blamed for their Babylonian captivity all contributed to the pain of not having *a place*, of not ever being able to enjoy the island's gentle sea breezes as the brutally scorching sun finally sets at the end of the day. Living in the in-between space where both sides - the capitalists to the north and the communists to the south - rejected Miguelito. He would never be accepted *aquí* because he would always be a spic and if he was to return *allá* he would always be a *gusano*, someone who betrayed his homeland in favor of the *yanqui* imperialists, a betrayal he is held responsible for even though he could barely walk or talk when it occurred.

Rejection from the object of his love and desire was reinforced the first time he ever strolled with pride and elation down *el Paseo del Prado*, a beautiful avenue containing a middle pedestrian way, guarded on either side by bronze lions. Shortly after turning fifty, almost half century after he left, he was able to amble down the picturesque boulevard toward the bay to watch the sunset and hear *el cañonazo de las nueve*.[*] A young, gaunt *jinetero*, street hustler, suddenly appeared out of the shadows, trying to get his attention. The young man began to first hawk cigars, then rum, and finally the services of a woman or a boy. After a few minutes, it became obvious Miguelito was not buying anything. But before the *jinetero* walked away, over his left shoulder he asked, "*¿de donde eres?* – Where are you from?" Miguelito replied a little too boastfully, sticking out his chest as it nearly burst with pride, "I'm from here, la Habana, I'm Cuban!" The young man immediately stopped, turned around, and sneered with indignation, "you might be from here, but you are no Cuban." He leaned in so close to Miguelito that when he spewed these

---

[*] Every evening at 9pm, across the bay in la Habana at the San Carlos Fort, an eighteenth century cannon is fired by soldiers in period uniforms.

venomous words, Miguelito felt a few drops of his spit land on his cheek.

This encounter was the first of many which would continuously happen every time he visited the island – and not just by *jineteros*. Held in contempt and suspicion on both sides of the Florida Straits, when *aquí* he is too Cuban to ever be American, and when *allá*, too American to ever be a Cuban, Miguelito felt himself neither. This trauma is one of never belonging, and the constant reminder of belonging nowhere prevents the healing of Miguelito's festering scar, an open wound kept fresh every time he is asked "where are you from," both on the streets of la Habana or on the avenues of the United States.

Dancing with Ochún

The one-bedroom apartment in the *barrio* was crammed to the walls that night by people who wanted to speak directly with Ochún. Miguelito, a middle-aged man, climbed up five tight flights of stairs and entered apartment 5C, somewhat winded. A few dozen people had already arrived, mostly Cubans, along with Puerto Ricans and Dominicans, and a couple of white folks who seemed very out of place – bless their hearts. Almost everyone in the apartment except Miguelito worked minimum-wage jobs. Many had rushed over right after work, still sweaty from the three block-long walk from the 181st street station which connected Washington Heights to their jobs – a very long commute north on the A train. Others who cleaned offices long after lower Manhattan emptied out of executives were planning to take that same train south to begin their night shift as soon as they finished consulting with the goddess.

The first thing Miguelito noticed in the cramped apartment was the fragrance of incense, scented candles, and *agua de florida*, blended with everyone's sweaty and perfumed body odors, creating a sweet poignant aroma which was not necessarily unpleasant, even though the smoke from the cheap incense made his eyes itch. Blaring over the radio was La Cocodrila's latest hit: *Oya's Funk*. Some people tapped their feet and swayed along with the rhythm as they chatted. As he walked by the kitchen on his way to the living room, he saw piles of dishes filled with the food of Miguelito's childhood – *arroz con frijoles negros, puerco asado, yuca, plátanos maduros* and of course *flan*. Every possible surface in the tiny kitchen was occupied. The apartment's walls, where lead-based paint chips delicately clung on, needed a fresh coat. The next generation of Latiné children awaited poisoning because slumlords seemed more interested in squeezing every last penny from their tenants than in recognizing the right for decent housing.

Miguelito had not attended a *bembe* since his teenage years. Tonight's *bembe*, a drum and dance festival performed in honor of an *orisha*, would attempt to bridge the gap between the spiritual and physical worlds, allowing *orishas* to borrow the body of a devotee and spend time in the flesh with their children. European gods often appear distant and aloof by comparison, thanks to the anti-body stoic philosophy which had infected Christianity during its early development. But Santería was different. There was nothing wrong, sinful, or wretched about a person's body whose flesh could experience and enjoy the fullness of their senses. In fact, being human was such a desirable state that African *orishas* incarnated themselves regularly, joining humans in their festivities by participating in plenty of drinking and dancing. In this way, one could speak face-to-face with African gods and goddesses who were always ready to guide their devotees.

Miguelito had fond memories of participating in many *bembes* during his youth. Latinos and Latinas, dismissed and discarded by polite white society would gather to celebrate different *orishas* on their special feast day. His parents had gone through the rituals and had eventually achieved the level of *santero* and *santera*. Like tonight, he remembered how thirty to forty people would squeeze into his parent's tiny apartment in Queens where one bedroom, *el cuarto de los santos* – the saints' room, had been entirely dedicated to conducting spiritual consultations. This meant Miguelito slept on a rollaway cot at the foot of his parent's full-sized bed, never having his own bed or room until his family moved to Miami when he was fourteen.

Marta, Miguelito's mother, was a devotee of Ochún, the deity of femininity. Although Miguelito himself was a child of Elleguá, the trickster, he decided to visit his mother's *orisha* this evening. His responsibilities at the theological school where he taught in Denver hadn't started yet, so he decided on making a quick trip up to New York City for the September 8th gathering and participate in a *bembe* at the home of a renown *santero*. He was also attending the party because he missed his mother who had died several years earlier due to lung cancer. She never smoked a cigarette in her life, but her husband – the old cop – who was a chain smoker, had been kind enough to give her, over the course of many decades, the gift of second-hand smoke.

Normally Miguelito would have taken the subway all the way up to the Bronx, but now he could afford to take an Uber. *El santero* Pepito, also a child of Ochún who tonight proudly wore the yellow neck beads representing his *orisha*, welcomed Miguelito to his home. Dressed all in white from head to toe, Pepito's salt and pepper hair gave him an aura of purity and wisdom. He had read one of Dr. De La Cruz's books, the one on Santería, disagreeing with many of the interpretations but nevertheless thinking it was a somewhat decent if not a naïve read. While on any other night he would have been honored to have an eminent scholar visit his humble abode, tonight the only guest of honor would be Ochún. Like most Cuban men who strive to be machos, Pepito was at first apprehensive when he discovered he was a child of a female deity. Why couldn't he be a child of one of the fierce warriors, like Oggún who thirsts for blood, or Changó who eats fire? The thought of Ochún mounting him, that is, taking possession of his body, was at first too much for his mannish sensibilities. He feared some people might think he liked men because Ochún is also the patron of gays, lesbians, bisexual, and transgender persons.

Pepito was too poor to afford an apartment big enough to have accommodated a dedicated *cuarto de los santos*, so the ceremony would be taking place in the living room, which had been emptied of furniture. This is where *el trono* – the throne –

would be erected to honor Ochún. Along the walls surrounding the cabinet hung huge thick yellow cloth drapes, Ochún's favorite color. A five-foot-tall white book cabinet which usually resided in his bedroom containing the *orisha*'s paraphernalia was brought out to serve as the centerpiece of *el trono*. A transparent fancy gold cloth was also draped over the top of the cabinet. Leaning against the cabinet was a peacock-feather fan, the common emblem of Ochún. Perched on top was Ochún's *sopera*, a large, yellow-lidded ceramic tureen which contained her sacred *otanes*, five pebbles chosen at dawn from the depths of a river. These *otanes* resonated with Ochún's *ashé*, discovered by Pepito who had been trained on how to listen carefully for the *orisha*'s presence in stones. There were also *soperas* belonging to other *orishas* present at the foot of *el trono*. Miguelito recognized a white *sopera* for Obatalá, an ocean blue one for Yemayá, and one made of cherrywood for Changó.

On the floor, before the other *soperas*, in front of the cabinet was an array of platters of prettily arranged fruits and cakes, including Ochún's favorites: rum cake, pumpkin, and honey. These treats served as food offerings whose *ashé* would be consumed by the *orisha*, although more than likely, if left out overnight, would be consumed by the apartment's rats and roaches. Also, the food offerings were flanked by many flowers, specifically her favorite, large sunflowers. In front of the cabinet was a small basket to collect offerings, copper pennies would suffice. Miguelito, more out of habit than respect, prostrated himself in front of the cabinet, dropped five copper pennies into the basket as a *derecho* – a tribute, shook the bell that was positioned next to the basket, and kissed the grimy floor's carpet. Shortly after he stood up, the *bembe* began.

Someone turned off the radio amid one of Santana's riffs as a loud slap of the leather drums signified the ceremony's commencement. At one corner of the room were the three sacred ritual drums called *batáa*. Through drumming, worshiper's messages reach the *orisha's* ear in the hopes of inducing Ochún to respond in person. Sometimes she would play coy and refuse to join the festivities held in her honor. Because the drums themselves are inhabited by an *orisha*, Miguelito, along with everyone else in the crowded apartment, made it a point never to turn their back to them. The first song booming throughout the tiny apartment simply honored the saint, so no one danced; instead, they all stood up and moved along with the rhythm to show respect. The drummers then played a rhythm inviting Ochún to possess one or more of the dancers. Anyone who went through the initiation ritual to become a practitioner can be possessed. The beat was now patterned into a seductive rhythm, with each slap of the drum tingling the innermost soul of those swaying to the beat. It was as if each slap sent a low voltage electrical shock throughout the body. The room heated up. Several people started to dance, slowly at first, then ecstatically, gasping for air. Sweaty droplets flew among the swirling and twirling bodies. Miguelito felt faint. Time melted and everyone breathed heavier as they danced, anticipating Ochún's arrival. Surely, she will visit tonight!

When an *orisha* delays in making an appearance, the drummers might begin to sing insulting songs, like how ugly Ochún really is. Offended, the *orisha* immediately possesses one of her children to rebuke the impudence. The drummers would then quickly switch to flattery to placate the angered *orisha*. At other times, someone might grow impatient and attempt to replicate a possession, collapsing to the floor enraptured. But those present with decades of experience can usually tell if someone is faking it, so they just ignore the imposter to their self-shame, who after some time must stand up with no assistance. Tonight, however, no one seemed to be playing games.

Among the dancers, Pepito, the host, stood out. He whirled around and around as if in a trance. Pepito, who works in construction, is a burly muscular man with a potbelly and leathery latte-colored skin caused by the *mestizaje* of his ancestors and reinforced by years of working beneath an unforgiving sun. As Pepito spun in circles, everyone in the room began to focus on channeling their *ashé* toward him. He danced in the manner of Ochún, sensual and suggestive, waving his arms so as to make his imaginary golden bracelets jingle. With his hands "she" began to rub his body as he thrust her hips in the direction of all the men in the room. This gender-bending sensuality fused the physical with the metaphysical, making it difficult to determine where Pepito ended and Ochún started. Miguelito stood there mesmerized, witnessing a transformation take place before his very own eyes. This macho of a man began to exhibit extremely feminine characteristics in a stylized, seductive dance. Then, Pepito started to laugh - a laughter which stretched into eternity. Ochún had definitely arrived. Many started to greet her with the words, *"yeye dari yeyeo."** Pepito may have started the dance, but Ochún finished it.

Accomplishing its purpose, the drumming ended with a loud slap to the largest of the three drums, the *iya*, which is surrounded by small bells. Silence filled the room as Pepito, now possessed by Ochún, collapsed onto the floor. Several rushed to help her. She was gently and respectfully lifted and guided to the adjoining bedroom to be prepared for her people. The rest waited with anticipation for her return. Because Ochún is the patron of gold, many had come to ask her for financial help. But she is also the goddess of love, so others came seeking help with their relationships. Whatever her children asked for, she was always eager and generous to grant their petitions. Unlike the others, Miguelito did not come in search of wealth or love. He came seeking wisdom concerning his own spirituality. Just because gods do not exist does not mean one should not believe in them. *Hay que respetar los santos.†*

---

* Ochún's arrival is always greeted with this salutation. Although difficult to understand its significance, it nevertheless connotes "the sweat, the kind."

† Saints must be respected.

Patiently they waited as time refused to be rushed. Eventually Pepito as Ochún emerged from the bedroom in full regalia. The drummers, the first to see her enter the living room, started to sing songs of praise. Everyone's eyes, including Miguelito's, were transfixed on Pepito-as-Ochún moved haughtily among them as queen, the grand dame of the domain. As she greeted everyone in the room, it became more difficult to see Pepito because the transformation was so complete. Ochún outshone the limitations of Pepito's body. All Miguelito saw was Ochún, gracefully gliding from one devotee to another, stopping every so often to whisper advice into the ears of some believers, flirting with others, admonishing some for their unfaithfulness, and demanding sacrifices from others seeking forgiveness.

Among the crowd was a petite young woman in her early twenties engaged in a torrid affair with an older married man of thirty-three who has several young children. She desperately wanted him to leave his family and be faithful only to her. He, on the other hand, was more interested in scratching a seven-year itch. If a Christian minister would have been present, they might have easily condemned the young woman as a whore and a wrecker of families, while ignoring the complicity of the man. But Ochún showed this tormented soul great compassion, because she knew what it is to be infatuated with a married man. Ochún is deeply in love with Changó, whose passion is always satisfied by others. And even though Changó was not her only lover, he was the one she pined for. Among her lovers there is the great diviner

Orúnla, to whom she was married until she met Changó. She also had an affair with the *orisha* of war, Oggún, who was Changó's arch enemy, not to mention romances with Ochosi, god of the hunt and Oko, god of farming. Her skills as a siren were indisputable. Because of her multiple affairs, Ochún possessed profound insight into the challenges and complexities caused by the difficult dynamics within relationships. Miguelito overheard Ochún tell the young woman who was standing next to him to write the name of her lover on a piece of paper and place it in a hollow pumpkin along with honey and other ingredients. After a certain amount of time, the woman should bring the pumpkin to the river as an offering.

Ochún's seductive powers are legendary. Through her ultra-femininity she was once able to save civilization. When Oggún, the god of metals, sought self-exile as a hermit after his incestuous offense, a great imbalance to the world's harmony resulted and civilization came to a standstill. Concerned, all the *orishas* tried to coax Oggún out of the forest but to no avail. With nothing else to lose, Ochún, the youngest of the *orishas*, decided to lure him out. She filled her gourd with honey, tied five silk handkerchiefs around her waist, and headed into the woods. Oggún could hear the jingling of her five golden bracelets from a distance, clanging against each other. Not wanting to be discovered, he quickly hid but was not fast enough. Ochún caught a glimpse of him ducking behind some bushes, all the same, she pretended not to see him. When she was close enough to detect his musky scent, she began to dance, swinging her sensuous hips from side-to-side, in perfect rhythm with the gentle love melody she was humming. Her enticing moves bewitched the mighty Oggún. Forgetting his commitment to live the life of a hermit as a self-imposed punishment for his incestuous sin, he popped his head out from behind the bushes where he was hiding to get a better view. But before he knew what happened, Ochún quickly dipped her long slender fingers into her gourd of honey and brushed them across his lips.

Who can resist the taste of Ochún's honey? Blind-struck with hot lust, Oggún began to follow the alluring temptress. Still pretending not to notice him, she sang and danced, ever so slowly moving toward the forest's edge. Whenever it appeared he was tiring, she would brush more of her honey across his lips. For five days she kept up this seductive dance until they finally arrived together at the forest's boundary. Smearing on his thick lips an extra dose of her honey, she led him out of the woods as if he was on an imaginary leash. For a moment in time, the hardness of iron yielded to the softness of water and all the other gods and goddesses celebrated, throwing a great party in the city of Ife. Oggún soon returned to his forger to work, allowing civilization to advance again. However, unable to forget Ochún's seduction, he has ached for her ever since, while he continues to labor unceasingly.

Pepito, now Ochún, started to flirtatiously dance, becoming the center of attention. Oh, how Ochún loved to dance! She would start with a man, then grab a woman and twirl her around, then dance with another man, at one point kissing him on the mouth. Amid her merriment, her eyes locked with Miguelito. Smiling, she slowly danced her way towards him. Taking a shining to Miguelito, Pepito's took him into his powerful arms made brawny by years of heavy lifting at construction sites. Then Ochún spun him around as if he were a small boy. Before becoming a religion professor or even getting married, Miguelito had been a prize-winning disco dancer during the '70s, renowned for his acrobatic moves; but tonight, he struggled to keep up with her, barely holding on to his balance because no one can ever out-dance Ochún, with the possible exception of her lover Changó.

Miguelito's *macho* culture conditioned him to feel uncomfortable dancing with another man, but when he gazed into Pepito's eyes, all he saw was Ochún's intelligence piercing the deepest recesses of his being. The beauty of her sparkling eyes shone through Pepito's dull ones. Miguelito felt reassured, loved, and a spiritual elation from the depth of her caring. Just at that moment, he remembered why he had come. As if reading his mind, Ochún purred into his ear, "*mi hijito* – my son, don't be so uptight. Loosen up. I know why you came tonight and have been anxiously waiting to chat with you." Taking his hand, she led him to the bedroom for a private consultation. They left the group to their merriment, going into the modest room cluttered with the furniture which once occupied the living room. Ochún provocatively spread herself on the bed, using a couple of pillows to prop himself up. Miguelito sat down on a wooden foot stool beside the bed.

He began by first politely expressing his gratitude for her taking time to speak with him, but then could not help himself and immediately dove into an intellectual discussion. Could anyone really blame him for his impertinence? Training to become a scholar of religion beat out of him the courteous small talk he had once mastered as a salesman. He began, quite rudely, asking why did she have to bleach herself to a lighter skin hue when she left Africa, then again when she left Cuba for the U.S.? Why had she become so white that statues to La Virgin de Cobre depict her as a pasty-shaded white woman with blue eyes? Was it so important for racist slaveholders to accept her? Shouldn't those who were not black learn to acknowledge her for who she is, black and beautiful? Miguelito was deeply concerned, both out of loyalty to his cultural roots and now as a trained scholar, over how Santería had moved further from its African roots and showed no sign of returning. If Africans who had converted to Christianity were simply expected to worship a white God, why can't whites just learn how to worship a black *orisha*?

Miguelito the scholar had read enough Critical Race Theory and Postcolonial books to be upset with Europeans, like his ancestors, appropriating the *orisha* traditions, easily bought with their cultural tourist dollars. What truly bothered Miguelito was how white colleagues, setting themselves up as experts, had interpreted – or rather "re"-interpreted - the Yoruban faith tradition through European-based definitions of what a religion should be. With each subsequent explanation they gave about Santería, they re-defined the faith into something that was farther away from its origins. Their privileged social location was so different from the marginalized who are devoted to the *orishas* that Miguelito feared his culture was being hijacked as the religious symbols with which he grew up were being re-signified, creating a possible danger of them eventually being used against his people.

Seeing right through Miguelito, Ochún simply answered, "Is your concern solely intellectual, or are you just upset with some of the criticism you received by some white folks about your writings on Santería?"

"I don't know. Maybe?" Miguelito sheepishly responded, annoyed by how quickly her retort had seen right through his motives. True, he did find the audacity of non-Cubans correcting his Cubanness down-right insulting. He has been a Latino a great deal longer than white colleagues who claimed they knew his culture better than he did.

"*Aye Miguelito, no quieras tapar el sol con un dedo*,"[*] Ochún continued, "Here you are, professing how deeply you are concerned about Santería moving away from its roots when you left this faith so long ago. When you yourself tried to become white. Didn't you become a Southern Baptist minister? Really, here you are, concerned about the faith becoming Anglicized and my skin color lightening, but then you join one of the whitest and anti-Latiné religions in the United States. Come on, this born-again conversion of yours is a very white

---

[*] "Don't try to obscure the sun with a finger."

concept, isn't it? Of course, white people have to be born-again, they never were brought up to be one with the terrestrial creation which surrounds them in the first place, looking instead to the sky for their gods. You complain about Anglicizing Santería, yet you are the one who uses white concepts of faith and teach others to do the same in that white liberal school where you teach. Don't you see how insincere your concerns are? Can't you see why I can't take you seriously?"

Ouch, that hurt. Miguelito felt cut to the bone. "*Coño Cachita* no jodas,*" Miguelito curtly responded. He continued his reply, somewhat agitated, "You know I did not abandon the religion of my parents, nor turn my back upon my heritage, of which Santería is a part. Just because I do not believe doesn't mean I do not choose to have faith.

With a glare strong enough to slice his soul, she let out a sarcastic laugh and sneered with a steel coldness in her voice, "*Mira Miguelito, no comas mierda.*" He instantly realized he had gone too far and probably should not have cursed at the goddess. Whether she existed or not was not the issue, he should have shown respect. She continued, "The secret to life is and always has been love! It is love which motivates my actions. What motivates you? Envy, greed, shame, guilt? Unlike you, because I love, I always strived to help everyone, regardless of whether they know me or not. All I want is for

---

* Cachita is an endearing nickname used by Cubans for Ochún.

you humans to live in harmony with your destiny. You really need to move beyond this "us versus them" mentality. All have the potential to be children of the *orishas*. Does it really matter if they know me personally? Or that they even believe? I stand ready to assist them in their trials and tribulations, whenever they look beyond themselves toward the otherworldly to deal with the difficulties which life brings. My love is greater than the ego of recognition. I really don't care if they call me Ochún, or La Virgen de la Caridad, or Aphrodite or Venus or Lakshmi. I don't care if they see me as black, *mulata*, white, or green. What is paramount are the needs and hardships of my children. For if there are no devotees, there can be no Ochún, or whatever else the humans want to call me."

"*Bien, bien, tranquila,*"* Miguelito tried to calm her, for it was obvious she was growing more agitated with the conversation. "All this makes sense, but why bleach yourself just to pass among whites? Don't you see the damage caused? Today, when your story is retold, you are often depicted as a white, blond-haired, blue-eye figure. And not only were you totally bleached, so too were the Taíno brothers in the rowboat who were transfigured into two white Spaniards with Rodrigo being changed into a balding, bearded, white-haired Spaniard also named Juan. The original story became the legend of *los tres Juanes*: one who is black while the other two are white, thus

---

* Ok, ok, calm down.

erasing Indians from the story and leaving a minor African representation in the form of a child."

"How can you hold me responsible with how others interpret reality?" Cachita asked. "Besides, I was not motivated to simply please white people. The copper skin hue I chose to wear was based on more than simple aesthetics. I made the conscious decision *not* to appear to my subjects in the same skin pigmentation as their white slave holders who were responsible for introducing so much misery and destruction upon my devotees. Instead, I appeared as the color of death and life. The color of death because it was the color of the copper being mined at Cobre responsible for the decimation of my children. But also, the color representing new life, those relegated to be the economic and racial outcasts, those who would comprise the new Cuban people, a literal mixture of whites and blacks." She had not rubbed her honey on Miguelito's lips, but he felt seduced anyways, tempted to follow her logic and explore the new intellectual possibilities her words presented.

He shook his head to clear his thoughts against the power of seduction emanating from her gold-clothed body. But what about her whitening, Miguelito stubbornly thought to himself. She responded by reminding him that she had no choice but to become La Virgen del Cobre so that all Cubans, including Miguelito's conquistador ancestors, could recognize her as their mother. "Do you honestly believe," she asked, "that the Santería you grew up in is in anyway the same as how I was worshiped in Africa? Of course not! Some 1,700 deities were worshiped in Yorubaland, but only a few of us, about twenty-five, accompanied our followers to the Caribbean. Of these, only a few continued the trek to the United States in the 1960s. Seven of us – Obatalá, Elleguá the trickster, Orúnla the diviner, Changó the warrior ruler of lightening, Oggún the god of war and iron, Yemayá the queen of the ocean, and I became prominent, known as *la siete potencias africanas*."*

"Don't you remember," she continued, "how during the 1970s Mariel boatlift, many among the mass exodus of black and biracial Cubans from the island were shocked by how Santería was being practiced by a predominately white Miami Cuban exile community? How much it had become commercialized? How many little stores opened all over the city to sell statues, robes, stones, beaded jewelry, musical instruments, incense, and live animals for sacrifice at a profit? Why should we be surprised by these white Cubans, who attempted to make Santería more mainstream by downplaying the African elements and highlighting concepts closer to Christian thought, even to the point of buying a church building so they can gather and worship me like Christians do? As if any structure can contain an *orisha*!"

"All religious faiths," she maintained, "are destined to change with each new generation to meet the people's needs as they live in different eras under unforeseen circumstances. Cuba was not Africa, so how the religion was practiced in Cuba has to be different than the way it was carried out of

---

* The seven African powers

Africa. The symbols, the rituals, and the beliefs must change to face the new conflicts which arise in a new environment. Just because your Spaniard ancestors influenced the religion so that I could be discovered by them did not mean I abandoned my African children."

She persistent with her analysis. "And you Miguelito are just as guilty of this too, which is why Pepito has some real difficulties with your book on Santería. This doesn't mean I will abandon white Cubans. So, you tell me: how can we *orishas* embrace the African and Cuban communities, as well as the Anglo community, if you refuse to deal with the cultural barriers which divide your very being or the racist and ethnic discrimination which is prevalent in your social interactions?"

Yes, her words were enticing, but Miguelito wasn't buying it. She seemed to be fine with whites, who have the power to interpret the faith of their slaves. He tried to press her on this point, but she continued her diatribe. "I know you are concerned with concepts such as liberation as the whites define it," she responded, "but frankly, my children are just trying to survive. You already survived and have a well-paying job as a professor so you can afford to leave behind gods and think of secular utopias. But look around you, look who came tonight to honor me. My children are just trying to put food on the table. Unlike you, I am present in their hardships trying to do something, not write about it from the security of tenure. Besides, haven't you insisted liberation is also for the oppressor? I agree. Not only am I here to restore the humanity taken from my devotees; but also restore the humanity of those who lost it because of what they stole. So, why question me when I extend my open arms to Anglos, and before them the white Spaniards? Don't be so quick to judge."

"*Ya*," she abruptly said, "let's bring this conversation to a close. I need to return to the *bembe* and minister to my devotees. They have physical needs to which I must assist, more important than your intellectual curiosities. I sincerely hope you found our dance enjoyable."

With that, Ochún immediately stood up, indicating the consultation was over, even though there was so much more Miguelito wanted to ask. As he was rising from his stool, she unexpectedly embraced him, holding him tight and close. In Pepito's strong arms, close enough to smell the aroma of cheap cigar on his breath, Miguelito suddenly lost himself in her gentle motherly hug. He was somewhat taken aback, mainly because like most, he usually dismissed Ochún as the quintessential love goddess, an *orisha* who is more interested with the sensual pleasures of the flesh. But as she rocked him in her arms, he felt her transform to Ibú Akuaro, one of the five avatars of Ochún which focuses on fiercely protecting children. Miguelito laid his head on her broad shoulder, similar to when he did the same as a child with his own mother, lingering there longer than he should. With eyes closed, he was again in his own mom's arms.

As they stood there, Ochún leaned into his ear and whispered, "I love and miss you very much." Warm tears began to roll down Miguelito's face. He held her tighter, not wanting the moment to pass. Yes, love can melt the rigid intellect. Eventually, she pulled away and left, leaving him alone in the empty bedroom. He again had to sit down on the little foot stool, quiet his sobbing, and gather his thoughts. He wasn't sure why he couldn't stop crying. Maybe it was because he missed his mother more than he realized and being in Ochún's presence brought back vivid memories of her. Or maybe he was just missing the roots of his culture more than he thought. He felt, after all, more comfortable at the *bembe* than he did at those stuffy faculty cocktail parties. But he was no longer that poor *barrio* street rat. He now had middle-class respectability and educational privilege. The cultural capital obtained by achieving a doctorate degree made it impossible to truly return to the old neighborhood. He stood out just as much as those few white folks attending tonight's *bembe*. He neither belonged among his own people nor would he ever be truly accepted by his white colleagues. And it was at this moment, in the darkened room of a rundown building in the Bronx, he realized that maybe the black goddess wasn't the only one who had been overly blanched.

Betrayals

Cain and Abel, Kulabob and Manup, Romulus and Remus, Oggún and Changó, all blood brothers in perpetual combat. The animosity between some brothers runs deep, as in the case of Oggún and Changó. The latter hates the former for raping their mother while the former hates the latter for seducing his wife. All too often, clashes among men are fought on the battlefield of women's bodies. Through women, men flex their muscles by trespassing upon each other's property. What better way to show dominance over an advocacy than to occupy their property, to replace them in bed, planting their seeds in another man's field? It didn't matter Oyá was a mighty warrior in her own right. She was seen as an extension of Oggún. For Changó to enter his garden and drink the sweetness of his most precious ripe fruit to quench his lustful thirst was a direct challenge to his brother's machismo.

But just because the world turns on patriarchal principals does not mean women sit by idly or innocently. Some, like

Ochún have learned how to manipulate men with the honey from her gourd, so that when she rubs men's lips with her syrupy sweetness, they become like putty in her hands. She did this not just to men, but also gods, even the most powerful deity in existence, Olodumare. Her manipulation of the Creator of all occurred when the *orisha* Babalú-Ayé faced Olodumare's wrath. Known during his youth to be an unalterable skirt-chaser, Babalú-Ayé spent his time indulging in licentious pleasures. "Babalú-Ayé, what gift would you want?" Olodumare asked when he was doling out powers to the different *orishas*. The immature deity frivolously responded, "I want to become every woman's lover." Disheartened with Babalú-Ayé's immaturity, Olodumare, nonetheless, granted his request, with just one stipulation, "You can never touch a woman on Thursday during Easter week."

What a minor restriction, Babalú-Ayé thought. He had no difficulty in faithfully obeying Olodumare's edict until the day he met the most beautiful woman he had ever set eyes upon, and it just so happened to be during Easter week. By that Thursday, they were relishing in unrestrained pleasures through each other's bodies. When news of Babalú-Ayé's defiance reached Olodumare the next day, the Almighty was outraged. In his wrath he unleashed illnesses, sickness, and all sorts of diseases and pestilence upon humanity. Because of Babalú-Ayé's disobedience, epidemics and plagues entered the earth, starting with the perpetrator himself, whose body was soon covered with boils and sores oozing with foul-smelling pus. Incurable buboes the size of chicken eggs developed on his groin, neck, and armpits making it difficult for him to move about. Soon the stench of decaying flesh hung over him. Everywhere the *orisha* went, he was followed by dogs licking his wounds. People recoiled in disgust and horror. He was repulsive to everyone, especially women. Although he felt guilt and shame for being the cause of diseases entering the world, there was little he could do for he was now struggling to simply stay alive. With time, the diseases were victorious over his body. People mourned his passing, more so the women.

The women of the world, saddened more by the absence of their lover than Babalú-Ayé's death, petitioned Ochún to find a way to reverse Olodumare's curse. If anyone could influence Olodumare to change direction it would be the great seductress. She made her way to Olodumare's hut on the pretense of seeking guidance concerning the wayward Changó. The unwary creator welcomed her to his home. While serving him tea, she reached for the pumpkin gourd hidden under her skirt, and dipping her two fingers in the stored honey, quickly spread the sweetness across Olodumare's lips. He was immediately aroused with overwhelming passions which had been dormant for eons.

"Give me more of your honey!" the enchanted and intoxicated Olodumare begged, "I have never felt so alive with my body tingling in areas I thought long dead to senses." She, however, held back her sweet elixir until her request was granted. "You can have your fill of my sweet sticky honey," she whispered, "if like the biblical Lazarus, you bring Babalú-Ayé back from the dead." Grateful to experience such delicious urges long forgotten, Olodumare immediately granted Ochún's request. Still, he refused to remove the *orisha's* sores. Healed, but still bearing the wounds of his folly, he made his way to Arará in Dahomey where he was proclaimed by the townsfolk as their king and ruler. No longer able to seduce women, he dedicated his life to nursing those afflicted by diseases. Though death was caused by his foolhardiness, Babalú-Ayé was reborn, getting a new lease on life due to Ochún's seductive powers.

But not all her gift of seduction was used for the good of others. She was also capable of incredible cruelty. Her cunning as the eternal temptress should never be underestimated. She not only gets her way through her sensual intuition but also through her crafty wiles. She could have had any god or human she wanted, yet she spent her days pining for the adulterine Changó, who was espoused to another. Memories of hours spent in her bed, pressing her nipples against the hardness of his slender muscular body while gently stroking his hair was sufficient to make her as wet as the morning dew. They may be passionate lovers, but he remained married to Obba, his lawful and legitimate wife, unwilling to leave or abandon her, even though the passion of that union has long been extinguished. The thought of him lying with that cold fish enraged Ochún more. Before he took the tempestuous Oyá as his mistress and made her his most favorite lover, Ochún was under the allusion she could have made Changó exclusively hers. But first, she had to remove Obba from the equation, by whatever means necessary. Afterward, she would concentrate on doing the same with Oyá.

Obba is the *orisha* whose domains are the still waters of lakes and lagoons. Like stagnant waters, her lovemaking consisted of laying tranquil in submissive obedience to her wifely duties until her husband was satisfied. Unfortunately for her, sexual release is not the same as satisfaction. Changó, the incorrigible philanderer, quickly tired of her, unfulfilled by the lack of sensual passion commonly experienced with his sexually adventurous mistress Ochún. With time, Obba began to feel neglected by her husband. Poor Obba, she failed to realize that one woman, regardless as to who she might be, would never be enough for her adulterous husband. Irrespective of his awful reputation, Obba – the ever-faithful spouse - truly believed she still had a wifely duty to honor and respect him. Yes, the gossiping of the townsfolk cut deeply, and the thought of her husband finding comfort between the legs of another woman crushed her heart. But what truly caused her inconsolable pain were rumors that Changó had also taken her sister Oyá as his newest lover. And yet because she loved him, she still yearned for his lustful hunger, now given so freely to other women.

Detecting her fiery husband's attention was cooling in their bedroom, the meek and unsuspecting Obba gathered what little courage she had and sought Ochún's counsel, completely unaware that the very person from whom she sought advice had also enjoyed trysts with her husband. Who else but the goddess of Eros, she reasoned, could provide sound counsel on how to satisfy her man? Hoping against hope, she thought she might learn how to incite passion in their monotonous bedroom. With honey dripping from her words, Ochún provided hope to the hopeless, "Tell me the desire of your heart and I'll make sure you achieve it," she cooed. How naive and sorrowful was Obba, not only to make a man the desire which could satisfy her heart; but to also trust in someone who had already betrayed her! Ochún, soothing her with flattering words, fooled the desperate Obba with a deceptive solution. First, they commiserated together on the unfaithfulness of the men they loved so dearly. Yes indeed, men were pigs – all of them. Slyly, Ochún promised the unsuspecting Obba that as her confidant, she was at the ready to do whatever she could to save the failing marriage. "Tonight," she advised, "prepare Changó his favorite meal, quimbombó, along with a side of fried cornmeal mush. For dessert, a fruit salad consisting of chopped apples and cactus fruit. And be sure to serve a glass of the finest red wine you can find. Now here is the crucial ingredient for the meal. Cut off one of your ears, finely mince it then mix it into the ram and okra stew. Once he eats you, he will forever be bound to you." She somehow convinced the gullible Obba that a woman's ear possessed aphrodisiac qualities.

Horrified by the suggestion, Obba nevertheless trusted Ochún, even if it meant imitating so many women who are forced to self-mutilate their identity for the sake of men's whims. That evening, Oba followed Ochún's instructions.

When Changó entered their home, ravenous after a night of carousing, he immediately sat down at the dinner table knowing his submissive wife would have a scrumptious meal already prepared, even though she was never sure if he would bless her with his presence on any given night. She may not be able to harden his resolve, he thought to himself, but by the gods, she sure could cook. His vision was so blurry from too much palm wine that he did not at first notice the bandage over the pale looking Obba's left ear protruding from under the low hanging pink head scarf she wore to cover the evidence of her deed. Halfway through his meal, as his hangover began to dissipate, he finally looked up to see his wife silently sitting across the table watching her husband devour her cooking. "Mmmm, you really outdid yourself dear wife," he said while chewing his food thoughtfully. Only then did he notice the compress over where her ear used to be. "What's wrong with your ear," he gruffly asked between mouthfuls. "An act of love," she shrewdly responded. But Changó was in no mood for elusive games. He repeated his question, only this time, sparks of fire rather than spittle flew from his mouth between words.

Fearful of inciting her husband's wrath rather than his passion, Obba confessed what she had done. Changó was shocked and disgusted, for he loathed any type of deformity. His shallow view of people measured the worth of a person more by their looks than their character. The once beautiful Obba was now hideous in his eyes, with a rugged stump where her ear once was. Thoroughly repulsed and appalled, he swore to never visit her bed again, declaring that he would from now on reside with her sister Oyá. There was no way Obba could ever again arouse him. They would officially remain married, but only in name. With streams of tears flowing from her eyes, she begged for forgiveness, but her entreaties fell on deaf ears. Still, he was no fool. He may have been revolted by Obba, but she was wealthy, a means of maintaining his life of leisure. Since that awful day, she came to be known as the patron *orisha* of the home, of marriage, and of neglected wives.

Hearts only break when they are carelessly given to others. Obba provides a cautionary tale of loving the one who is unfaithful and confiding in the one who is untrustworthy. Miguelito may have been accustomed to punches and kicks, but more painful were cunning betrayals. A lifetime of double-crossing and double-dealing has taught him not to trust white people. While being hailed as "a credit to your race," they shortchanged him when it came time to compensate his services. Even though as a prolific professor publishing more books than all his institution's white colleagues combined, when they discovered he was the highest paid faculty member due to the remuneration formulas designed years before by a previous generation of white educators to privilege whiteness, they quickly decided – in the name of justice – to rewrite the compensation package. The fact he was so prolific only meant he could not really be scholarly. As one colleague observed: "There is a problem when some publish too much for the short-term financial benefits of generating more publications vs. those of us who commit to the long-term benefits of pursuing a complex research agenda that might not result in a publication every year." A barrio dog, an illegal dirty spic whose only option was to attend a community college, can never be allowed to outshine white folk who sport Ivies pedigree.

Expecting the worst makes acceptance easier. While Miguelito was always guarded in the presence of white people, especially those professing to be his allies, the emotional ache caused by betrayal from one's own community proved more excruciating, more unbearable. What was it that early twentieth century author Zora Neale Hurston wrote? "All my skinfolk ain't kinfolk." Miguelito was always willing to bend backwards to help other Latinés wishing to become scholars and professors. He was quick to serve on their dissertation committees, provide publishing opportunities, write strong letters of recommendation, and provide introductions for employment opportunities. One particular student, Reinaldo , whom Miguelito treated as a son, caused such great heartache that it almost led the not-yet-old professor to take early retirement. Reinaldo was unbelievably tall and thin, in reality quite emaciated. He begged Miguelito to take him on as a student and with words dripping of honey, buffed up Miguelito's fragile ego. Like most Latinés constantly hearing from white colleagues that they do not belong in the hallow ivy towers of academia, Miguelito developed an imposter syndrome. Regardless of him being prolific, he lived in unjustifiable fear whites would accuse him of lacking scholastic rigor. He unwisely placed too much stock on what his white colleagues thought.

Obba believed Ochún was a friend, a sister, this is why she was devastated by the betrayal. Even as the look of disgust came across Changó's face, and Ochún's treachery began to dawn on Obba, she still clung to the myth of sisterhood. At first Miguelito failed to comprehend what was occurring. He was honored when his academic guild elected him as their president. He gave the customary plenary address based on a book published several years earlier on a theorical concept he was further developing. When he widely presented his scholarship to his peers, Reinaldo's true colors were exposed. For about a year, he was passing off Miguelito's published research as his own. Rather than admitting his failure to properly document his source, Reinaldo chose an easier and more cowardly path, starting a whisper campaign that Miguelito was the one plagiarizing his work. Gaslighting to save face, an attempt was made to destroy Miguelito's reputation, honor, and career. Earthly treasures can be stolen; but one's reputation and honor are the only commodities that when taken, leaves one poorer.

Of course, anyone with an internet could have discovered that five years before Reinaldo made his accusations, the arguments Miguelito supposedly plagiarized were already published in at least two of his books. But for some, the whiff of scandal was more tantalizing to the ears than the boredom of facts. Several white colleagues who could not stand Miguelito for multiple reasons – some of course justified –

found the accusation a reason to damage his character. His own colleagues at his institution, rather than insisting on conducting an investigation, allowed rumors to fester, even assuring Reinaldo would eventually graduate. Of course, if Miguelito would have been white, a different response would have ensued. Reinaldo would have been expelled for plagiarism.

For many years Miguelito refused to take on any new doctoral students. The cut was too deep. With time he learned that protecting his heart by not assisting other Latinés succeed was more damaging to his soul than the broken heart caused by betrayal. Still, he wrestled with trying to comprehend why those suffering due to white supremacy willingly pull-down members of their own community to the cheers and applause of the dominant culture. Why are the oppressed like crabs in a bucket?

One of the joys of living in Miami during the 1970s was land-crabbing at Matheson Hammock, the first park gifted to what would eventually become Miami Dade County. A forest of naturally occurring mangrove trees served as a hedge for this charming little cove, providing a cool and breezy escape for families during Miami's eight-month summer season. Because of the beach's petite size and relatively shallow waters, parents could relax and let their kids run around unsupervised to build soggy sandcastles out of the ugly gray sand by the warm lapping waves.

Along the long and winding road leading to the boiling asphalt-covered parking area, which served to announce one's arrival at the hammock was an unadorned snack bar and adjacent boat marina. There were a few road-shoulder areas where cars could pull over to attempt a picnic. Only when you got out of the car and faced the swamp were you able to see that there were dry paths leading deep into the quiet forest. For much of the hotter months it was impossible to walk too far into the trees because by nine o'clock in the morning the heat of the sun bearing down upon the still waters trapped between the long legs of the trees made the stifling air reek. Three types of trees grew in the brackish mud: red, black, and white mangroves, which appeared to walk on land as their long pipe-like roots literally lifted the tree's trunk out of the stinky mud. The leaves of these vertically erect trees with aerating branches excreted salt. The seeds of the red mangrove in particular were foot-long and pencil-shaped. With an astonishing reproductive system, the "live" young remained connected to their parents until they could live on their own. A vibrant ecosystem around the roots would collect a dense mixture of fallen leaves, twigs and branches, live fish, small land creatures and decaying animal remains, which together with drying sediment would, over time, form dry land.

For many decades it had become an annual tradition for locals to go to Matheson Hammock during hurricane season to hunt for blue land crabs. Before dawn, cars would quietly turn off dimly lit Old Cutler Road and head east in the pitch-blackness toward the ocean. A few minutes later, the car's headlights would reveal millions of crabs as far as the eyes could see, and the earth itself appeared as if to be heaving with the clickety-clacking of legs and claws climbing over each other in enormous acts of migration. Due to the morning high tide, it took some maneuvering to park safely on top of the moving ocean of crabs, being sure to turn the tires inward against the slope and getting out of the car on the driver's side away from the marsh, for opening the passenger door meant falling into the water full of snakes and who-knows-what else. There were so many crabs that it was easier to scoop them up by the bucketful than with a shovel. Collecting half a dozen buckets of crabs was a brief enterprise lasting less than ten minutes. The crabs, waving their claws angrily, would inadvertently grab onto their captor's pants legs by mistake and hold on for dear life not understanding that their survival depended on letting go.

One could easily tell who the expert land-crabbers were because they arrived in old and battered vehicles. Regardless of how many crabs one could eat that night for dinner, it seemed ridiculous to drive all this way for only one bucketful when you could have filled up hundreds of buckets just as easily, not to mention the exorbitant prices restaurants charged for the very same meal. Seasoned land-crabbers brought their kids along to help with the scooping task, and after dumping their buckets of crabs into the back of an old pickup truck, the youngest member of the family was given a stick to smack down would-be-escapees on the drive home. It wasn't too surprising, then, to find a flattened blue crab in the middle of Dixie Highway or even on the better-kept side streets along Coral Way, several miles away from the beach.

Seagulls and crows would feed on the heroic carcass that had opted for a squashed getaway. After scrambling out of the speeding truck and plopping onto a suburban pavement, the crab would at least have the satisfaction of one of its claws puncturing a tire instead of having to endure the indignity and death by soup-pot. Other escapees, however, would enjoy the ultimate revenge by hiding under their captor's driver's seat, only to be discovered when the seat was lurched into position. The sudden crunch would be followed by a bloom death-stench, bringing the mangroves to waft forever more throughout the vehicle.

Some of the crabs, however, seem to have a mean disposition toward their own kind. While they were all being scooped into the white bucket of their collective doom, crabs relegated to the bottom would pinch the legs of those trying to escape and drag them back down. Why would these crustacean-brained creatures play the role of Judas and betray their own? Maybe it's because the white bucket is an artificial imposed environment. The lure of survival trumps the wisdom of cooperation. In their natural habitat, among the odorous legs of the mangrove trees, near the rocks where ocean waves come crashing down, crabs work together to pull each other up to safety.

Ochún could have helped Obba, or at least warned her. But her betrayal smacked down their bond of sisterhood in favor of keeping Changó in the driver's seat, a role which demanded the requirement of betrayal. Oyá might have become Changó's beloved, but he could never stop resisting the unmediated passion of Ochún. If she could seduce the great creator of all, Changó didn't have a chance. Changó may have moved in with Oyá, but this did not bring an end to his womanizing. His numerous rendezvous with Ochún humiliated Oyá, but at the same time Oyá could not tolerate his visits to her sister. But with those who intimately live together, Oyá soon began to learn some of Changó's most hidden fears. His braggadocious machismo may have masked his insecurities to others, but Oyá quickly learned what he feared most - death. One night, Changó put on his finest red vest, showering himself with expensive cologne. "Where are you going?" Oyá asked icily, already knowing the answer. "Out" he curtly responded, "don't wait up." She knew damn well he was going to again seek comfort in Ochún's embrace. Oyá's temper began to boil. Enough was enough she thought. *¡Basta!*

Knowing his fear of death, and being the keeper of cemetery gates, Oyá summoned a platoon of the departed to arise from their graves and posted them as sentries surrounding her house. When Changó, well dressed and perfumed, opened the front door to leave for a pleasant evening, he was confronted, face-to-face, with the *Ikú*, the dead. Horrified, he slammed shut the door, bolted it, and went to hide in their bedroom. Smugly smiling, Oyá accomplished her goal, keeping her lover home and away from that whore Ochún.

Meanwhile, Ochún started to worry when Changó failed to show up. Yes, he was irresponsible, but until now, he had never stood her up. Soon she heard from Elleguá what happened. This was simply unacceptable. She had saved Changó from Obba, and now it was time to save him from Oyá's clutches. She stationed herself outside of Oyá's house and patiently waited until she left to conduct errands. When the coast was clear, Ochún approached the house. The *Ikú*'s orders were not to let Changó leave, but nothing was commanded prohibiting anyone's entry.

When the door opened after gently knocking, she greeted her lover with *Kawo Kabiesile.** As soon as she entered the home, they fell into each other's arms. There and then, on Oyá's bed, they made up for lost time. As they laid enjoying the warmth of each other's body after a rapturous explosion of passion, Changó, almost in tears, lamented being held captive, a prisoner in his own home. "Don't worry *ifemi* – my beloved, I'll save you from Oyá." With that, she jumped out of bed, slipped on her yellow skirt, adjusted her hair, and went to work. First, she went to Oyá's closet and pulled out a multicolor skirt and black blouse. "Put these on," she barked at Changó. Taken aback, the macho warrior hesitated. "I said, put these on," she repeated. Not willing to argue, he sheepishly obeyed.

Once Changó was in drag, Ochún took some of Oyá's makeup she kept on the dresser and applied it. With eggshell powder she lightened his face. Taking a pomegranate from the

---

* A salutation of praise given to Changó which means that the king (Changó) did not hang himself, did not die, connoting that Changó became an orisha before death.

kitchen, she grounded the seeds and applied it to his lips, giving them a ruby shade. Laying hold of some beet roots from the garden, she grinded them, added some saffron, and created an orangey-red shadow powder which she brushed on his eyelids. Then she did the unthinkable. With a pair of scissors, she cut off locks of her hair which she added as extensions to his. The virile Changó was transformed into a beautiful woman. Fortunately, his smooth babyface made the transition seamless.

With Changó all dressed up, Ochún implemented the second phase of her plan. She always knew she could seduce gods and men, but could she entice the dead? There was only one way to find out. Opening the front door, she summoned the guards to draw near. They hesitated at first, not wanting to abandon their posts. But her soft words, batting eyes, and flirtatious smile made it difficult to ignore her request. As the *Ikú* approached the goddess of lust, she quickly dipped her two figures into her honey and brushed it across where their lips had once existed. Even the dead are inebriated by her beauty, able to feel the tinkle of arousal within decaying flesh. Momentarily ecstatic, they forgot why they had been summoned to the house. At this moment, Changó in drag stepped onto the porch, but the dead barely noticed the disguised *orisha*. Their full attention was laser-focused on Ochún. Locking arms with Ochún, like sisters going shopping, Changó walked boldly through the unsuspecting *Ikú* who barely glanced his way.

When Oyá returned and discovered Changó escaped, she was furious. A whirlwind storm erupted toward the *Ikú* for their stupidity. Even when men are dead, they still have their heads turned and act like total *comemierdas* when in the presence of a pretty woman. Not wanting to wait for her wrath to descend, they hastily made their way back to their graves, hoping to rest in peace. Oyá remained angry for some time, but that too passed. Even passionate lovemaking grows tedious after a while. Once Changó had his fill of Ochún, he returned to Oyá, who stimulated more than just his groin. They remained together because Oyá learned to ignore his womanizing. At the end, betrayal fell short, but unfortunately, patriarchy won, and the white bucket of supremacy created for crabs endured.

In Elleguá We Trust

In the village of Kétou there were once some contentious neighbors who lived across the street from each other. They would always find a reason to be disagreeable. They fought over the latest decree issued by the king, they argued over which *orisha* was the most powerful, and they quarreled over which type of sacrifice contained the most *ashé*. They even bickered over the weather, almost coming to blows. It was only a matter of time before one of the neighbors would kill the other out of anger. They would sit on their respective porches glaring at each other from across the street, murmuring curses under their breaths. One day, the young and playful Elleguá walked down the middle of the street between the two homes, turning neither to his right nor to his left. Later that afternoon, the two neighbors had a conversation but as expected, their words soon became heated. "Did you see Elleguá walk by this morning?" one asked, "He was wearing a red hat, a black shirt, and red trousers." "You blind idiot!" retorted the other. "Yes, that was Elleguá, but he was wearing a black hat, a red shirt, and black trousers." "*Comemierda!*" was the response. "*Hijo de puta!*" the other shouted back. Just as both sides were reaching for their machetes, Elleguá appeared before them eating candy. The neighbors looked upon Elleguá who was now facing them and noticed the oddness of his attire. His hat was of two colors, black on the right side, and red on the left side. His shirt was the opposite, red on the right side and black on the left, while his trouser matched the pattern of his hat, black on the right and red on the left.

Both neighbors were right, and both were wrong. That day, they learned a valuable lesson about truth. It often depends on one's particular point of view. Reality – like religious traditions and memories – are often ambiguous, depending on where one stands, from which side of the street one gazes. Being fooled by the trickster led the neighbors to admit their silly arguments and for the first time, harmony was established between them.

The impish Elleguá, a contradictory figure who hates those who are engaged in acts of injustices, is said to exist everywhere, sitting at every crossroads of life, offering lies to discover truth, stealing to create equality, and disrupting the status quo in order to establish harmony. Early missionaries dismissed Elleguá as the African incarnation of Satan, unaware that all religious traditions, even those found in their precious Bible, has trickster figures. Tricksters like **Elleguá** realize that within oppressive structures, the only way for the powerless to radically counter those profiting at their expense is to *joder* - fuck with the system. Lying, cheating, joking, and deceiving unmask deeper truths obscured by oppressive moralists. Miguelito, who had faced physical violence as a child and institutionalized violence as an adult discovered Elleguá provided a way when none existed.

Besides serving as a means of disrupting the life-denying harmony of those in power, the trickster provides a way to flourish. Once, when Olodumare was ill and close to death, all the *orishas* gathered in hope of finding a cure. Elleguá just a young lad at the time, was dismissed because he was always playing youthful tricks and silly games, so naturally the elder *orishas* neither invited nor consulted him. But what they failed to realize is that because he is everywhere, hiding behind every door, he is always seeing, hearing, learning. Years of observing had provided him with a wealth of wisdom and knowledge. As a result, when he heard of the symptoms caused by Olodumare's infection, he immediately knew what combination of herbs would cure him. Uninvited, he showed up at the great Creator's home where all the elder *orishas* had gathered. Even the *orisha* of illnesses, Babalú-Ayé was dumbfounded by the ailment and could not discover a cure. Seeing Elleguá at the door they burst into laughter at his hubris. "This child thinks he can succeed where those more powerful have failed," they scoffed. As they were shooing him out of the house, the weakened Olodumare, in an almost inaudible whisper, instructed them to leave the youngster alone since everyone deserves a chance.

The young *orisha* ran to Olodumare's bedside and helped him drink a concoction he crafted. Within minutes, color returned the Olodumare's cheeks. Half an hour later, his fever broke, and he ate some food for the first time in days. Within an hour, he was out of his deathbed, walking and laughing among the other *orishas*. He was grateful for the cure which he might not have taken due to the arrogance and pride of the other *orishas*. So appreciative was Olodumare he proclaimed from that day forward, Elleguá would be the first to be honored at every ceremony and sacrifice. No petition would be granted by any *orisha* without first obtaining Elleguá's approval, regardless of how insignificant the request might appear.

Elleguá may hold a high position of esteem among the *orishas*, but at the end of the day, does it matter if he even exists? Or if the *orishas* are real? Maybe like humans, all gods must also one day dance with Ikú, death. Gods exist as long as humans remember them and feed them *ashé*. Once they are ignored, they fade into nothingness, leaving behind buildings where they once dwelled as tombstones, tourist-traps to be visited not by pilgrims, but by those recognizing how these once powerful beings were crucial in forming and informing a culture. After decades living in the belly of an industrial empire which has no god but capital, maybe the old gods of Miguelito are simply dying of hunger as years pass without them being fed. Elleguá, like all the other *orishas*, and like every other god which has ever existed, is only real as long as there are humans who claim them. But even when humans insist on forgetting them, they still stand in the breach to serve and protect.

"Will pick up in 30," was texted to Miguelito. He looked at his phone and grunted. He was getting too old for this. With some forty plus published books under his belt, and much in demand, he was forced to reduce the number of speaking gigs to just three a month. As a professor of religion and ethics, there were many issues on which to speak about: critical race theory, health care, ecological degradation, or the abuses of neoliberalism. Today's talk at the college was on immigration. He has given this talk many times before. Approaching his mid-sixties, Miguelito began to contemplate retirement, so naturally, he started to muse over what his last lecture would look like. Surely it would not be the one he was giving today, a standard talk which while important, only touched on one aspect of his intellectual pursuit.

The hotel room was nice. Usually, colleges arranged for pleasant accommodations. If he had to be over a thousand miles from home, the least they could do is make him as comfortable as possible. He was already dressed. All he needed was to put on his bow tie, button up his vest, and slip on his boots. The bowtie had become the drag he wore, a transethnic act to appear whiter, not for the purpose of assimilation, but an accessory for survival. As much as Miguelito spoke and wrote against white supremacy, he nonetheless understood the closer he appeared to the white male ideal, the less were the struggles. When one thinks of the characters who usually wear bowties, from old stuffy professors to the nutty professor, Miguelito – channeling Elleguá - was playfully subverting how whites saw him, covering the brown body whites saw as inferior with the symbols of white intelligentsia. Could he wear "whiteness" not only as a form of self-defense, but also as a means of dismantling how he is usually seen and defined?

A meticulous dresser, Miguelito understood that what he wore negotiated not only how he expressed himself, but also served as a visual identity where his Latino body acted as a canvas, a mediator, to the outside world. If clothing is indeed a language unto itself, an attempt to obtain status and social acceptance, was it possible to dress his brownness in the image of power. Cross-dressing into whiteness sought acceptance into the scholarly community which saw him as an intruder but upon which his livelihood depended. Other white male professors at his institution, in a feeble attempt to look as young as their students, wore T-shirts and jeans instead of jackets, believing that the neckties worn were a barrier distancing them from their student. They sought creating a state of eternal adolescence, a wistful attempt to remain the same age as their students.

As a young professor, Miguelito tried imitating his white professors' dress code. But the end-of-course evaluation (upon which pay-raises and tenure depended) had multiple comments about students not "feeling safe" with him, especially from his white female students. Years being taught to be afraid of brown men – greasers, rapists, thieves, and gangbangers – did not dissipate when they found themselves in the classroom under the tutelage of a brown man. The image of the dangerous Latino man was too much for them to simply set aside. So many negative evaluations, threatening his livelihood, forced Miguelito to conduct an experiment. He performed whiteness by wearing a bowtie to soften him. Immediately, by the end of the next semester, his course evaluations shot up to be among the highest in the school.

By appropriating the costume historically worn by white men with power within the academy, Miguelito – playing the trickster - destabilized and disrupted how his students gazed upon him. His lectures did not change, just his clothes. Due in part to this gaze, fused by centuries of ethnic discrimination, this Latino man was forced to dress better in order to be recognized as having the proper academic credentials to teach predominately white students. While his white colleagues can be seen as "cool" for teaching in a t-shirt, Miguelito, who constantly had his credibility as a professor questioned, would simply be disrespected and dismissed. No, he wasn't trying to assimilate; he simply wore a professor's costume which provided cover, a survival tactic against rude treatment from students and colleagues whose bigotry easily allowed them to write off the Latino as being a credible professional in the classroom.

One last look in the mirror. *¡Bello como un camello!*[*] He grabbed his notes and headed for the lobby where his host was already waiting. "Boo-eeno day-iss," his guest greeted him in

---

[*] "As pretty as a camel!"

a mutilation of the language of angels. "Good afternoon," Miguelito responded, having heard this type of gesture so many times before. "I am grateful for your kind invitation." Small talk followed on the drive to the college. Always with the small talk. How Miguelito hated this part of his trips. By the time they arrived, the auditorium was packed with noisy undergrads. Even though the days of social distancing were a thing of the past; still, years of masks and quarantines has left him somewhat apprehensive whenever he found himself in large public gatherings. Soon after arriving his apprehensiveness escalated for other reasons. Unlike other speaking events, this time he was greeted by the campus police, who quickly whisked him to an adjacent room. It was certainly strange, and he was a bit disappointed not to have been able to mingle with some of the students before his presentation. "Good afternoon Dr. De La Cruz," the officer began. "Forgive the show of force. In an act of overcautiousness, we have decided to attend your talk. Because this is a public lecture on such a controversial subject, we thought it wise to be present."

"Immigration is only controversial because of the anti-Latiné hysteria" Miguelito thought to himself. Hatred toward Latinés had become even more acceptable since the former President, during the launch of his political career, referred to them as having lots of problems, of being criminals and rapists. It provided an excuse for all the closeted haters and nutjobs to come out of the woodwork. Once in office the president had quickly moved to tear brown children from their parent's arms at the border and had them placed either in cages or camps like the one in Tornillo, Texas. The response of the white Christian community had been a simultaneous yawn. White Christianity had now exposed itself as a rotting corpse whose allegiance to an antichrist, meaning a person who is the anti, the opposite, of the gospel teachings of Christ, now operated as Ikú - death masquerading as an angel of light. Since 45 began his term, there had been such an increase in hate crimes directed at Latinés that it was beginning to make Miguelito apprehensive whenever he traveled, especially to those red states where support for the former president remained at a fever pitch, states like the one where he found himself today.

"The police picked up some chatter on the dark web about today's lecture," the school security officer continued. "We suspect someone, or several persons may attempt to disrupt your talk. That is why the police posted an officer at every entry point and have several officers in plain clothes sitting in the audience. I will constantly be present to your stage left. If anything was to happen, you would need to quickly make your way to me."

"Was a threat made on my life?" Miguelito asked, not entirely surprised. After all, he had been placed on a professor watchlist by a conservative group labeling him a dangerous teacher because of what he taught.

"Well, yes," the officer admitted. "But such bravado is common. Although we're not taking the death threat seriously, to err on the side of caution, we feel that our visible presence will have a calming effect." Leave it to those in power to think more guns in a room is calming.

This was not the first time Miguelito received a death threat. His calls for social justice have a way of attracting kooks, like flies to light. He had learned to take such verbal acts of bravado from the far right in stride. Maybe years of physical beatings from whites have made him callous to their threats? When he shared these threats with his colleagues, a few commented on his courage for speaking up. Such responses were both naïve and unhelpful. To lift one's voice for those who are voiceless should never be considered as an act of courage, for it is simply an act of human decency. One's humanity is claimed whenever they stand in solidarity with the world's disenfranchised and dispossessed, with those relegated to the margins of white supremacy.

"You will not be able to mingle with the students after your presentation nor autograph books. Instead, you will immediately exit the stage where your driver will be waiting to take you back to your hotel."

"Get me off campus as soon as possible," Miguelito thought, "so I need no longer be your responsibility." Not being able to chit-chat with students, the part of the gig he did enjoy, was disappointing, but he grudgingly understood. So, he just sat in the nondescript dull grey room with his bodyguard waiting for when it was time to give his presentation.

At the back of the auditorium filled with several hundred students sat Charles Sweat, but his friends – when he had friends - simply called him Chuck. Even though he was in his late twenties, his baby face struggled to grow a raggedy blond beard, allowing him to easily fit in with the crowd. He decided to see for himself what the fuss was all about when it appeared on one of his alt-right websites, announcing yet another pro-immigrant spic was going to give a lecture about needing to tear down the wall the former president supposedly built, this life-saving wall keeping out the brown barbarians who threatened the lives and safety of hard-working white Americans like himself. Americans were being replaced by a mongrel people – and it had to stop – by whatever means necessary. There were several posts from other like-minded men and women who also planned to show up and cause trouble. "Cause trouble, what exactly did that mean?" Chuck thought to himself. He was growing impatient with so-called defenders of white civilization that were all talk but no action. "If we are going to make America great again, then we need to take bold and aggressive actions, like the patriots of old once did in 1776."

Ironically, Chuck never thought much about race issues growing up. He was raised in a politically moderate family. His father leaned toward conservative Republican ideas, attracted to their low tax platform. His mother, on the other hand, leaned toward liberal Democrats due to their commitment to reproduction rights. Neither, however, were fanatics, always willing to find compromise somewhere in the middle. What if their votes cancelled each other out? - politics were never that important to them. They were quick to remind anyone who would listen that they did not harbor a racist bone in their bodies. Their colorblindness could be verified by the fact that they had a dear and close black friend who always had an open invitation to whatever social function they hosted. Sure, his father would at times let loose with the occasional n*gger or ch*nk joke when those kinds of people played the race card to gain some unfair advantage, but overall, they didn't see color and taught their son likewise. There were good people on all sides. So, for most of his life, Chuck was like most other white people, embracing all races. But the realities of adulthood began to change his mind.

He was able to find a job as assistant manager at a local fast-food outlet after barely finishing two years of community college. The money wasn't great, but at least he would never starve, and could eat all the hamburgers he wanted. Although socially awkward, he was romantically involved with a girl who was months away from turning eighteen. People thought she was too young, but they didn't know Molly like he did. She was really wise, and sensitive, and not too bad looking, almost pretty. And while they had been hooking-up for only five months, she had been his first sexual encounter. Until Molly, he was an incel; without her, he probably would still be. They were going to be together forever, he thought. That had been the plan until Pablo started sniffing around. Pablo, just a year older than Molly, thus closer to her age, started working at the same burger joint. One day Chuck caught the two of them talking to each other. He just couldn't understand how a nice white girl like Molly would even talk to that kind of guy. Pablo was everything Chuck wasn't. Where Pablo was lean and took care of his health, Chuck was paunchy and ate poorly. Where Pablo was well groomed and took pride in his personal hygiene, Chuck was unkept, going days without showering, with constant dirt under his fingernails. Chuck felt generally satisfied, settling with this job, but Pablo seemed to have bigger dreams, like wanting to become a doctor, and was saving his money for college. First Pablo and Molly got together for coffee, then for dinner, and finally got together to watch Netflix and chill. At first Molly had snuck around, but soon enough broke it off with Chuck.

Chuck was devastated as his world shattered. No one would ever love him again like Molly did, he thought. "Fucking wetback," even though Pablo had been born in the same county hospital as Chuck. He decided to wait until Pablo made a mistake so he could fire his ass. Soon enough, a customer complained that Pablo got their order wrong, apparently forgetting to add fries to the burger meal. Without first checking to see if Pablo was at fault, Chuck instantly yelled and fired him. Pablo protested that other employees had gotten orders wrong also but had never been terminated. He was smart enough to realize that his dismissal had nothing to do with the forgotten fries but was because Chuck was mad over losing Molly. The more he complained, the angrier Chuck got. How dare this foreigner question him, wasn't he the boss? Chuck unwisely yelled out, "What's wrong with you. Can't you speakit-the-eeenglish? Goddamn spic, you're fired, get the fuck out!"

When headquarters learned of the incident due to a racial discrimination complaint filed by Pablo, it was Chuck who was let go. Being fired for having a race-based complaint on his employment record made it even harder to get another managerial job. He had lost the love of his life, the job of his dreams, and soon he would lose his apartment and his car would be repossessed. He was running out of money and would have to go back to living in his parents' basement.

With time on his hands, Chuck started living online, cruising the web for sites that helped him better understand why he lost his job. He found himself drawn to websites where other white people were saying the same things that he felt but had difficulty putting into words. He began to understand that his loss was not his fault as he read the angry rants people posted. "This is so true," he found himself saying, over and over again as the words and images he saw became more insistent, even violent. These spics are taking over, taking over our jobs thanks to affirmative action and taking over our women. Something radical had to be done. At first, he found comfort in a president who spoke of building walls to protect Americans from roving caravans of brown people. He rejoiced when the airports were closed to Muslim terrorists. "If that wall had been built decades ago, people like Pablo would not be illegally in this country, taking away the women and jobs of white people – replacing us" he said to himself, as image after image of angry young white men rolled by on his computer screen. It did not matter that Pablo had been born in Charlotte. The fact that he had a funny sounding name and immigrant parents – meant that he didn't belong. "They all should go back to the shithole countries where they came from," he found himself agreeing.

Chuck decided to get involved and felt better and better with each new meeting or event he attended. He became active in taking back his country, marching in Charlottesville to unite the right; appearing before State Capitols demanding to liberate states from the Democratic governor's usage of the COVID hoax to limit his civil liberties; waving a Blue Lives Matter poster at rallies demanding justice for what everyone knew. He fumed against what the fake news media kept hidden; how George Floyd, a known criminal, got what he deserved for resisting those sworn to serve and protect. With time on his hands, he even joined other Proud Boys in DC protesting the stolen election on January 6th, hitting one of the Capitol police with the pole upon which hung the thin blue-line flag.

Once again, he was an incel, unable to find another girlfriend. Just as devastating, he was unable to land another job. Chuck's fury blinded him to reality. So, when he saw the announcement that some highfalutin' beaner was going to speak about opening the borders and let in all the drug pushers, murders and rapists, Chuck knew this could be an opportunity to rally real Americans to the task of finishing that damn wall. A dramatic gesture was necessary. He wrote a manifesto full of spelling and grammar errors, just in case something was to happen to him, and had it ready in his email outbox, where he could hit send once he took advantage of whatever opportunity might present itself.

That morning, as he sat in the audience waiting for the greaseball to speak, he tried to eavesdrop on some of the conversations occurring around him. Some people sounded like fangirls - for christsake. "Such dumb fucking assholes," he thought to himself. "Too much education just makes you more stupider." But he overheard a few comments about being tired of "race hustlers dealing in white guilt." He looked around the room and noticed the number of police personnel. "Fuck," he said to himself. Those guys are definitely on the wrong side, and they're gonna mess me up," he thought. "Crap, what a waste." Maybe he should just leave, but decided instead to stick around for a while, just to hear what kind of lies the speaker was going to spit out of his deceitful spic mouth.

At 1pm on the dot he noticed a slightly older man with graying hair approach the podium. He's probably using that Just For Men formula, Chuck thought. He didn't look like a spic. In fact, he looked pretty white. But if there was any hesitation about where the speaker was from, the very first heavily accented sentence, which enraged Chuck, gave him away: "All white Christianity is detrimental to communities of color. For the survival of Latinés, it must be rejected!" "Fuck! The nerve, the gall, goddamn!" Chuck thought. These professor types are dangerous. There's a reason that Hitler gathered the university professors and got rid of them first before tackling the Jewish problem. "That fucking critical race theory shit was ruining this country." The more he heard from

Dr. De La Cruz, the angrier Chuck became. At the end of the lecture came the punch line: "When one nation build's roads into another nation – through gunboat diplomacy or establishing banana republics – to steal their raw material or cheap labor, why should we be surprised when people from those invaded countries take those same roads following everything that has been stolen from them."

Chuck could no longer just sit there and hear this diarrhea of words. He suddenly stood up. Fists clenched, he glared at the speaker. Students sitting around him looked up curiously, noticing his angry red face. The security personnel also shifted their attention to him. The glare of indignation continued. But the speaker, reading from his notes, did not notice the young man. Not to be noticed was just one more slight felt deeply by Chuck. The security guards began to move toward him. With no real option available, he headed for the back door murmuring something about "blut und boden." Once he was gone, the guards relaxed and went back to their sentry posts as Dr. De La Cruz brought his lecture to a conclusion.

Outside Chuck was self-flagellating for his cowardness. Here he had come to make a grand gesture, and few people had even noticed his pathetic act of defiance. Like the others on those websites, he had failed to walk the talk. Leaning against the passenger door of his father's Chevy he smoked a cigarette and tried to calm down. A joint would be much more smoothing, he admitted to himself. Not much to do but head home, he thought. That's when from the corner of his eye he caught a glimpse at opportunity. As students were leaving the auditorium, a blue sedan drove by. Sitting on the passenger side was the speaker, grinning and laughing with the driver. No doubt he was mocking Chuck for forcing him to just sit there in the back of the auditorium and take his racist insults. Chuck quickly hopped into the car, turned the ignition, and without thinking it through, started following the car. Once they drove off campus, the security detail went their separate ways.

Chuck followed for less than four miles to the fancy hotel close to campus. It was the type of hotel Chuck would never be able to afford, a hotel than in a simpler time would cater just to whites like him. He quickly parked and slipped into the lobby, just in time to see the professor enter through the same automatic sliding doors. Chuck moved quickly to get to the elevators ahead of Dr. De La Cruz. As the professor approached, Chuck noticed he had undone his bowtie. As soon as the elevator doors opened, a small black boy, about eight-years-old, ran out, bumping into the prof's legs and smearing on his pants, with sticky chocolate hands, the candy bar he just finished eating. The boy just looked up, grinned, and ran off. Trying to wipe the chocolate off his pants, Miguelito simply chuckled, relieved he packed an extra outfit. Before he stepped into the elevator, Chuck had already slipped in, pressed the button for the top floor and leaned against the back wall. Dr. De La Cruz followed, lost in his own thoughts, and pressed the sixth-floor button, standing with his back to Chuck, facing instead the front of the elevator. He didn't really notice the other passenger, except for a momentary whiff of an unwashed body.

As the doors began to close, the professor was engrossed in mentally rewriting a difficult paragraph for an essay he was just finishing, Chuck touched the Smith and Wesson M&P BodyGuard .38 special revolver in his pocket for courage. The doors shut and the elevator began its upward journey. The ride to the sixth floor would take less than three minutes. Somewhere while passing the third floor, Miguelito was arriving at a better way to academically articulate his point. Chuck, meanwhile, was lost in delusional thoughts of glory, envisioning how he would finally make a name for himself, celebrated as a true patriot and hero for encouraging other oppressed whites to take action against those contributing to their subjugation.

To anyone on the sixth floor waiting to ride down, the ding of the bell announced that the elevator arrived. The bell vainly tolled for no one was waiting. The doors opened, revealing to no one in particular, anything amiss which might have occurred during the upward trek. Out stepped Dr. De La Cruz, leaving behind a passenger to continue his journey. So insignificant was the other passenger to Miguelito, that he barely noticed that he was not alone during the ride. But maybe if he would have paid attention, he might have observed an expression of pain and shame on the face of his fellow rider. As the doors closed behind him, Miguelito was simply unaware that left behind was more than just Chuck, for unbeknownst to both, another silently rode with them, and fortunately for Miguelito, it was not Ikú.

Miguelito may no longer believe in Elleguá, but Elleguá continued to believe in Miguelito. Reason and science may rule the professor's mind, but the spiritual continued to dictate his heart, regardless of his attempts to intellectually reject gods to guide his feet. It would have been easier to die a martyr, for living by one's convictions is so much more difficult, proven by how consistently Miguelito fell short of the ideals he teaches. Elleguá the trickster, always upsetting preordained endings, simply prevented a simple and expected conclusion to the story. At the moment Chuck was resolute to act, sometime before reaching the fourth floor, Elleguá – even though anemic by not being fed by Miguelito for decades and thus low on the necessary *ashé* needed to protect him - brought to the angry young man's mind all his feelings of self-doubt and self-loathing, flooding his mind with memories from his childhood, of his parents, of his teen years, of not being able to satisfy Molly. Fortunately, this task was not too difficult to accomplish and not much *ashé* needed to be expended. Chuck's eyes glazed over and his body momentarily relaxed while his mind wandered away in a swirl of misty thoughts and emotions.

Miguelito, like all Latinés within the United States, would continue to face the dangers of occupying a Latiné body, no matter how light his skin pigmentation might be. Being Latiné is rewarded with disproportionately higher unemployment and greater poverty. When pandemics ravished the land,

Latinés were more likely to become infected and die. Their children are more likely to be tossed into cages. Bowties are insufficient to protect the silent genocide occurring on the nation's borders. And while Chuck will go down in history as another nobody, Latinés will continue to more likely die at the hands of all the other Chucks in the world, itching for some apocalyptic race war driven by a learned hatred which provides a simple answer to their downwardly economic mobility. Miguelito walked to his hotel room, very pleased with himself and a bit proud for finding a conclusion for his next academic thesis.

There will one day be a final lecture, but not today. There will one day be a final dance with Ikú, but not today. Unlike his father, he will be surrounded by those he has loved and who have loved him as he lays on his death bed. Maybe Elleguá will be there to greet him and maybe not. Maybe there will be a tunnel with a light at the end, or friends to guide the way or maybe not. Maybe this life he has lived is all there is, and there is nothingness as his consciousness slips into oblivion. But does it really matter? In the hopeless existence faced by so many people in the world due to their horrific suffering, due to violence, due to starvation, due to forced displacement, due to institutionalized racism, due to ignorance, carelessness and indifference, maybe the only thing that matters, that makes life worth living, and that provides purpose and meaning, is to continue to struggle for justice - a justice that will never be realized - to continue resisting all who would belittle Latinés, to simply end it all

with a yell: *"Lo que me dio Elleguá no hay quién me lo quite -
¡Ashé!"**

---

* That which Elleguá gave me, no one can take away. Ashé!"

Miguel A. De La Torre is a religion professor who teaches ethics, specifically the intersection of faith with oppressive structures, specifically racism, classism, sexism, and heterosexism. Author of over forty-three books, he is probably the most published Latinx religion scholar.